Only
Ever
Christmas

Only EVER Christmas

SHAELA KAY

 Blue Water Books
Richland, WA

For everyone who, like me,
wishes it was Christmas all year long

Prologue

When I was in first grade, I wanted to be a squirrel. You know how at the start of the school year you'd make an All About Me booklet, with your name and age and family members in it? On the page that asked *What do you want to be when you grow up?* I wrote *a skwurl* and drew a picture of a squirrel in a tree. My teacher gently tried to guide me to something more practical, like a doctor or teacher or mom. But I was insistent. If I was a squirrel, I reasoned, I'd never have to leave my beloved trees.

And that's all I really wanted—to stay in the trees forever.

Chapter 1

The rich smell of damp earth fills my nostrils as I dig, bringing a smile to my lips. Sophie would have a fit if she could see the state of my fingernails at this moment, but I always prefer planting without gloves. There's just something about digging into the dirt with nothing but my bare hands and a spade that makes me feel so *alive*.

Finished with the hole, I select the last green sapling from the wheelbarrow and pull it out of the flimsy black pot. Loosening the rootball a bit, I set it in the hole and fill in the gaps, tamping down the earth until it's even and firm.

"There you go, little one," I murmur, spreading a spadeful of fertilizer around its base. "Grow up big and tall, now, like your brothers and sisters. But watch out for budworms; they were bad last year."

I sit back on my heels, looking down the row of saplings planted between the 6-year-old Noble firs with a satisfied smile. The method of overlapping fields like this saves space, but it also means we can't use an automatic planter—we have to do it all by hand. But I don't mind. I love planting days.

Getting up from the ground, I brush my hands off on my jeans and throw my tools into the now-empty wheelbarrow. Taking it by the handles, I head down the access road to the barn. The air is a bit more crisp than is typical for May, but the sun is warm on my face, and there's hardly a breeze to make the trees in the surrounding forest dance. I breathe in the cool, clean air with a relish, letting it filter into all the gaps of my soul.

I put away the tools, lock up the barn, and head for the house. "Mmm, something smells good," I say, coming into the mudroom from the garage. I pop my head around the corner into the kitchen, seeing my dad stirring something on the stove. He glances up and gives me a grin.

"Emmy-girl! You done for the day?" he asks, the deep timber of his voice a comical contrast to my mother's floral apron, tied around his tall frame.

"Yup. Just the yearlings to go."

"That's great."

After taking off my boots, I wash up in the mudroom sink, scrubbing at the black underneath my fingernails with the stiff bristles of a brush. I give up after a few minutes, resigned to the fact that they've been more or less black for weeks already. Sophie will have my head for sure.

Heading into the kitchen, I look over Dad's shoulder at the stew simmering on the stove. "Is there cornbread, too?" I ask, looking up at him hopefully.

He chuckles. "As if you can't smell it already."

I smile, stretching up on my toes to give him a quick kiss on the cheek. "Merry Christmas, Dad."

He smiles. "Merry Christmas, sugarplum. Dinner will be ready in about twenty minutes," he says.

4

"Okay. Where's Mom?"

"She's dozing out on the front porch."

I find Mom asleep in the rocking chair, and I shut the screen door carefully, not wanting to disturb her. I watch her face for a long moment, bittersweet feelings of love and loneliness warring for dominance in my heart. I love watching Mom when she's sleeping because her face and brow relax, making it easier to imagine that she's young and healthy again. But I know it's just an illusion—the black walker beside her is a stark reminder of the reality we now live in.

I brush a soft kiss on Mom's forehead and sit down in one of the old wicker chairs, looking out across the small lawn to the fields and forest beyond. Growing up in the woods and hills of western Washington always felt like a fairy tale. When I was a child and read the stories of Hansel and Gretel or Little Red Riding Hood, I always pictured the stories taking place here, in the Mt. Baker-Snoqualmie National Forest. It's about as perfect a place as you can imagine—unless you don't like the rain. Or trees. Or moss that grows on everything. But I love the cool damp that never quite goes away, even at the height of summer. To me, this is paradise.

A bushy gray squirrel with quick feet and sharp claws scampers down a tree, clinging to the bark with gravity-defying ease. He pauses, sniffs the air, then with a flash of his tail disappears around the other side of the trunk.

Mom stirs beside me, and I watch her for a moment before laying a hand gently on her arm. "Hey, Mom," I say softly. "How are you feeling this evening?"

"Walter?" Her eyes are unfocused, her voice quiet.

My heart cracks a little. "No, Mom, it's Emily."

"Emily?" Her voice is unsure, but slowly her eyes focus,

concentrating on my face until recognition dawns. "Oh, Emily. Hi sweetie."

I give her arm a little squeeze. "Can I get you anything, Mom? Do you want a drink?"

She nods, and I head back into the kitchen. "Mom's awake," I say to Dad, now setting the table.

"Oh good, would you help her inside? I'll let Chase know we're about ready to eat."

"Yup, she just wants a drink first."

I take one of the Stanley knock-off mugs from the drying rack and fill it with water, then attach the lid. Letting the screen door bang behind me, I step back onto the porch and beside the yellow rocking chair—painted by my mother years ago to "bring a little sunshine" to the porch.

"Here you go, Mom," I say, holding out the mug.

"Thanks, sweetie." She reaches for the drink, her tremor more pronounced in her groggy state. She grabs the handle but I hold onto the cup, helping guide the straw into her mouth as she drinks. When she pulls it away, I take the cup from her and set it on the little table beside the wicker chair.

"Thank you," she says. "Now, why are you here and not out working?"

A puff of laughter escapes me as I smile. "I was," I say, "but I'm finished for today."

"Hmm," she says, turning to look out across the nearest tree field. "Was it a planting day?"

I nod. "For 2021."

"How are they?"

I grin. "Anxious. Nervous. Excited. They couldn't wait to leave the nursery and find their places in the field."

Mom's look softens. "I bet they chattered at you every time you went near, wondering when their day would come."

The smile on my face eases the ache in my heart. We know, of course, that the trees don't *actually* talk to us, just like we know there's no cure for Parkinson's disease. But I grew up speaking to the trees, and it's not something I plan on giving up anytime soon.

"Dad said it's about time for dinner," I say.

She nods and I help her rise, but when she starts to move past me I gently grasp her arm. "Hang on, Mom, you need your walker," I say.

She scowls. "No, I don't. I haven't fallen in ages; I don't know why Walter insists on that horrible contraption."

I have learned not to argue with her when she gets like this. It's been nearly thirteen years since her diagnosis, and her fading memory and lack of awareness is merely a progression of the disease. There's no point in reminding her that she had a minor fall only last week—it will only confuse and anger her.

Instead, I grab the nearest handle of the walker and maneuver it next to her. "I know, Mom, but it will make Dad feel better if you use it."

She grumbles, but thankfully takes the handles and shuffles to the door. I hold it open for her, then follow her slowly into the kitchen.

Chase and Dad are talking quietly at the table when we come in. My twin brother stops mid-sentence when he sees us, and I wonder what they're talking about. Chase looks sober, and Dad's forehead is creased in a collection of worried lines.

"Hey, Em," Chase says, standing. "Mom, how are you feeling?"

She waves him back down into his chair. "Fine, fine. No need to get up."

Dad helps her sit at the table, ignoring her grumblings about the walker and setting it out of the way for now. I take the seat on her other side, and once she's settled, Dad sits beside her. He bows his head to say grace and we all follow suit.

"For what we are about to eat, may the Lord make us truly thankful. Amen," he says.

"Amen," I murmur.

The stew is delicious, as I knew it would be. Dad's always been the better cook, which is something Mom used to joke about when we were kids. *"I always heard that the way to a man's heart was through his stomach,"* she'd say, *"but if I would have followed that advice Walter would never have married me."*

I watch my brother out of the corner of my eye as we eat, trying to read him. We're obviously not identical, but we still look incredibly similar. Same dark brown hair, same slight build. Chase is taller and more muscular than me, owing to his love of sports, and my hair is long while his is short. But otherwise our features are the same.

Dad carefully spoons stew into Mom's mouth, wiping her chin when needed, and helping her when she picks up a piece of cornbread. After a few minutes he asks Chase if he called the bank today, and my brother nods.

"They'll meet with us tomorrow at nine," he says. They share a look, and an unspoken tension slinks into the room, cold and dark as a shadow.

My eyes search out Chase's, but he's focused on his food. I wait, willing him to look up at me, and finally he does. We stare at each other for a moment, the unspoken language of twins passing between us, and my heart sinks.

Something is wrong. Very wrong.

The meal passes without much conversation, and when Mom is done eating, I take her dishes and my own to the sink. Dad finishes his stew, then helps my mother into the other room, where I hear their gentle voices rising and falling as they talk.

Chase brings his dishes to the sink. "We need to talk," he says.

I reach over and place a bowl in the dishwasher. "I'll say," I respond. "The air is thicker than a winter fog in here. What were you and Dad talking about before dinner?"

"The farm."

"What about it?"

He takes a deep breath. "Emily, we're in trouble."

I scrub another dish and place it next to the bowl. "We've been in trouble before. But we always pull through, don't we? We'll do it again."

"Not this time, Em."

I stop washing dishes and look up at him. He runs a hand through his hair, not meeting my gaze. "I talked to Dad. Earlier today. He wasn't able to make the full mortgage payment this year. The bank agreed to a three month extension for the balance, but Dad hasn't been able to make that deadline, either."

Our farm, like most others, makes only one mortgage payment a year—usually after the harvest comes in and the crops have been sold for the season. For us, that means January. But if Dad got an extension, it would have been due last month, in April. I frown.

"Why hasn't he paid off the balance?" I ask.

"Money, Em. He said it was either pay the mortgage or pay

the doctors, so he opted to pay the bills for Mom's treatment and services."

We lapse into silence, my thoughts turning to our mother. She was once the life of this place. She adores Christmas and loves gardening, and the Kenworth Christmas Tree Farm combines the best of both. I remember following her around the property when I was only five or six years old as she checked on all the trees. She talked to them like they were people, and I remember asking her once why she did.

"They're alive, just like you and me, Emily. Why shouldn't I talk to them?"

But Mom hasn't been out tending to the trees in years. The sicker she got, the less able she was to get around, and the more time Dad spent taking care of her instead of taking care of the farm. Chase put off going to med school last year and came home to help out, but neither one of us knew how bad it was.

How bad it *is*.

"So are we going to lose the farm?" The words taste sour in my mouth.

He picks up a dish from the sink and loads it into the dishwasher. "I don't know. Dad and I need to talk with the bank to see if there's anything else we can do."

"Which is on the agenda for tomorrow, it sounds like."

He nods. "You want to come with us?"

But I shake my head. "No, I've got to finish the planting. Besides, I'd just be an extra body—you know I'm terrible in those situations."

We finish cleaning up from dinner in silence. I follow him out of the kitchen, pausing before turning out the light. "Chase?" I say, and he looks at me. I try to swallow the rock lodged in my throat. "The farm... the trees... it's home. We can't lose it."

He sighs. "We might not have a choice, Em."

"But if we do, even if there's just a slim chance of saving it, will you take it? Please, Chase. Please tell me you'll take it."

He looks at me for a long time. I stare right back into his blue eyes, a mirror of my own, knowing I don't have to say anything in order for him to understand. Finally he nods.

"I'll do what I can."

Chapter 2

Dad and Chase leave for town after breakfast the next day, so Mom and I spend the morning playing SkipBo. It was one of our favorite games when I was growing up, and it brings back fond memories. The game takes longer than usual, since Mom has a harder time picking up and holding the cards, but it's good exercise for her. I make us peppermint hot chocolate (her favorite) and bring a cozy blanket for her lap.

"Have you done much drawing lately?" she asks, placing a seven on one of the piles.

I shrug. "Not really. I've drawn a few things since Christmas, but not much."

"What kind of things?"

"I sketched Mr. Tumnus—the big squirrel who lives in the tree nearest the front porch?—eating a nut last week. And some of the year three saplings."

"Oh, that sounds lovely. Can I see it? Your picture of the trees?"

"Sure," I say, getting up from the table. I retrieve my current sketchbook from my room, flipping through the pages as I walk back into the kitchen. I find the page and hold it open, handing it to my mom.

"Oh honey," Mom says, reverently touching the page. "It's beautiful. It looks just like them."

Her comment makes me smile. The sketch is rough—all harsh lines and sharp angles. But it is unmistakably a picture of three young saplings. *Which* saplings, however, is impossible to tell. There's no way anyone would ever be able to pick them out of the hundreds of others just like them on the farm. But of course, Mom feels like she knows every single tree, from seed to sale.

We continue the card game, sipping our cocoa and chatting about whatever comes to mind. We reminisce about family vacations and holidays, favorite traditions and almost-tragedies. It's a "good" morning for her, and if it wasn't for her trembling hands and the ever-present walker at her side, I'd almost believe she wasn't sick at all.

Shannon, Mom's home health aide, shows up just as we finish the game. "Hi Shannon," I say, opening the door for her. "Come on in."

"Thanks, Emily. How's your mom today?"

I smile. "It seems to be a good day."

"Glad to hear it. Is she napping?"

"No, we just finished a game of SkipBo, and I was about to make some lunch. Would you like to join us?"

"No thanks, I already ate. I'll check on Kathy while you put that together."

She moves toward the living room while I head into the kitchen to make some grilled cheese sandwiches. While they're cooking, I pull out my phone and send a quick text to Chase.

Shannon is here, so after lunch I'm going to
run a couple errands. How's it going?

He hasn't responded by the time we've finished eating, and I'm not sure whether that's a good sign or a bad sign. I try not to worry.

"I've got some things to do in town, Mom," I say, giving her a kiss on the cheek. "I'll see you later, okay?"

"Alright, sweetie," she says. "Merry Christmas."

I smile. The phrase *Merry Christmas* has become a verbal catch-all in our family. It means hello, goodbye, I love you, good luck, etc. Sort of like *Aloha* in Hawaii.

"Merry Christmas, Mom," I say. "Merry Christmas, Shannon."

"See you later, Emily," Shannon says, giving me a smile.

Pulling on my boots, I head out into the damp air. Spring in the Cascade Mountain Range is pretty wet, and the sky overhead looks as if it can't make up its mind whether to rain or not. Climbing into my old Ford pickup, I turn the key and buckle my seatbelt. Usually I like to roll down my windows, but since it's a bit chilly this morning I keep them up. The radio hasn't worked in years, but I don't mind—the silence feels comforting, like an old blanket. I wouldn't be able to hear much over the rumble of the engine, anyway.

It's a twenty-minute drive into the heart of Echo Ridge. Main Street makes an elongated S through the town, with small streets and side avenues winding off of it. Though the area must have been cleared to make way for the town initially, it hardly feels like you've left the woods at all. Tall cedars lean over the roads like nosy neighbors, their branches intertwining to form a loose canopy overhead, while clumps of daisies and foxglove add splashes of color amid all the green.

Pulling into the parking lot of McKinley's Ace Hardware, I park the truck and cut the engine. My list isn't long—just some twine and a few other odds and ends—so this shouldn't take too long.

"Hi, welcome in," a teenage girl calls as I enter the store. I wave in greeting and grab a hand basket, heading for one of the far aisles.

I know my way around McKinley's Ace almost as well as I know my way around the farm. It's been a fixture in Echo Ridge for as long as I can remember, and owning a farm means our family is on a first-name basis with the owners, and most of the employees, too. I find what I need without any trouble, then head back up to the front.

Aerosmith wails over the sound system as I place my purchases on the counter. The teenager who greeted me is busy with another customer, so it's the owner, Mr. McKinley, who helps me.

"Hi there, Emily, how are you today?" he asks, scanning my purchases.

"Hi Steve. I'm fine, thanks," I say.

"How're your parents doing?"

"They're good."

"Glad to hear it. And Chase? Is he doing all right?"

"Yup. We're all good."

Mr. McKinley finishes ringing up my items and gives me a total.

"I never heard whether your brother got in to med school or not," he says as I pull out my wallet to pay.

Inwardly I sigh. I really hate small talk, even with people I know. I mean, who really likes talking about boring stuff like that, anyway?

"He did, but was granted deferment in order to help out on the farm for a bit," I say.

"I bet it's nice to have him home." His lined face creases as he gives me a smile, which I return without hesitation.

"It is. I really missed him when he was at school."

"I'm sure you did. Say, did you hear that Jackson is coming home, too?"

"He is?"

"Yep, his flight gets in this afternoon."

"That's great. Did he get a job locally?" I ask, tapping my credit card to pay. The sooner this transaction is done, the sooner the conversation will be, too.

"Nah, he's still looking. But we figured he could apply for jobs online just as easily here at home, and then we're not paying double rent. Besides, maybe he'll find a job in Seattle." He looks hopeful as he hands me back my receipt.

I smile. "I'm sure your wife would love to have him close by."

"She's certainly looking forward to it. Say hi to your folks for me."

"Will do. See ya."

I take my purchases and head back out to my truck. A light drizzle is now falling, but the clouds are patchy and I don't expect it to last long. I glance at my phone—still no message from Chase. I consider swinging by the bank on my way home to see if he and Dad are still there, but I talk myself out of it, deciding instead to stop in and say hi to Sophie.

I drive a few blocks down Main Street and turn into the Safeway parking lot. *The Jitterbug* is a hip little coffee bar that sits in the northwest corner of the lot, and Sophie is the assistant manager. The proximity to the high school makes it a popular haunt with the younger crowd, but it wasn't until Sophie started working here that I actually began patronizing it.

The bell above the door jingles merrily as I pull it open, the rich aroma of coffee filling my nostrils and making my mouth water. I spot Sophie behind the counter, mixing up a drink for the customer on the other side. I wave as she glances up, and walk over to wait by the till.

"One tall vanilla cappuccino for Richard," she says, handing the drink to the waiting man. He smiles and thanks her, and she comes over to greet me. "Hey you," she says. "Coming up for air?"

"Almost finished with the planting," I say. "Then I'll be free."

She laughs. "Liar. After the planting it's what, fertilizing? Weeding? You've always got something going on."

"Guilty as charged," I say with a light laugh.

"So what'll it be?" she asks.

"I'll just have a regular iced tea to go."

"Are you sure? I could make you a gingerbread latte..." She waggles her eyebrows at me, her short black hair falling across her dark forehead into her eyes.

"But it's not in season," I say, surprised.

She dismisses my excuse with an impatient wave of her hand. "Oh, please. We promote things seasonally, but we can make stuff year round. Mamá is always asking me to make her horchata cappuccinos."

"Really? So you can make anything you offer, anytime?"

"Well, not everything—we can only get eggnog in

November and December, but pretty much everything else is an option."

"This is dangerous information," I say, and she laughs.

"One gingerbread latte, coming up," she says, ringing me up. I tap my card on the reader, and she gasps.

"Emily Noelle Kenworth, what have you done to your nails!" she howls. I pull my hand back quickly, but she snatches it before I can hide my fingers. She *tsks* as she examines my short, dirty nails. "*Ay, qué fuerte!* How many times have I told you to wear gloves, Em? Your cuticles are a mess!"

"Sorry, Soph—planting season, remember?"

"It's no excuse," she says, giving me a dirty look as she heads off to make my drink.

I watch her in silence for a few minutes, searching for something to say. "Oh, hey, did you know that Jack is coming back to town?"

"Who?"

"Jackson McKinley."

"Where'd you hear that?"

"His dad told me when I was at the store this morning."

She adds whipped cream and a sprinkle of nutmeg to the top of my drink. "Is he just coming for a visit?" she asks.

"No, his dad said he's coming to stay. At least for a while."

"Huh. I didn't think he'd ever come back. He couldn't *wait* to get out of here after high school."

I roll my eyes. "Him and everybody else."

She gives me a look, holding out my drink. "*I* didn't take off, did I?" she says.

I smile. "No, you didn't, and for that I am eternally grateful." I reach for the cup and she glares at my fingernails.

"You're getting a mani *stat*," she says.

I sigh. "Not until I finish the planting."

She rolls her eyes dramatically. "Fine. When will that be?"

"I should be done this week."

"'K. I'm off next Friday. Put it on your schedule—I won't take no for an answer."

"Yes, ma'am," I say, with a tiny salute.

She narrows her eyes at me, but it softens into a grin a second later. The bell above the door rings, and we both glance behind me. A middle-aged couple comes in, signaling the end of our visit.

"See ya later, Em," she says.

"See ya, Sophie. Thanks again for the drink."

"Wear your gloves!" she calls.

I wave and head out the door.

The rain shower has cleared by the time I hop back into my pickup and head up the mountain to the farm. Patches of brilliant blue sky are visible between the clouds, hinting at summer and higher temps. I watch the sky with a mixture of delight and concern. I need to get those saplings in the ground before it gets any warmer.

Chase and Dad are standing in the kitchen talking when I come in the back door. "Hey, sugarplum," Dad says when he sees me. "Did you get what you needed in town?"

I hold up the bag from Ace. "Yup. And stopped in to see Sophie."

"Bring me anything?" Chase asks.

"I would have," I say, lifting an eyebrow at him, "but you never responded to my text, so I didn't know you'd be home."

He makes a face. "Sorry about that. We were busy."

"Have you been at the bank all this time?" I glance between him and Dad, who sighs heavily.

"Yes, we were at the bank. Have a seat, Emmy-girl, we need to talk." He indicates the kitchen table across the room, and we make our way over.

A quiver of fear twists inside of me. "Your promise?" I ask Chase in a low voice. He nods but won't meet my eye, which hardly helps me feel any easier.

The three of us take our seats at the worn oval table. I can't remember a single family meal that didn't take place in this room. Sunday dinners, birthday celebrations, holiday meals—sharing food around the table is something our family has always done. We shared grief here, too. Mom's diagnosis. Grandpa's fall. Even when our old border collie Scout died, we gathered around this table to mourn, drawing comfort and strength from one another.

Now, as I look between the faces of the two men I love and respect more than any others on Earth, a rope of anxiety coils in my gut. Whatever they have to say, it's not good news.

Dad pulls his hat off and drops it on the table, running a hand up through his thinning, salt-and-pepper hair. "Chase said he told you that we weren't able to make the mortgage payment earlier this year," he says.

I nod. "He said there wasn't enough money; it was either pay the mortgage or pay the medical bills."

Dad nods. "That's what I did, sure enough. But now the bank is threatening to foreclose on us."

I glance at my brother, then back at my dad. "But you talked to them, right? What did they say?"

Dad doesn't answer, his eyes fixed on his hat resting on the table. I look to Chase, who's watching Dad. Finally my brother faces me.

"Legally, they have every right to foreclose the mortgage and repossess the property," he says, "since we're more than ninety days delinquent."

The blood drains from my face. "Please tell me that's not going to happen."

"It might still happen," Chase says, "but I was able to buy us some time."

"How?"

Dad has been quiet while Chase explained, but now he scowls. "I still don't know how I let you talk me into that, son," he says. "It ain't right."

"What's not right? What did you talk him into?" I ask, my eyes darting between them.

Chase sighs. "I pulled the money we've been saving for med school out of my account." He glances at Dad, who's staring at the table, his mouth set in a hard line. "I got us caught up on the payment and late fees, but the bank said if we can't make the mortgage payment on time next year, they're going to foreclose."

I'm so shocked I don't move. My parents have been pinching and saving practically our entire lives to send us to college. It was quite a relief to them when I didn't show any interest in leaving the farm, because then it could all go to Chase and his plans to become a doctor. He managed to get his undergrad with scholarships and grants, so there's been a big chunk sitting in the bank, waiting for med school. But apparently not anymore.

"How much?" I ask, half afraid of the answer.

"Almost all of it," Chase says quietly, not looking at me.

Dad balls his hand resting on the table into a fist, his eyes misty. "I never should have let you touch that money," he says, his voice heavy with regret.

"We didn't have a choice, Dad," Chase says. Then, turning to me, "Dad's been dipping into their savings for years, trying to keep the farm afloat. Then when Mom got worse..." He shrugs. "There's nothing left."

"I should have taken better care of y'all," Dad says, his voice husky.

I reach out and cover his hand with my own. "You have taken better care of us than anyone else in this world ever could," I say. "You and Mom both."

Chase nods beside me. "She's right, Dad. Now it's our turn to take care of you. You never intended to run the farm yourselves forever anyway, did you? We're just cashing in on our inheritance a little early." He gives Dad a smile, then looks at me. I nod and smile as well, squeezing Dad's hand.

"It'll be okay," I say. "You take care of Mom—Chase and I can manage the farm."

"And how do you plan to do that?" Dad asks. "Even if we can make the next payment, the farm's been bleeding money for years. We're doomed."

Chase looks determined. "We're not giving up yet, Dad— we'll do everything we can to save the farm." He glances at me. "I promise."

Chapter 3

I manage to get the rest of the saplings planted over the next week. Chase and I don't talk much about the plan going forward—he's been spending all his time in the office with Dad, looking through the books—so I've been doing what I do best: tending to the trees.

Taking care of the trees has always been what I loved best about owning the farm. Gathering the seeds, planting the saplings, shearing, fertilizing, and pruning—caring for the Christmas trees is what fills my soul and brings me joy. I talk to them, too, just like Mom used to. And though I'd never admit it to anyone, I feel like they talk to me, too.

I head toward the house for lunch one afternoon and see my brother sitting out on the front steps. He's not doing anything, just staring out at the woods, which isn't a good sign. He watches me as I walk up to sit on the step beside him.

"So how does it look?" I ask.

Chase blows out his breath, leaning his elbows on his knees. "Pretty bad, Em, I'm not going to lie."

My stomach drops. "Really?"

"Yeah. Mom used to keep the books, you know—she was always better at numbers and math than Dad was. But all that came to a screeching halt when she got sick. I think Dad did what he could, but there hasn't been any budget for years—invoices are unpaid, accounts are backed up; money's been going out but there hasn't been nearly enough coming in." He sighs, dropping his head into his hands. "I don't know, Em. It might be too late. We might lose the farm *and* all my money for school."

"We won't let that happen," I say, rubbing his back. "We'll figure it out."

"We're going to need professional help to figure it out, Em. We can't do it on our own."

"What do you mean?"

He sits back, looking at me. "From a business consultant. Someone who can take a look at the big picture and tell us what to do to turn things around."

I stare at him. "You can't be serious."

"Of course I'm serious."

"You want to let a stranger come here, pry into our personal business, and tell us everything we're doing wrong?"

"That's not what they do."

"That's exactly what they do." I get up from the step, dusting off my jeans. "Besides, we don't even know any business consultants."

"That's what the internet is for."

I roll my eyes. "See? A stranger."

I step up on the porch, intending to walk past my brother into the house, but he catches my arm. "Please, Em. I can't do this without you."

It's the 'please' that gets me. Usually my brother tries to

tease or cajole me into going along with whatever scheme he's cooked up for us. *"Come on, Em,"* he'll say, with that devilish half smile that tells me I'll be missing out on something grand if I don't give in. It only works about half the time, but that doesn't bother him—even for as close as we are, Chase has always been an independent soul. He certainly *wants* me to tag along with him, but he's always been fine on his own. So when he says *"Please, Em,"* in the voice he never lets anyone hear except me, I know he means it. He doesn't just want me to come along, he *needs* me.

I look out past the sparse lawn, to the trees and woods that come almost right up to the edge of the house. Towering pines with trunks as big around as tires stand like sentinels all around us, the ground thick with fallen needles. I sigh. I love this place. It's home, and I would do anything to save it.

"All right," I say. "What do we need to do?"

I hate to admit it, but Sophie was right: there's always something going on at the farm. But it's not fertilizing or weeding just yet—with the planting and transplanting done for the year, I turn my attention to the shearing.

Before Chase and I were old enough to help, Dad used to hire extra hands to assist with the shearing. The shearing knives are long and incredibly sharp, and more than once Dad had to take an employee to the ER for stitches. It became a rite of passage in our family, being allowed to learn how to shear the trees, and for several years the four of us were able to get the work done ourselves. But then Mom got worse, Chase went off to school, and it was just Dad and I. This year I'm working practically by myself, so I'll need to hire some help to get it all done in time.

Whenever someone unfamiliar with the Christmas tree business hears the term *shearing* they think of sheep. It works in much the same way, except instead of shaving the trees bald, shearing is merely trimming them into a more conical shape, to coax the tree to grow thicker and fuller rather than rounder or taller. Aside from harvesting, it's one of the most labor-intensive and time-consuming tasks on the farm, *and* we've only got about a month to get it all done.

I make some calls, and bright and early on Monday morning, four guys are waiting by the barn for their instructions. Mario and Josh have worked with us before, but the other two are new. Not new to the Christmas tree business, thank goodness—I'm busy enough as it is without having to train any newbies on safety or proper technique. Dad helped me sharpen all the blades last week, so once I let the men know which rows and fields to shear, we get to work.

The shearing goes smoothly for the next three days. The men are good, hard workers, and the rows get done quickly. On Thursday morning I take my shearing knife and shin guards to one of the far fields to work on the ten-year-old trees. Most of them will be harvested come autumn, which makes me feel more protective than I do about the trees that have a few more years to grow. A bad shearing on a tree with two more growing seasons can be overcome, but if you botch a shearing on a tree slated for harvest, you're worse off than a snowman in a sauna.

I've been working for nearly an hour when I notice my brother in the distance, coming down the hill with another man. Chase calls out my name, and I lift a hand in acknowledgement before making another swipe down the branches.

I've finished two more trees by the time they reach me. "Hey, Emily," Chase says as the two men stop beside me. "I've brought reinforcements. You remember Jack, don't you?"

I hadn't recognized him from a distance, but as I look into the face of the man standing in front of me, my heart stutters. He's an inch or two taller than Chase, with dark hair, a clean shaven jaw, and nearly perfect teeth. *Jackson McKinley!* my heart seems to sigh. Jack was an all-star athlete at our little high school back in the day, which is how he knows Chase—and the reason I know him, too, I guess. Every girl in school was crazy about Jack at one time or another, and Sophie and I used to ~~drool over~~—*ahem*—admire him politely from a distance.

"Jack." I say, glancing at his polo shirt and slacks. "You look a little overdressed to be shearing trees, but we'll take all the help we can get." I grin, but confusion clouds his face.

"Um..."

"Not that kind of help," Chase says, rolling his eyes. "He's going to help us with the business."

Now it's my turn to look confused. "I thought you were going to hire a business consultant?" I say, looking between them.

Chase grins, clapping Jack on the shoulder. "Which is exactly what I did."

My eyebrows shoot up as I look at Jack. "You're a business consultant?" I ask.

"Not exactly. But I just graduated with my MBA, and that's what I'm hoping to do."

"So we get to be the first client on his resume," Chase says, tossing him a grin. Jack returns the smile, then holds out his hand to me.

"It's Emily, right?" he asks.

I nod, shaking his hand. "Yeah."

"When I heard that Jack was back in town, I called him up to see if he'd be interested in helping us out, or if he knew someone who could. We met up for coffee this morning to talk things over, and lucky for us, he's willing to take the job."

"Sounds like a plan, then," I say. "What does Dad think?"

"Haven't talked to him yet—I thought you might want to do it together. Can you come up to the house?"

I glance at the long row of trees I still have to shear and sigh. I turn, an excuse on the tip of my tongue, but the look in Chase's eyes stops the words from leaving my lips. *Please, Em,* they say, and I swallow.

"How long do you think it'll take?"

"Not long," Chase says, at exactly the same time Jack says, "I can come back another time."

We all look at each, laughing quietly. Jack clears his throat.

"I never meant to impose," he says with an apologetic smile, "but Chase was so insistent that I come back and talk with you all right now that I couldn't refuse. I didn't know we'd be interrupting your work."

I lift an eyebrow. "You, I believe, but Chase knew darn well that I'd be working," I say, giving him a look. Chase rolls his eyes.

"You're *always* working, Em," he groans, "but you can take a break whenever you want." A grin splits his face, revealing the dimples I didn't inherit. "Besides, it's not like you can get fired."

I shake my head at him, but the smile tugging on my lips tells him he's won. "Fine," I say, "but I want it noted that there's not really a reason for me to go. I trust you on this, Chase."

Chase's look softens. "Come on," he says. "Dad's expecting us."

With another sigh I sheath the long shearing knife and tuck it under my arm. "One hour," I say. "And I don't promise to actually pay attention."

Chase grins, throwing an arm around Jack's shoulders. "Noted. Let's go."

Dad is waiting for us in the living room when we get up to the house. "Welcome back, Jackson," he says, extending a hand to Chase's friend.

"Thank you, sir," Jack says.

"Please, call me Walter," Dad says.

Jack nods. "Walter." He looks around. "Is Mrs. Kenworth here?"

"Kathy is napping at the moment," Dad says, indicating the sofa and chairs. "Come in and have a seat."

I slip quietly up the stairs to my room, the murmur of men's voices a low hum as they situate themselves. Grabbing my sketchbook and pencil, I head back to the living room and curl up on one end of the sofa. Chase sits at my feet, while Jack and Dad sit in the two armchairs opposite.

"So what have you been doing with yourself?" Dad asks Jack.

"School, mostly. Got my undergrad at UW, then went to Michigan for my MBA. I had an internship in Arizona last summer, like a lot of my classmates, but with the way the economy is right now, not many of those turned into job offers."

"I'm sorry to hear that," Dad says, his voice sincere.

I've been listening to the conversation while scrutinizing the sketch of Mr. Tumnus when a movement outside the window catches my eye. A robin has landed on the sparse grass beyond the house. He hops and pecks intermittently at the ground, searching for food. I flip to a fresh page in my book and quickly sketch out a rough outline of the bird.

I tune out the voices around me while I flesh out my drawing. The robin darts here and there on the grass until, with a flash of wings, he alights on the branch of a nearby pine tree. I look down at his likeness, adding some texture to his feathered breast and shading to his bright eye, but when I glance up from my sketchbook he's gone.

"That sounds like a fair idea," Dad is saying. "What do you think, Emily?"

I look up when I hear my name, a faint blush painting my cheeks. "Sorry, what was that?"

Dad chuckles, but Chase frowns. "Jack has offered to consult with us about the farm for half the going rate," he says.

Surprised, I look to Jack. "That's very generous of you," I say.

He smiles, making his angular jawline look almost square. "I can't guarantee anything, of course," he says. "But until I find a permanent job, I'm happy to help. The stipulation is that when I *do* find employment elsewhere, I'll need to leave off my work here," he says.

"How long do you think until that happens?" Dad asks, placing his hands behind his head and leaning back in his chair. Jack shrugs.

"With the current market, it's anyone's guess. A month? Two? It could be next year for all I know." He lifts a hand as if to run it through his hair, but stops and brings it down again. "At the moment, I don't have any interviews set up and hardly any leads. I'm applying to jobs blind."

Everyone is silent for a moment, and I wonder if that's what will happen to me if we lose the farm. Will I be looking for a job this time next year? What can I even *do* if it comes to that? The trees are all I know.

I look down at the half-finished sketch in front of me. A quick glance out the window confirms the robin hasn't come back, and I bite my lip, trying to remember where exactly the feathers changed colors. I add more shading to his underside and wings, sketching a bit of the grass he's standing on, too. I'm so absorbed in my work, I practically jump when I hear Jack's voice right next to me.

"Did you just draw that?" he asks.

I resist the urge to cover the picture with my arm, feeling suddenly exposed. "Um, yeah, I did."

"Wow. That's amazing. I didn't know you were an artist."

I laugh lightly and unfold myself from the couch, using the movement as an excuse to close my sketchbook. "Not really. It's just a hobby." With a bit of alarm, I realize that we're alone in the room. Where did Dad and Chase get off to?

Seeing my look, he offers me a smile. "Your dad went to check on your mom. Chase wanted to grab something from the office to show me."

"Oh."

We stand there awkwardly—well, *I* stand there awkwardly, Jack stands there looking like a supermodel—until he clears his throat. "So, you didn't seem to be paying much attention to the conversation earlier," he says.

I grimace. "Sorry, it's nothing personal, I just..." I shrug. "I don't pay much attention to the business side of running the farm. My knowledge and expertise lies in the more physical aspect of doing things around here. I told Chase I support the idea of hiring a business consultant to help us, but I don't really even know what that entails. I was planning to leave it all up to him."

He looks bemused. "I appreciate your honesty. And I hope you'll be more comfortable getting involved as we move forward."

I don't really know what to say in response to that, but thankfully Chase walks back into the room carrying a large folder. He gives me a look, but I merely duck my head and sidle out of the room. I return my sketchbook to my bedroom, and when Chase doesn't call after me, I head back out to the fields to continue the shearing. He can lecture me later.

Chapter 4

Coming downstairs the next morning, I walk into the kitchen and abruptly stop short. There, sitting at the counter, is Jackson McKinley. He looks up at my entrance.

"What are you doing here?" I blurt out.

He gives me a sarcastic half-smile. "Good morning to you, too."

I frown. "Sorry. Um, good morning?" I pause. "But seriously, what are you doing here?"

He chuckles. "Your dad let me in. Judging from your reaction, you didn't hear that part of the conversation yesterday?"

A flash of embarrassment warms my neck. "Um, no. Sorry."

He shrugs. "I'm here for a tour of the property, to get an idea of the 'hands on' aspect of the farm before going over the books with Chase. He said you know more about the day-to-day business, and since you like to get up and get going, we should do it first thing in the morning."

"Oh."

He falls silent, and I glance at my watch. My brother's not

usually an early riser, but if he was expecting company he should have been up by now.

I stand there shifting from one foot to the other for a moment, wondering what I should say or do. Jack and Chase were friends back in high school, but my brother and I ran in different circles, so Jack and I didn't interact a whole lot. I feel strangely tongue-tied with him sitting casually in my kitchen.

"Um, would you like some coffee?" I finally ask.

He brightens. "Coffee would be great, thanks."

I let out a breath, shifting into my usual morning routine, trying not to think about—or care—that his eyes follow me around the kitchen. After starting the coffeemaker, I excuse myself to ~~strangle~~ find my brother. As I suspected, he's still in bed, fast asleep. I jostle him awake.

"Hey sleepyhead," I say, shaking him, "in case you weren't aware, Jackson McKinley is currently sitting in our kitchen."

Chase rolls over, rubbing his eyes, then sits bolt upright. "Jack! Oh man, what time is it? I overslept!"

"Calm down, it's fine."

He runs his hands through his hair, looking around to see how much getting ready he has to do.

"Why didn't you tell me he was coming today?"

He gives me a hard look. "If you'd have been listening to the conversation yesterday, you would have known."

I fold my arms across my chest. "That's not fair. I told you I was going to let you handle getting a consultant—I don't understand why I had to be there in the first place."

"And I told you that I needed your support."

He pulls back the covers and swings his legs over the side of the bed. I huff a sigh.

"Fine, I'm sorry. I should have paid more attention yesterday."

He grunts and picks up a t-shirt from the floor, smelling it before pulling it on. Getting up, he grabs a pair of jeans lying near the door. "Do you mind?" he says sharply, glancing at me.

I frown. "I'm sorry, Chase. Honest. I'll do better."

His look softens, and he sighs. "Thanks, Em. I really do need your help."

"I'll do my best." I clear my throat. "So we're giving him a tour of the place?"

"Yeah, Jack said yesterday that he'll need to see the whole farm and look over the books before he can put together a business plan for us."

"Okay."

He pauses in the act of putting on his deodorant. "What?"

I grimace. "I just wasn't expecting to lose a day's worth of work today."

"The shearing?"

"Yeah."

"I thought you hired some help?"

"I did, but I don't want to just leave them by themselves. I was going to work with them. Besides, you know I always shear the ones slated for harvest myself."

He rolls his eyes. "They know what they're doing, Em, they'll be fine for a day."

"It's not them I'm worried about," I grumble, thinking of my trees.

"Tell Jack I'll be down in a few, okay?"

"Fine. But don't take too long—you know I'm terrible at small talk."

He mumbles something unintelligible and I leave the room, shutting the door behind me.

I head back to the kitchen and my unexpected guest. Jack isn't sitting at the counter anymore—he's wandered over to the wall full of framed photographs. I go to the cupboard and pull out three mugs.

"Is this you?" he asks.

I look at the photograph he's pointing to. It's one of me holding a small drawing with a blue ribbon attached.

"Yeah. Fifth grade art show."

Glancing at a small framed sketch of a deer standing in a grove of trees on the same wall, he asks, "And is this it? The picture you're holding?"

"Yup."

"Wow. That's pretty good—especially for fifth grade."

He looks around the room. There are a few more framed pieces of mine gracing the walls, and he studies them. Most of them are inked and watercolored, but a couple are only in pencil. I watch him, feeling strangely uneasy, until he finally turns back to the photographs.

I follow his progress along the wall, taking in our family's story one picture at a time. The photos haven't been updated in years, so most of them are of me and Chase as kids and teens. There are a lot of pictures of my brother playing on his various sports teams, a few of my Mom and I out on the farm, one of me playing chess with my dad, and lots of the four of us grouped together in various locations—usually somewhere on the farm or on vacation.

"Your family seems to be really close," he says.

I nod, then realize he isn't looking at me and clear my throat. "Yeah, we are."

"How come there aren't any pictures of you playing sports?"

"Probably because I don't play any sports."

"Really?" He turns to look at me. "Huh. I just assumed since Chase was so athletic, you were, too."

I shrug. "My brother and I are very different, actually."

"Is that why you didn't really hang out with us at school?"

"I guess. Chase and I are very close, but we had different friend groups in high school because our interests weren't the same."

I pull out the creamer from the fridge and put the sugar bowl on the counter with a couple spoons. Jack comes back and sits down on a bar stool. I pour coffee into the three cups and hand him one. "Thanks," he says.

"Chase said he'll be down shortly," I say, taking a careful sip from my mug.

"You like it black?" Jack says, his eyebrows raised.

"For a few sips, yeah. It wakes me up faster."

He chuckles. "I might have to try that sometime. I'm not much of a morning person."

I smirk. "Neither is Chase. He's lucky we live on a tree farm instead of a dairy farm or he'd be toast."

"But you like mornings?"

"I don't mind them. It's quiet in the morning. I can be alone without being seen as antisocial."

Jack stirs his drink, takes a sip, then adds a bit more sugar. "You consider yourself antisocial?"

I take another sip. "Antisocial is probably the wrong word. But I like to be alone."

He chuckles. "Fair enough. So you like mornings—spent alone, preferably; you're a talented artist, and you take your coffee black. Anything else I should know about you?"

My teenage heart swoons at his interest, but my adult brain frowns. "Why do you need to know anything about me?"

"Well, if we're going to be working together, it'd be nice to get to know you a bit. I know Chase pretty well, but I hardly know you at all."

He gives me a look, as if he'd *like* to get to know me, and my heart rate kicks up a notch. Keeping my face neutral, I add a bit of creamer and sugar to my cup and stir, wondering what to say. I've already spoken more to Jack in the last fifteen minutes than I have with anyone besides my family in ages.

Thankfully Jack changes the subject. "Did Chase get into med school? I thought he was on track to become a doctor, so I was surprised to see him in town. I thought he'd be in school forever."

"He was accepted to UW School of Medicine, but we needed his help at home, so he's deferred for a year."

"I'm sorry to hear that."

I lift a shoulder. "It happens. You'd probably do the same for your family, if they needed you."

He laughs. "I don't know about that. It'd take something pretty drastic to keep me in Echo Ridge for an extended period of time."

"What makes you say that?"

The sound of footsteps on the stairs makes us both turn, and a minute later Chase comes around the corner into the kitchen.

"Sorry I overslept, man," he says to Jack.

"No problem. Emily and I have just been getting reac-quainted."

I lift an eyebrow at him over the rim of my cup. That's

stretching it a bit, since I still don't know anything about him, and what he knows about me isn't interesting or relevant.

"Great. So are we ready to get started?" Chase asks.

I hand him the remaining cup of coffee. "Caffeinate first— then we'll get going."

I finish my own mug and rinse it out in the sink, then sit down on the little stool in the mudroom and put my boots on. Grabbing my rain jacket from its hook, I look back at my brother through the doorway. "I'm going to get the men started on the shearing," I call to him. "Come find me when you're ready."

I breathe a sigh of relief as I leave the house, rolling my shoulders in an effort to dislodge the tension held there. It's been a long time since I've had to carry on a conversation with a virtual stranger, and I'm out of practice. I walk toward the barn, pausing as I pass an ancient cedar. I press my hand against the trunk and look up into its branches,

"If only people were like trees," I murmur, "I wouldn't worry so much."

I blow a kiss upwards and pat the rough bark, then continue on my way to start the shearing.

I'm just finishing my first row of trees when I see Chase and Jack walking toward me. Sheathing my shearing knife and unbuckling my shinguards, I set them down and go to meet them.

"You ready?" Chase asks.

I shrug. "Guess so. Where are we starting?"

"Wherever you think is best," he says.

"Let's head up to the greenhouses, then."

The three of us walk in relative silence to the southern edge of the property. Jack now carries a clipboard, and every so often he asks Chase a question and makes a note. The morning started out overcast as usual, but by the time we get to our destination the clouds look as if they'll be breaking up.

"Here we are," I say, pulling a wad of keys out of my pocket and unlocking the door to the far greenhouse. Jack raises his brow.

"You worried about much theft, way out here?"

I give him a humorous smile. "From the local critters, yes."

"Oh." He writes something down.

"So this is it," I say as we step inside. "We start the seeds in here, and grow them until they're ready to be hardened off."

Jack starts walking down one of the long aisles, taking notes. "How many different species do you grow?"

"Only three," I say. "Two firs and a spruce. The seedlings stay in the greenhouse for one to three years, before being transplanted to outdoor beds."

"Any electrical usage in here?"

"Lights and fans occasionally, but mostly we just need access to water."

He makes a note and we head back outside. We walk along the south road toward the barn. "These are the transplant beds," I say as we go past them. "The seedlings come from the greenhouse and stay here for another year or two before being planted in the fields."

"We used to buy seedlings and transplants from a nursery," Chase adds. "But then we built the greenhouses, so now we grow them all ourselves."

"Why did you make the switch?" Jack asks. "Is it more cost effective?"

Chase and I look at each other. "Yes and no," I say. "It's probably a wash, honestly. But this gives us more control *and* flexibility when it comes to planting. We don't have to wait for shipments to arrive—"

"—or rush to get them planted when they do," Chase finishes.

"I see," Jack says.

Passing the transplant beds, we come up to the barn. Contrary to what the name implies, our barn houses equipment rather than farm animals. We spend more than an hour inside, going over the various pieces of machinery and tools: what they're used for, how much they cost, the maintenance required, when they'll need to be replaced, etc. Chase holds his own at the onslaught of questions, which I appreciate. He's always been better at conversation than me.

From the barn we cross the south road, passing through another patch of transplant beds and my dad's old workshop. Coming abreast of the dilapidated building, Jack stops.

"What's this?" he asks.

"Just an old workshop," Chase answers.

"Workshop?"

"Yeah. Our dad had a woodworking hobby when we were younger, and this is where he kept his tools and made everything. But he hasn't used it in years."

Jack steps up to the window and peeks inside. "So what's it used for now?"

"Nothing," I say.

"Not even storage?"

"No—it's not fully finished on the inside."

"Hmm." He looks through the window again, then walks around the small building. "Can we take a look inside?" he asks.

I shrug. "Sure." I dig through my keys to find the right one, then unlock the door and step aside. Jack enters first, followed by Chase and myself.

"What gives?" I murmur to my brother, but he just shakes his head.

"Beats me."

The workshop has been locked up for years, and it shows. Though it was cleaned out before doing so, a few random blocks of wood still litter the floor, which bears evidence of mice. A beat-up workbench and small, broken table are the only pieces of furniture in the room. The grimy windows barely let in any light, and piles of dirt and old sawdust cover every surface. Jack flips on the light switch, but nothing happens.

"Dad had them shut off the electricity when we cleaned it out, since it wasn't going to be in use anymore," Chase says.

"But it's wired for electricity?"

"Yeah, he just never got around to finishing the interior after doing that," Chase says, indicating the exposed studs on all but one wall.

Jacks nods, crossing the room. "Do these doors open?" he asks, indicating the double barn doors at the back of the room.

Chase shrugs. "Don't see why they wouldn't."

Jack continues making notes as he paces out the room. We go back outside and he looks up. "Does the roof leak?"

"It shouldn't," I say. "It was replaced the same time as the roofs on the house and the barn, about seven years ago."

Jack nods, making another note, then looks up at me expectantly. "Ready when you are, Emily."

We take a quick stop at the seed orchard on the far side of the workshop, which helps to block the house from view of the highway, then make our way down the main road to the parking lot. "This is where our customers park," I say. "We set up a temporary office at the far end—there, by that little shed —and the trimming block and baler go beside it."

"What else do you sell besides Christmas trees?"

"In past years we've made wreaths from cuttings to sell, but other than that, nothing," I say.

"We have complimentary coffee and cocoa for our customers when they come," Chase pipes up, "and candy canes."

Jack gives him a smile and jots something down. "Are there any other structures on the property?"

"No," Chase says. "You've seen it all but the tree fields now."

"And how many employees does the farm have?"

"Two full-time employees—Dad and myself," I say, "and anywhere from two to ten part-time employees throughout the year. Usually seasonal or temporary, depending on the farm's needs."

Jack nods. "Alright. I think I have what I need from Emily, and the rest—acreage, utilities, taxes, and whatnot—I can get from Chase when we take a look at the office."

"Great," Chase says. "Should we grab some lunch and then look over the books?"

"Sounds good to me," Jack says.

"You two go ahead," I say. "I'm going to finish the row I was on before lunch."

I wave goodbye and head off in the opposite direction.

Chapter 5

J ack said he'll need a few days to put a business plan together, so until then, work continues as usual. The shearing is coming along well, and on Friday I'm finishing up my tenth tree of the day when my phone rings. Pulling it out of my back pocket, I see Sophie's face on my screen.

"Hey Sophie," I say. "What's up?"

"Hey yourself," she says, in her I'm-trying-not-to-be-annoyed-but-I'm-actually-very-frustrated voice.

"Uh-oh," I say. "What's wrong?"

Her response is to sigh deeply and loudly. "Our mani appointment?"

I groan, closing my eyes. "Oh Sophie, I'm so sorry. I completely forgot."

"I assumed as much," she grumbles.

I glance at how many trees I've finished, then look at how many I have left to go, and my heart sinks. "Can we maybe do it another day?"

"If we postpone, you're just going to forget again."

I sigh. "I'm sorry. It's just that..." I let my voice trail off, realizing that no excuse is a good enough reason for bailing on my friend. "Never mind. Let me put this stuff away and I'll come right over. I should be there within the hour."

"You mean it?" The incredulity in her voice is hard to miss, and I grimace.

"I mean it. I'm sorry I haven't made time for you sooner. But I value your friendship and I'm going to do better. Starting now."

"Thanks, Em. I'll see you soon, then?"

"You will. I promise."

Forty minutes later, I pull into the tiny parking lot of the fourplex where Sophie lives. Echo Ridge has only one large apartment complex, and it was built within the last five years, so while they're very nice, they're also very expensive. Which means that rather than spend the entirety of her meager salary on rent, Sophie shares an apartment with her cousin Maria, in a fourplex owned by her uncle. It's a bit run-down, with moss growing along the edges of the roof and large potholes in the parking lot, but the rent is cheap and she can still afford groceries. And nail polish—which she insists is more important than bread and milk anyway.

Cutting the engine, I grab my wallet and phone and hop out of the truck. It rained all night so there are puddles everywhere, but I manage to avoid the worst ones as I pick my way to Sophie's front door. She opens it wide after my first knock.

"You came!" she says, ushering me inside with an airy kiss on each cheek.

"I told you I was coming," I say, taking off my jacket. She gives me a look.

"I know how you are about your trees, Em. I'm lucky your guilty conscience got to you today."

As soon as I set down my stuff, she grabs my hand and examines my fingertips. I finished the planting several days ago, so a lot of the dirt under my nails has been cleaned out. But they still look a fright.

"Come," she says, pulling me with her to the small table tucked into the dining area. "Your hands are atrocious."

Sophie loves her job at *The Jitterbug*, but her real passion is nail art. She has almost as many bottles of nail polish as I have trees on the farm, and that's hardly an exaggeration. And not just polish—she has stamping plates and dotting tools and all sorts of things needed to create stunning manicures. I once asked her why she didn't go to school and become a nail tech, but she just shrugged and said she worried it would steal the joy out of it for her. So instead, she collects nail polish like rare coins, and offers anyone with two hands and a heartbeat a free manicure. I've given up trying to understand her. She's a mystery to me.

"You didn't wear your gloves, did you?" she accuses, pushing back the cuticles on my left hand.

"You know I didn't," I say, "so why even ask?"

She huffs dramatically. "One day I'm going to stop offering to save your poor hands from your deliberate neglect, you know."

I grin at her. "Empty threats, Sophie, empty threats."

She rolls her eyes, but her lips pull into a grin. "So how's your mom doing?"

"She's fine," I say. "Good days and bad, as usual."

"And Chase?"

"Up to his eyeballs in paperwork, I assume. Did I tell you he hired a business consultant to help us with the farm?"

She lifts her brow. "Things are that bad, huh?"

"Yup. And you'll never guess who he hired."

She picks up her cuticle trimmers. "Who?"

"Jackson McKinley."

"He hired *Jack?*" she says, her mouth dropping open. I nod. "Yup."

"Is he going to be sticking around, then?"

I shrug. "For the time being. I guess he hasn't been able to find a job since getting his MBA, so he agreed to help us out for now. He came over yesterday to get a tour and go over the books with Dad and Chase."

"Wow," she says, "Jack McKinley." A sly smile slides across her face. "Is he as hot as he was back in the day?"

"Sophie!" I say, choking on a laugh.

"What? You can't tell me you never thought he was attractive. I *know* you did. What was it that we called him? The MVBOC?"

"Most Valuable Body On Campus," I say, trying to hide my smile. "Yeah, okay, you're right, I did find him attractive. But he was so out of our league, you know?"

"At least you had an in," she says, switching to my other hand. "He and Chase were pretty good friends, weren't they?"

I shrug. "They did sports together and hung out at school, but it's not like he was ever over at our house."

"That's because you live so far out of town," she says matter-of-factly. "Still, you had a connection."

"I guess. But it doesn't matter. He's only here until he finds a real job somewhere else. And besides, I hardly know anything about him."

"You know he's hot," she says, waggling her eyebrows. I laugh.

"Looks can only take you so far, Soph. He might have a girlfriend for all we know."

"Not likely, if he's hanging out here instead of wherever she might be," she says. "But enough about Jack—what do you want on your nails today?"

Sunday mornings on the farm are as slow as the sap running through the trees. I sit at the kitchen table, my feet tucked underneath me, admiring the glittery pink polish I let Sophie talk me into putting on my nails. Dad's humming to himself as he flips pancakes—our traditional "family breakfast"—and the smell mingles together with the rich aroma of brewing coffee.

Chase helps Mom into her place at the table while I get up to gather the plates and utensils.

"Mm, did you make buttermilk syrup, too?" Chase asks.

Dad looks over his shoulder and grins. "Of course."

We chat idly about sundry topics while we eat—the new fertilizer I want to try, Dad's plans to set traps for the gophers in the north field, and my brother's non-existent love life. Mom helps me clean up a bit after breakfast, and then everyone wanders off to follow their chosen pursuits.

I collect my sketchbook and sit back down at the kitchen table to work on a new likeness. This one is of a porcupine that lumbered through one of the transplant beds last week. I had to chase him off so he wouldn't make a feast of the Douglas fir saplings, but not before I snapped a picture with my phone so I could sketch him later.

A car coming up the drive catches my eye. It pulls up in front of the house and Jack McKinley gets out. By the time I stash my sketchbook in my room and do a quick check in the mirror, he's knocking on the door.

"Hey Jack, come on in," Chase says, stepping back to let him into the house. Mom, reading on the couch, brightens at the sight of him.

"Jackson McKinley, is that you?" she says.

"The very same, Mrs. Kenworth," he says, giving her a smile. Dad turns off the tv and stands, shaking his hand.

Mom beams up at him, her head only slightly ticcing to the side. "When Chase told me you were helping us out, I almost didn't believe it. When did you get back in town?"

"Just last week."

"And how long are you staying?"

Jack blows out his breath. "I'm not exactly sure. My internship didn't pan out quite like I expected, so I'm home until another employment opportunity comes along."

"Well, we're certainly glad to have you here. Although it's hard to believe you're so grown up! I can still see you and Chase in my mind's eye as little boys, running around the baseball field with grass stains on your knees. Do you still play?"

"Not since high school, I'm afraid. I wasn't as good as your son, so I didn't get to play in college."

Mom gives Chase a fond smile, who clears his throat. "Come on into the kitchen, Jack, we're anxious to hear what you have to say.

Dad helps Mom into the kitchen and sits her at the end of

the table, then takes the seat beside her. I follow and sit on Dad's other side, opposite both Jack and Chase.

"First of all," Jack says, looking around the table, "I want to let you know how much I appreciate that you've asked for my help. I know how much this place means to your family, and I'm honored that you trust me enough to share with me the details of your lives."

Mom and Dad exchange a smile, and Dad squeezes her hand before looking back at him. "You're welcome, son. We appreciate your help."

Jack nods, then takes a deep breath. "I'm going to be honest—things look pretty bad. After going over all the accounts with Chase, it's clear that the business has been in trouble for a while. Without intervention, the farm will fail within the year."

His words feel like a slap in the face. Were all business consultants this blunt? Besides, the farm isn't just our family's business—it's our home, our life, our entire world. I glance at my father, whose face is grave.

"Thank you for your honesty," Dad says. "What do we need to do?"

"The business plan I've put together is a drastic one—you might even call it a Hail Mary, since we're honestly at that point," Jack says. He hands each of us a printed sheet of paper. "I've made a list of the biggest changes we need to make in order to turn things around."

"We?" The word tumbles from my mouth in surprise. I stare at Jack, who nods.

"I don't intend to throw you a lifeline and not haul you in," he says. "I plan to work beside you every step of the way. I want to see this place succeed and thrive right along with you.

Besides, I haven't got much else to do right now; it will be nice to keep busy."

I glance at my brother, whose look reflects my own. Clearly he wasn't expecting this kind of commitment from his friend, either.

When no one else comments, Jack continues. He takes us through, point by point, explaining in more detail all the major adjustments needed. The first few items relate to the overall management of the farm and how things are run in the office: updating our inventory and payroll systems, establishing a stricter budget for expenditures, hiring an accountant, etc. But soon enough we get into the hands-on changes.

"What's this about opening an artisan market, and what does it have to do with the farm?" I ask.

Jack lights up. "I'm glad you asked, because it's one of the things I'm most excited about. The plan is to fix up the old workshop and turn it into a boutique, where you can sell items related to the tree farm: pine-scented soaps, lavender sachets, Christmas ornaments, that sort of thing. Ideally we'll be contacting local artists and vendors for permission to sell their items as well."

"But why?"

"It's a way to increase revenue year-round. Right now all of your income is loaded into the final quarter of the year, which makes annual budgeting and planning for emergencies more difficult. Having an artisan market will bring people to the farm throughout the year."

"Do you really think they'll come all this way, just for a little boutique? You can find those all over," Chase adds.

"I do," he says with confidence. "We'll be selling handmade goods and one-of-a-kind items that they can't get anywhere else. Plus, they won't be coming just for the market, they'll be coming throughout the year to participate in the various events you'll be hosting."

"Events?"

"Yes. The two most obvious will be a Christmas in July celebration and a winter carnival type thing, in December. But I wanted to brainstorm about some other events we can host—preferably something in the spring and another in the fall.

"Springtime is for planting and shearing," Dad says.

"Is there any way we can get the public involved in either of those activities?" Jack asks.

"Not with the shearing," Chase says. "Way too much liability for all involved."

"What about the planting?"

The table is silent as we consider the question. My stomach clenches at the thought of getting strangers involved in any portion of the farming, but I have an idea.

"What if," I say slowly, "we invite people to sponsor a tree?"

Four pairs of eyes swivel my direction.

"What do you mean?" Jack asks.

"Well, I don't know exactly," I say, shifting in my seat. "I was just thinking about the field trips we used to host up here for the elementary kids around Arbor Day. It was a sort of hands-on science lesson, do you remember?" I direct my question to Chase, who nods. Turning back to Jack, I continue. "We'd take them on a tour of the farm and explain the lifecycle of a tree, starting with the seed orchard and the greenhouses, then the grow beds and fields. The kids got to plant seeds into pots and take home a yearling sapling to plant in their yards."

"Do you still do the field trips?" Jack asks.

"We haven't for a few years," my brother says.

"How come?"

Dad speaks up this time. "I had to turn down a few school requests due to staffing and family reasons," he says, glancing at Mom. "I think word got out and the schools quit calling. We haven't bothered to set anything up with them since."

"Field trips sound like a great way to get some free advertising and tax credits," Jack says, "but you said something about sponsoring a tree, Emily. Can you elaborate on that?"

"Well, like I said, I was thinking about the field trips. What if we did something like that, but for individuals and families? We could offer short tours of the farm, explain what we do and some of the costs involved, and then ask people to sponsor a tree. They could pay a small fee to help cover the costs of fertilizer and maintenance, for example. And we can still have them plant seeds so they feel some ownership."

"Em, that's a great idea!" Chase says, sounding excited. "And for a certain amount pledged in the spring, maybe we can give them a coupon discount for a fresh cut tree in December."

Jack has been scribbling in a notebook as we speak. "Excellent. This is exactly the kind of thing I was hoping for. Any ideas for an event in the fall? It doesn't have to be something big—July and December will be the big events."

"In the fall we're usually tagging trees for harvest and collecting cones and seeds," Chase says, leaning back in his chair with his arms crossed. "By Thanksgiving we have to be ready to go."

Mom clears her throat. "Maybe we could offer classes on wreath-making? Or pinecone crafts, or something like that."

I give her a smile and reach out to squeeze her hand. Jack nods and writes it down.

"That could work," he says. "Any other ideas?"

No one speaks, and eventually he moves on. "Not a problem. But if any of you think of something else, let me know."

"So are we going to be doing all of this now? This year?" I try to keep the panic out of my voice.

"Not at first, no. I mean, we should definitely do a Christmas in July and a winter event. But spring and fall events can wait for a year or two."

"How much do you think all this is going to cost to implement?" Dad asks.

Jack grimaces. "Quite a bit. But you have to understand that the investment of time and money now is necessary to establish a more productive business going forward." He glances at my brother, who nods. "I'm working on a budget with Chase, but we should have enough to pay for everything we need."

Dad and I say nothing, knowing the only money available is the rest of what Chase was saving for school.

"And if we can't?" I ask.

Jack looks at Chase again, who blows out his breath. "We can sell off the forty-five acres west of the main fields," Chase says.

"But what about our plans to expand?" I protest.

"Em, we can't even manage the size of the farm as it currently stands," he says. "We'll all have to make sacrifices if we want to save the farm." He gives me a hard look and I swallow, knowing the sacrifices he's already made.

"We're not planning to sell anything just yet," Jack says. "But it's an option if it comes to that. In the meantime, Chase will have a lot to sort through in the office—"

"I'll help you with that, son," Dad chimes in.

"—but the most pressing project is going to be getting the workshop sorted and ready to use."

"And lining up vendors and artists to fill it, right?" Chase asks.

"Exactly," Jack says. He looks around the table at each of us, his eyes lingering on my face a moment longer than the others. "I know this is a lot to take in," he says quietly. "But I promise you, this is your best chance at saving the farm."

"Thanks, Jack," Chase says. "We appreciate the advice."

"Yes, thank you," Dad says, standing from the table. It's the cue we've all been waiting for that the meeting is finished. "Why don't you and Chase and I head over to the office and get started on some of those things on your list?"

"Of course," Jack says. "I just need to have a word with Emily real quick."

I had just helped Mom up from the table when I hear what he says. "With me?" I ask.

"Yes, if you have a minute."

"Sure, just give me a second."

I help Mom walk back to her room so she can lie down for a nap. When I come back, Jack is alone in the kitchen.

"You wanted to talk with me?" I ask.

"I did." He offers me a smile. "Your brother is going to have his hands full in the office for a while, so I was hoping you and I could tackle the workshop together."

"Oh. Um, sure. I have some shearing I still need to finish, but if we can work around that it shouldn't be a problem."

"Great! I've got to put some hours in at the hardware store, so how about we meet together on Friday to start cleaning it out?"

"Sure, that would be fine."

He smiles, extending his hand as if to shake mine. Surprised, I put my hand in his, but instead of shaking it, he turns it over to examine my fingers. "Nice nails," he says with an appreciative grin.

The sparkly pink looks boldly feminine on my short, stubby nails. "Thanks," I say, secretly pleased that he noticed, even as my face turns red.

"Friday, then?" he says, still smiling. I nod.

"Friday."

Chapter 6

JACK

Are we still on for tomorrow?

This is Jack, btw. Chase gave me your number.

The texts come as I'm getting ready for bed on Thursday night. I groan. I'd honestly forgotten all about our meeting, so I guess it's a good thing he reached out.

EMILY

Sure

JACK

Great! Does 10:30 work for you?

EMILY

Yup

JACK

See you then

Feeling irrationally annoyed, I save his number in my phone and head across the hall to Chase's room. His door is ajar, so I don't bother knocking, and he looks up from his desk when I push open the door.

"Hey Em," he says, "what's up?"

"You gave Jack my number?"

"Yeah—in case he needs to get ahold of you. Makes sense, you know, to have all our numbers. Now that he's working for us."

"You mean *with* us," I say, sitting cross-legged on his bed. He swivels his chair around to face me.

"That surprised me, too," he said. "But he's not charging us extra for it, so it can't hurt, right? We can always use more hands to help around the farm."

I frown, picking at a thread on the old, worn bedspread. "About that..." I say, not looking at him. "Are all these changes he's suggesting really necessary? I mean, I know he talked about increasing revenue throughout the year and stuff, but we're a Christmas tree farm—do we really need a fancy boutique and seasonal events, just to sell Christmas trees?"

"That's kind of the point, Em," Chase says. "Just selling Christmas trees isn't enough anymore. More and more people are opting for artificial trees, or grabbing a pre-cut tree from a corner lot. The market just isn't what it used to be, and if we don't adapt, we'll fail."

I sit in silence, letting his words sink in.

"Are you worried about the extra cost, or the extra work?" he asks.

I shrug. "More like, the extra people. You know I'm not crazy about strangers and crowds."

He chuckles. "Yeah, that tracks. You won't worry about the extra work, but if you have to talk to people? Heaven forbid!"

I throw his pillow at him, trying not to smile. He catches it, laughing, and gets up to put it back. He sits down beside me, so close our arms are touching. I lean my head against his shoulder.

"I know it's kind of scary, Em," he says, "changing stuff around here and all. But it's going to be okay."

"I just... don't like change very much," I say. My mind goes back to when Mom got sick, and how *everything* changed. Chase nudges my arm.

"Not all change is bad, Em," he says softly, reading my thoughts. After a moment he adds, "I'm kind of excited, actually. Jack's ideas are going to breathe some new life into this place. When all's said and done, I bet we won't even recognize it anymore."

"That's what I'm afraid of," I grumble.

He chuckles again. After a moment I unfold myself and head back to my room. "'Night, Em," he calls.

"'Night, Chase. Merry Christmas."

I don't sleep well that night, and the morning comes far sooner than I want. Dad is taking care of Mom, and I'm too anxious and tired to get much work done myself, so once I set the men to shearing I head back to the house to wait for Jack. Taking my sketchbook and watercolor paint supplies to the kitchen, I fill two jars with water and set to work.

I've worked with other paint mediums before, but watercolor has always been my favorite. Dipping my brush into one of the jars, I pick up some pigment and swirl it onto the paint tray, watching it bloom like spilled tea. Mr. Tumnus looks up at me from the page, frozen in the act of eating a nut. I start with soft washes across his fur—warm gray for his back and tail, a stroke of burnt sienna along his belly. The water makes the colors dance and blend, blurring together in unpredictable ways. His face is tricky, and I take extra care as I paint, making sure to leave a ring of white around each eye. I add a dab of russet to his cheeks and ears, then pause to let the page dry, my breath catching as the image begins to come alive.

I'm so caught up in my art that when my phone pings from its place on the table I jump.

JACK

Did you want me to come up to the house, or will you be coming down to the shop?

I groan, realizing I'm late.

EMILY

Sorry, lost track of time. Coming now.

I quickly rinse out my brush and pull on my boots. Grabbing a jacket, I rush out the door and sprint down the hill.

Jack gets out of his car as I jog to a stop in front of the small building. He's wearing jeans and a UW sweatshirt and looking *far* too attractive to clean out a dusty old shop.

"Sorry," I say, breathing heavily. "I should have set an alarm."

"No problem," he says. "I thought you'd be out in the fields, but it looks like you came down from the house."

I step up to the door, fishing for the right key. "Is there a question in there?" I ask, fighting to keep my voice level. I'm still winded from the run.

He laughs. "Sorry. I guess I'm just nosy. What have you been doing this morning?"

I shrug. "Not much." I finally locate the correct key and unlock the door. "You sure about this?" I ask, stepping inside. I can't picture anything in this space besides my dad and a mess of wood and tools.

"Positive," he says.

"It's going to take a lot of work."

"True, but I don't think it's anything you and I can't handle."

He tosses me a grin and then puts his hands on his hips. "First things first," he says. "We need to haul out the old table and see if that workbench can come out as well. Then we need to clean things up and check on the state of the windows, floor, and doors."

I unlock the double barn doors at the back of the shop and open them wide so we can drag the table and workbench outside. After that, we head up to the barn to get brooms and cleaning supplies. We load everything into the back of the ATV wagon, then I grab the keys and climb onto the four-wheeler it's attached to. "Hop on," I say, looking up at Jack.

He looks taken aback. "Um, are you sure? I don't mind walking back to the shop..."

I frown. "Why? Are you afraid I'll crash or something?"

"No, it's not that, I just... won't it be awkward for you if I ride double?"

Well *now* it feels awkward. But I press my lips together. "Just get on, Jack," I say. "This is a farm—we do what we need to to get stuff done."

"Can't argue with that," he says, climbing up behind me.

He puts his hands lightly on my waist, sending a jolt through my insides. I honestly didn't even think about riding double with him until he mentioned something, but now I'm hyper aware of Jack on the seat behind me.

"I'm ready when you are," he says.

I pull away from the barn and head down the drive, telling

myself not to go too fast, which would cause Jack to hold on to me tighter. I try to distract myself from the feeling of Jack's hands resting on my hips by singing *The Twelve Days of Christmas* in my head. But somewhere along the way the pipers got mixed up with the swans, and one of the dancing ladies ran off with a drummer who looked suspiciously like Jack.

Yep. Definitely distracting.

Thankfully we arrive at the workshop without incident, and I breathe a silent sigh of relief as soon as he lets go of me and climbs off.

"So Chase went to Western to work on his undergrad, but what have you been up to since graduation?" Jack asks, grabbing a broom and heading through the double doors.

"Nothing much," I say, following him inside with another broom. "Mostly I've just been here working with my dad."

"You didn't go off to school?"

"I went for a semester the year after we graduated, but decided not to continue after that."

"Why not?"

I shrug. "It felt like a waste of time and money, when I already know how to raise Christmas trees. Chase wants to be a doctor, but all I've ever wanted to do is run the farm."

"Seriously? You've never wanted to do anything else?"

"Not really."

"What about your art?"

I pause. "What about it?"

"You never wanted to pursue that further?"

I don't answer right away, going out to the trailer to retrieve a dustpan in order to buy myself some time. I don't know why I feel so hesitant to discuss my art with Jack, but it somehow feels too personal. "It's just a hobby," I say, when I come back inside. "Tuition is too expensive to throw away on something like that."

"Oh, I don't know," he says. "I don't think any education is wasted. Even for hobbies. Besides, going to school would have given you a chance to get out of Echo Ridge."

I give him a quizzical look. "What makes you think I wanted to get out of Echo Ridge?"

"You didn't?"

"No. I love it here."

He seems to chew on that for a moment before asking, "What do you like about it?"

I almost laugh. What do I like about breathing? What do I like about eating or sleeping? How do I explain that what I love about home isn't really something I *can* explain; that Echo Ridge and the tree farm are as much a part of me as an arm or a lung. I can't imagine life anywhere else, because it wouldn't *be* a life anywhere else.

Instead, I draw a deep breath, then immediately start choking on the dust. I sputter and cough, hacking like a reindeer choking on a candy cane.

Jack's brow creases in concern. "You okay?" he asks.

I nod, coughing and sputtering as I fight to clear my lungs. Finally, after several sips of water and clearing my throat a dozen times, I manage to regain my composure.

"Sorry about that," I say, my voice raspy.

"You sure you're okay?" he asks again. I nod, and we both go back to sweeping. We clean in silence for a few moments, and about the time the red has faded from my face he clears his throat.

"So, you were about to tell me what you like about living here?" he prompts.

Oh. Right. I chew the inside of my lip. "It's kind of hard to explain. I guess it just feels like home, you know?"

"You don't mind the rain?"

"I love it."

"The small town?"

"One of my favorite features."

He stops and stares at me incredulous. "Seriously?"

"Seriously."

He laughs lightly, shaking his head, which makes me frown. "Why does that surprise you?" I ask.

"I don't know. It just feels so... restrictive to me here. There aren't nearly as many opportunities as there are elsewhere."

"That may be true, but Seattle's only an hour away—what you can't get here you're sure to find there."

He shrugs. "Yeah, I know. But I honestly couldn't wait to get out of Echo Ridge. I much prefer life in the city."

I don't know how to respond to that, so I say nothing. A few minutes pass in relative silence, save for the sweeping and banging of the brooms as we try to clean up five years worth of dirt and dust.

"So what was it like, growing up on a Christmas tree farm?" Jack asks, breaking the silence.

I smile. "Like it's Christmas all the time."

He grimaces. "That's too bad."

A startled laugh escapes me. "You don't like Christmas?"

Jack lifts a shoulder but doesn't look at me. "It's fine. Just not my favorite holiday."

"Why not? Everyone likes Christmas." I spray one of the windows with glass cleaner and start wiping it.

He turns to face me, leaning against the broom with a smirk. "Not those of us with Christmas birthdays."

"You were born on Christmas?"

"Christmas Eve," he says, resuming his cleaning. "So no one remembers—well, besides my parents. And as a kid, my birthday was always lumped together with the holiday. I had Christmas-themed parties and combined gifts. I just felt like I missed out on having my birthday be about *me*."

"I know the feeling," I say, tossing dirty paper towels in one of the trash bags we brought.

"Oh that's right, you had to share with Chase." He chuckles. "Guess we both got the short end of the birthday stick growing up."

"I didn't mind," I say. "At least, not as much as he did. We had combined parties until we were about ten years old, but after that, Chase wanted his own. One year he had a paint-balling party with a bunch of friends. It sounded like a lot of fun."

"Sounded like? Didn't you go?"

I shake my head. "I could have, of course. But I was too scared about getting hit. I've always kind of regretted it, actually." I clear my throat. "Anyway, we had separate parties for a couple years, until we were thirteen."

"What happened then?"

"That's when I quit having parties altogether. No one came, so there didn't seem to be a point."

Jack stops and stares at me. "No one came to your birthday party?"

"Nope."

"I would have come," he says, frowning.

I grin. "That's sweet, thanks. But don't feel too bad for me— no one came because I didn't invite anyone."

It takes him half a second to realize what I said, and I laugh at the face he makes.

"So wait—you sabotaged your own party?" he asks.

"I was shy! Every time I tried to invite someone, I got tongue-tied and bailed on the conversation," I say, starting on another window.

"What about your friends?"

"I didn't have many friends."

"Why not?"

I huff a laugh. "Didn't you hear what I just said? I was shy—meeting new people stressed me out, so I mostly just kept to myself."

He gives me an appraising look. "You don't seem shy to me."

I shrug. "I kinda grew out of it, I guess. I still don't really like being around new people, though. I never know what to say."

"Huh." He grabs the dustpan and sweeps up a big pile of dirt and sawdust.

We've made good progress on the shop. The floor is a lot cleaner, and you can actually see out of the windows now.

"Should we bother doing more with the walls?" I ask. "We're just going to be covering them up."

"I was thinking about that," Jack says. "The stud walls we can leave—we'll need to insulate them and cover them with sheetrock. But this wall here should be dusted off at least."

I retrieve a small hand broom from the trailer. "Here, this will get you started," I say, tossing it to him.

"Gee, thanks," he says with a sarcastic grin. But he starts sweeping it along the wall.

"How come you didn't go into construction or general contracting?" I ask. "This seems right up your alley."

He shrugs. "You pick things up when your family owns the

only hardware store in town," he says. "But construction never really interested me."

I take the cleaning spray and paper towels and start on the inside surface of the front door. "So what was it that made you interested in business management?" I ask.

"It seemed a good, solid choice," he says. He gives me a wry grin. "At least, it did until I graduated."

"What do you think happened?"

"Who knows? Politics. Economics. There just aren't a lot of jobs with the current market recession. Half my class was unemployed at graduation, even after our internships, and that's practically unheard of."

"Yikes. I didn't realize it was that bad."

He shrugs. "It is what it is. It might take a while, but I'm sure I'll find a position as a manager or consultant eventually. And hey, in the meantime, I get to hang out with you and Chase." He winks at me, flashing the smile that made every girl in our high school swoon. Myself included.

I turn away, noticing the stir of attraction I feel inside. Nothing could complicate this situation more than falling for my brother's friend. And not only that, but he's also our business consultant. *Besides,* I think to myself as I scrub the door clean, *he'll get a job and move away before too long. There's no point in getting attached to someone who won't be sticking around.*

I sneak a glance at my co-cleaner across the way. He ditched his sweatshirt a while ago and is working in just his jeans and a white t-shirt. The thin cotton does nothing to hide his trim waist and clearly defined muscles. I look away before he catches me staring, sighing to myself.

It's going to be a long summer.

Chapter 7

We spend the rest of the morning and into the afternoon getting the workshop cleared out and cleaned up, but without any electricity we have to call it a day when the sun goes down. Jack agrees to come back the next morning, and at dinner that evening Chase offers to help out as well.

"Do you know when the power will be hooked up again?" I ask him as we head down to the shop after breakfast the next morning.

"I called the utility company yesterday—we should have it back on by Monday or Tuesday."

Jack's car is parked next to the building when we arrive, and he climbs out as we walk up to the door.

"Hey, Jack. Why didn't you come up to the house?" Chase asks.

"I didn't want to bother anyone," Jack says. "I don't mind waiting." He turns to me and smiles. "'Morning, Emily."

My heart does a little twirl, tugging at the corners of my mouth until I smile back. "'Morning, Jack."

"You ready for phase two today?" he asks.

"Ready and willing," I say, pulling out my keys to unlock the door.

"What does phase two entail?" my brother asks.

"Well, we managed to get the shop all cleaned out yesterday," Jack says, "but we need to insulate the walls, add sheetrock, mud, texture, and paint."

Chase blinks. "And I thought this would be the easy part," he mumbles, following me inside.

"You can always go back and work in the office," I tease.

He gives me a withering look, and I chuckle.

"Before we get started," Jack says, surveying the empty room. "What do you guys think we should do about the floor?"

We glance down at the slab of concrete we're standing on. "Any chance we can just leave it?" Chase asks.

Jack makes a face. "If we were going for a modern industrial look we could, but I was thinking more quaint and rustic. Country chic, if you will."

"You'll want a wood floor, then," I say. "With wide planks. And maybe instead of sheet rock, we can use wood paneling on the walls. Or something to make it look more like a cabin in the woods, you know?"

"That's not a bad idea," Jack says. "What if," his voice kicks up a notch, and he takes a few steps into the room, spreading his arms out, "we do2 wood plank floors, as you suggested. Then finish most of the walls with sheetrock and mud and all, but this wall—" he indicates the long eastern wall with two widows, "—we cover in reclaimed wood."

"Oh, that's a great idea!" I say. "It would be the perfect aesthetic for this space."

"Do you know where we can get a bunch of old wooden planks and slats?" Jack asks.

I smirk. "This is a farm, remember? We've got old wood lying around everywhere."

"Perfect. Different sizes and colors will be best, and we can stain the floor to match one of them."

"What color are you thinking for the walls?" Chase asks.

"Cream," Jack says.

"Antique white," I say at the same time.

We look at each other and laugh.

"Cream is too yellow," I say. "If we're going for country chic, we're going to want an off-white, soft ivory color. Antique white is usually what they call that."

"Sounds good to me," Jack says. "How should we paint the exterior?"

I grin. "Red with white trim, of course. This *is* a Christmas tree farm, after all."

He chuckles, shaking his head. "Of course." He gives me a sly grin. "Should we make a sign that says 'Santa's Workshop' to hang out front?"

I fold my arms, thinking. "No, because that's not really what this place will be. 'Mrs. Claus's Closet?'"

"Nah, that makes it sound like we're selling clothes. 'Mrs. Claus's Boutique?'"

I snap my fingers. "'The Candy Cane Boutique!'"

Jack grins. "Perfect."

"So, why did you need my help again?" Chase asks, shoving his hands in his pockets and grinning at us. "You guys seem to have everything figured out."

Jack and I look at each other before he gives my brother a

sheepish smile. "Sorry, Chase," he says. "Do you have any feed-back on what we've discussed?"

Chase rolls his eyes. "None whatsoever. Em is better at aesthetics than I am anyway. But if we're just going to discuss the latest trends in decor, you're probably better off without me."

"Don't get your tinsel in a tangle, Chase," I say. "We just had to figure out what we're going to do with the space before the real work begins."

"Exactly," Jack says. "But now that we have a plan, we can head into town for the building materials. We just need to check the windows and doors first." He looks between us. "Any chance we can run a hose out here and spray the widows down from the outside to check for leaks?"

"I can bring the water tank down to do that," Chase says.

"Great. I'll check all the doors and hinges, then take measurements for flooring and sheetrock."

"I can help you in here," I say, "and once you guys go to town, I'll start collecting wood."

Chase heads up to the barn to get the water trailer, while I help Jack measure the walls and check all the doors. One of the large barn doors leans a bit when it's open, but otherwise they look good. Jack makes some notes, and then we measure the floor. By the time Chase arrives and hoses down the windows, I'm heading out to find wood.

The day is overcast but warm, and I take the same ATV with the trailer attached that we used yesterday to haul supplies. I grab a pair of heavy gloves from the barn, where Dad is tinkering.

"Hey sugarplum, watcha up to?" he asks.

"Jack and Chase are going to town to get materials for the

shop, and I'm off to check all the junk piles on the property for old wooden boards."

"Boards? For what?"

"We're going to cover the long wall in the shop with reclaimed lumber. To give it a rustic look. It's very 'in' right now, plus it will lower the overall cost of supplies."

Dad chuckles. "I'll have to tell your mother I was right not to throw away all that old fencing."

I smile. "How is she today?"

His smile falters. "It looks to be an off day, I think. Shannon is with her right now."

I reach to give him a hug, and he holds me tight for several moments. "I'm sorry to put so much on your shoulders, Emmy-girl," he says, his voice husky. "You and your brother deserve better."

"Don't talk like that, Dad," I say, stepping out of his embrace. "You and Mom are the best parents we could ever hope for. It's nobody's fault that Mom got sick and the farm took a backseat. That's how it should be—people always come first."

He looks down, shaking his head. "I still wish I would have asked for help before we got so desperate. Maybe we could have saved the farm if I didn't wait so long."

"We *will* save the farm, Dad," I say as firmly as I can. "Jack knows what he's doing, and Chase and I will do everything we can to turn things around. You just take care of Mom. We'll take care of everything else, okay?"

He gives me a long look before letting himself smile. "When did you get so strong, Emmy-girl?"

I climb up on the four-wheeler and smile back. "It's something I learned from my dad," I say. Lifting a hand in farewell, I call "Merry Christmas!" and and take off down the road.

I make several trips around the property to fill the trailer with old planks and slats of wood. When it's full, I dump it in a pile outside the workshop and head out for more. By the time I drop my second load, Chase and Jack have returned from town and begun sheetrocking the walls. Dad comes down to join them, so I sneak away to check on the shearing. We only have a few weeks left before it will be too late in the year to get it done, and I don't want the work on the farm to fall behind with all the new projects Jack has planned.

The men we've hired to help have done a good job. It still feels wrong to leave the work to others, and I have to remind myself that the work we're doing on the shop is going to help the farm, too. But Chase was right to tell me not to worry—Mario and the others have it well under control.

I stop a few trees away from where Mario is working, fingering the soft, lime-green growth on the tips of the branches. As a child I used to pluck them off and play with them, not realizing the damage my innocent delight was doing. When my father caught me and explained that doing so could damage or disfigure the tree, I cried for an hour, convinced I was responsible for any of the trees that died. I wasn't, of course, but it was a lesson I never forgot.

"Hey, Emily," Mario calls. "Did you need something?"

I drop my arm, turning to face the man as he walks up beside me. "No, I just wanted to check on your progress. How's it going?"

"Good." He adjusts his baseball cap, looking out across the

field. "We're more than two-thirds finished. We might even be done next week."

"That would be fantastic," I say. Kicking at a clump of grass beneath my feet, I chuckle. "Just in time to start on the mowing."

He laughs with me. "It never ends, does it?"

"Never," I say. Then, thinking about the possibility of losing the farm, I sober. "At least, I hope it never does."

He doesn't respond, just looks out across the trees with me. Thousands of trees representing decades of work stretch out before us, rising and falling with the terrain like waves across the sea. Shaking off my melancholy, I turn to him with a smile.

"Since you seem to have things well in hand, I think I'll start prepping the mowers. That way we can start the mowing as soon as we finish the shearing."

He answers with a nod, turning back to his work while I head up the rise to the barn.

It takes two more days before Jack and Chase have all the walls finished in the workshop. I should probably be helping them, but that little spark of attraction I feel for Jack has me worried, and I decide to keep my distance. Instead, I get the mowers ready for the season while they prep the shop for painting,

Rather than managing weeds between the rows of trees with harsh chemicals, my grandfather planted grass. It certainly helps with weed control, but it requires constant mowing through the warmer months. If the grass gets too long, it will steal nutrients from the soil that the trees need to stay healthy and strong.

Two of the mowers only need oil and gas to coax them into starting up, but the engine in one of the large mowers won't turn over. I have it half apart on Tuesday afternoon when Dad joins me in the barn.

"Mower not working?" he asks when he sees me.

I huff, propping my hands on my hips. "Nope. The blasted thing won't start, and I can't figure out why."

"Have you checked the spark plugs?"

"Yup."

"Oil and gas?"

I give him a look, and he chuckles. "Alright, alright, I'm sure you've done all the things. But aren't you supposed to be helping at the shop?"

I press my lips together. "I can't just leave off my chores to work on the shop," I say. "The farm still needs to run smoothly, and right now that means fixing this mower. Chase is helping Jack; they'll be fine."

Dad crouches down and pokes at the engine. "If I recall correctly," he says, not looking at me, "Jack asked *you,* not Chase, to help him with the shop."

I don't respond, and he finally looks at me.

"Let me worry about the mower—you go help the boys, I think they're painting today. Besides, the other mowers are working; we have time to sort this one out."

I sigh. "Fine. But if they have things under control, I'm coming back to help you."

Dad shrugs noncommittally, and I take off down the hill. The sun warms my back, and I almost consider taking my coveralls off, but if they're painting I'll want to keep them on. Besides, they are most definitely *not* flattering, and if I can keep

Jack from finding *me* attractive (not that he ever would), that would help ensure a completely platonic summer.

My hopeless little heart pouts at the thought.

I hear the sound of someone singing along to Ed Sheeran as I get closer to the shop. At first I think it might be Chase, but as I step up to the open door I realize it's Jack. He has his back to me as I come in, so he doesn't notice me at first. I pause and lean my shoulder against the doorframe, listening. I'm impressed—I don't remember hearing that he ever participated in choir or anything, but he's got a good set of pipes. He starts in on the chorus a second time, but as he leans down to fill up his roller with paint again, he spots me.

"Emily!" He sounds more surprised than embarrassed, but a hint of pink creeps up his neck. Apparently he's not used to singing for an audience.

"You're a regular Harry Styles," I say, coming into the room. He laughs self-consciously.

"Not really. But sometimes you just have to sing along, you know?"

I nod, looking around. "Where's Chase?"

"He got a phone call he had to take and went up to the office. I think it was from the new accountant."

That sounds about as fun as taking a bite of peanut brittle with a toothache. "Better him than me," I say, making a face. Jack chuckles.

Looking around, I let out a low whistle. "Wow, you guys have done a lot."

Jack looks around as well. "Just need to finish the painting and then we can lay the floor," he says, sounding pleased.

I run a hand gingerly along the reclaimed wood wall, the varied slats of wood a myriad of brown and gray hues in all different sizes and shapes. The texture is rough and uneven, but it's a beautiful contrast to the creamy whiteness of the newly finished walls.

"You like it?" Jack asks, watching me.

"I love it. It's exactly how I pictured it."

He grins. "Good. I love it too. Chase thought maybe we should sand it down to make it smoother, but I like the rustic touch it adds."

I nod my head. "Agreed. It's perfect."

Jack goes back to painting the final wall, and I look around for something to do. "I didn't realize you guys were almost finished," I say. "How can I help?"

"The trim still needs painting," he says, indicating a small cup of paint with a paintbrush balanced on top. "Chase was about to start when he got the phone call."

I pick it up and start on the trim around one of the windows. Ed's voice keeps us company from the bluetooth speaker in the corner, but this time Jack doesn't join in. I'm almost disappointed.

We paint without saying much for the next forty minutes, and when I finish the last of the trim, I step back to survey our work. "Looks good," I say.

"It does," Jack responds, setting the roller down. "Even if you did make a bit of a mess of yourself."

I frown and look down, trying to see if I got paint anywhere. "What do you mean?"

"You've got some paint on your face," he says.

"I do? Where?"

He reaches over and smears a streak of paint from his finger onto my cheek. I gasp.

"Right there," he says, grinning.

Narrowing my eyes, I swipe at him with my paintbrush, but he leans away from me, laughing. I lunge toward him, but as he jumps backward, his foot tangles in the drop cloth and he trips. Thrown off balance, he lands hard on the floor, hitting the edge of the paint tray as he falls. Creamy white paint splatters all over his arm and side, coating him like a yogurt-covered raisin.

My hand flies to my mouth. "Jack! Are you okay?"

He lifts his dripping arm, grimacing. "Aside from being covered in paint, you mean?"

"I'm so, so sorry." The words tumble over themselves in my haste to apologize. "I didn't mean to make you fall."

"It's alright," he says, looking himself over.

"Are you hurt?"

"Just my pride," he says, forcing a laugh. "But this shirt is toast."

He's right. The entire left side of his torso is coated with paint, the thick white substance weighing down the fabric and dripping onto the floor. Gingerly he pulls his arm out of the shirt, then eases it over his head.

My already flushing cheeks burn even hotter. "What are you doing?"

"Trying to avoid making a bigger mess," he says, carefully wadding up the shirt to contain as much of the paint as possible.

Growing up with a twin brother, it's not like I haven't seen a guy's bare chest and back before. Chase ran around in nothing but shorts nearly every summer when we were kids, and I'm used to seeing the men we hire occasionally working without a shirt on. But it's been years since I've seen the bare torso of a man that I find attractive.

Very, *very,* attractive.

Jack tries to wipe off the paint on his arm with the shirt. I stare at the defined lines of his shoulders, at his flat stomach and smooth skin. He's not overly muscular, nor is he tan, but his trim torso and athletic build are certainly easy on the eyes. It doesn't register that I'm oogling him until he smirks at me.

"If you wanted to see me with my shirt off, Emily, you didn't have to go to such drastic measures."

I turn abruptly away, as much to hide my flaming face as to give him some privacy. "Sorry. Um, let me get you something to clean yourself up."

I head toward the corner where the supplies are and grab a roll of paper towels, then hurry back to hand them to him.

"Thanks."

He tears off a few and rubs the paint from his hands, then wipes at the spots where it got on his pants. I follow his hands with my eyes as they clean off his elbow, then hover in the air as he pauses.

"Did I get it all?" he asks.

My eyes snap back to his face, aware that I've been staring again. "Yes," I say, flushing again. "I mean, no. You have some in your hair, from taking off your shirt."

He curses quietly, and guilt washes through me again. "I'm really sorry," I say.

"It's not your fault," he sighs. "If anything, it's mine. If I wouldn't have smeared that paint on your face, this never would have happened."

Oh. I had completely forgotten about that. I lift a hand and gently touch my cheek, feeling the sticky paint beneath my fingertips.

"Here," he says, handing me a paper towel. I reach out and take it from him.

SHAELA KAY

"Thanks."

"I guess we're even," he says with a half-hearted grin.

I let out a breathy laugh. "I'd hardly call us even," I say, eyeing his bare chest. Realizing how dangerous that could be, I quickly avert my eyes.

"Then here, help me get the paint out of my hair before it dries to make up the difference," he says.

I glance at the small white globs clinging to his dark hair. "Let's go outside," I say. "We can use a bottled water to help rinse it out."

We trek outside, blinking in the sudden brightness. It's pleasant in the sun, but a light breeze keeps it from feeling too warm. Jack bends forward so his head is hanging down, and I unscrew the cap on the water bottle. I pour it slowly over the spots of paint in his hair, rubbing gently with my fingers to get it all out. His dark hair is smooth and slippery, and not as thick as I had expected. I lift the bottle and step back.

"I think that's all," I say.

He straightens up, and as he does the remaining water on his head runs down his body. He tenses, and I see the faint outline of the muscles in his abdomen.

"Ah, that's cold!" he says, sucking in a breath.

Another wave of heat courses through me, my thoughts careening wildly out of control. I close my eyes, since I can't manage to tear them away from his abs, and take a deep breath.

"Hey, you okay?"

I open my eyes to the sky to ensure I can keep them under control. When I finally drop my gaze to his face, he's watching me with concern.

"I... yes, I'm fine." I force my lips to smile, determined not to let my eyes wander, however sorely they are tempted.

80

"You sure?"

"Yeah, I was just—" A flash of inspiration sparks in my mind. "I was just thinking I could run up to the house and get one of Chase's t-shirts for you to put on."

"That's a great idea," he says. "I'll come with you."

My frantically beating heart kicks up a notch, but I shrug, feigning indifference. "Sure. You can clean up in the mudroom while I find you something to wear."

"Do I look that bad?"

I glance at his face and he winks at me, effectively disarming my crumbling self control. I laugh in embarrassment, then look pointedly at his chest, letting my eyes wander across his shoulders and down to his stomach. I feel my cheeks warm, but force myself to look back into his eyes.

"Not bad at all," I say. Then, with a grin of my own, I add, "for a city guy."

He laughs, following me up the hill to the house.

Chapter 8

I take my time finding Jack a t-shirt, willing the blush to fade from my cheeks and desperately trying *not* to think of him without clothes on. I finally manage to locate the baggiest, rattiest shirt of Chase's for Jack to wear, hoping it will help with my wildly inappropriate thoughts. Unfortunately, Jack somehow manages to still look hot in the faded, oversized advertisement for *Bob's Fish Hut*.

We're on our way back down to the shop when we hear Chase calling to us from behind. We stop and turn, waiting for him to catch up.

"Sorry Jack," he says. "That took longer than I expected."

"Everything okay?"

"Yeah, she just wanted—" He blinks. "Is that my shirt?"

Jack tosses me a grin. "We had a little accident with the paint, so Emily got it for me to borrow."

"Huh. Okay, well, do you still need help?"

"Just with cleanup," Jack says. "Emily and I finished the painting."

The three of us continue down the slope and into the shop. Chase gives a low whistle when he sees the mess.

"Do I even want to know what happened?" he asks, glancing between us.

"It was an accident," I say, feeling the heat creep back into my cheeks. "Let's just get it cleaned up."

We work together to clean up as much as we can, then put away the painting supplies for the night.

"We'll do another coat tomorrow," Jack says, "so we can get started on the flooring Thursday."

"I think Chase should help you with that," I say, more than a little concerned about the growing attraction I feel for Jack. Especially after today.

Jack looks at me, surprised. "You don't want to help?"

"I just need to catch up on some other things around the farm," I say, avoiding his eyes.

He looks disappointed, but Chase pipes up, oblivious to the unspoken conversation happening between Jack and I.

"Sure, I can help," he says.

"Thanks, Chase," I say. "I have a list of chores a mile long, including a greenhouse inventory so we can make sure to order enough potting soil and containers for the Adopt-A-Tree event."

"That reminds me," Jack says, "you and I need to have a meeting, to plan out what we're going to sell here in the boutique."

I barely hold back a sigh. Guess I won't be avoiding him, then.

"My mom has some great ideas," I say, thinking she'll at least be a good buffer. "Let's include her as well."

"Great. How does Friday afternoon sound?"

"Works for me."

He flashes me another smile, and the butterflies in my belly swirl in response. Pulling out my keys to lock the door, I say, "You guys go ahead, I'm going to lock up and then walk down to get the mail." Hopefully some distance from Jack will calm my frenzied pulse.

Jack darts a glance at my brother, who's already moving back toward the house. "I think I'm going to head out, actually," he says.

Chase turns around. "Sure. Just don't forget to bring me back that shirt—it's a classic."

Before I fully register what he's doing, Jack pulls the shirt up and over his head. He wads it up into a ball. "Here, catch!" he calls, throwing it to Chase, who catches it easily. Chase lifts an arm in farewell and continues up the hill. Grinning, Jack turns to me.

My mouth is agape, and his smile widens. I snap it closed.

"Want a ride down to the mailbox?" He hitches a thumb over his shoulder, indicating his car parked in front of the shop.

I turn away and shrug, trying not to let him see how ~~sexy attractive hot~~ *frustrating* I find him. "Sure," I say.

So much for finding distance.

I text Sophie later that night.

EMILY

Well, I can confirm that Jack is not only the MVBOC, he's also now the MVBOF

SOPHIE

??

EMILY

Most Valuable Body On the Farm

SOPHIE

Is there a story behind his promotion?

EMILY

She calls me a moment later, and I tell her everything.

"He did it on purpose," she says when I'm finished. "He wanted to show off for you."

"I don't know about the first time," I say, "but I think you're right about the second time. He wouldn't stop grinning at me. I was mortified."

I think about how he looked, and remember wanting to kiss those wicked, smiling lips. But Sophie doesn't need to know that. *No one* needs to know that.

"So what's next for the boutique?" she asks, breaking into my reverie.

"Oh, um, he and Chase are going to work on the floor. And he's coming over Friday to talk with me and Mom about what to sell."

"Well, he'll have to keep his shirt on around your mom, but you could go down to the shop while he's working and ask him to take it off for you again. And be sure to snap a picture for me this time."

"Sophie!" I choke on a laugh.

"What? I need evidence that his promotion is warranted."

"You can't just take my word for it?"

85

"I mean, I *could,* but I'd much rather have a photo."

(I don't blame her. I'd like a photo of that myself.)

Despite Sophie's suggestion, I do *not* ~~sneak~~ walk down to the shop to see how Jack and Chase are getting along with the flooring. Instead, I busy myself with my chores and try not to remember how Jack looked with his shirt off.

I'm cleaning up in the kitchen when Jack knocks at the open front door Friday afternoon, and I holler at him to come inside.

"Emily?" I hear him say.

"In the kitchen," I call.

He comes around the corner and stops short. "Whoa," he says, his eyes widening, "what happened in here?"

What happened is what usually happens when I cook: meaning there's more flour on me than in the cookie dough, and more dishes in the sink and on the counters than in the cupboards. I laugh at the stunned look on his face.

"This is nothing," I say. "You should see what happens when I help with Thanksgiving dinner."

He chuckles, shaking his head.

"You know, as long as you're working for us here on the farm," I say, washing my hands, "there's no need to stand on ceremony whenever you come over. If the garage is open, just come on in through the mudroom."

"Are you sure? Won't your parents mind?"

"Mom's the one who told me to tell you. Besides, we don't always hear when someone's at the door, and I wouldn't want to keep you waiting."

"Alright, then. Thanks—I'll do that from now on."

"Have a seat," I say, indicating the table. "I'll get my mom."

I dry my hands on a towel and start down the hall. Mom is sitting on her bed, reading, when I open the door.

"Hey Mom," I say. "Jack is here—he wants to talk about the boutique."

"Wonderful," she says. Sniffing suspiciously, she asks, "Are those cookies I smell?"

"They are. I figured it might help us brainstorm if we have something sweet to munch on."

"Always a good idea," she says, smiling at me.

I help her up from the bed and spend five minutes trying to convince her to use her walker. "I don't want you to fall, Mom," I say, trying to be patient.

"I am *not* going to fall," she insists, her illness making her belligerent.

"At least take my arm, then," I say, "so I can help you down the hall."

"So you can trip me, you mean," she says angrily. "I'm not going anywhere with you. Just leave me alone. Where's Walter?"

I sigh, knowing it's time to give up. "Alright, Mom, I'll leave."

I make a show of walking out of the room, but I leave the door slightly ajar so I can watch her. Experience has taught us that she shouldn't be alone when she gets like this, so I pull out my phone and dial Dad's number. I watch from the hall as she mumbles to herself, walking around the bed and back again.

"Hey, sugarplum," Dad says, answering his phone.

"Hey, Dad. Can you come sit with Mom?"

"Sure. Is everything okay?"

"Yes, she's fine, just not cooperating." I sigh. "We're supposed to meet with Jack to talk about what to sell in the boutique, but when I tried to get her to come down to the kitchen, she didn't want to use the walker, and things escalated from there."

In the half beat of silence that follows, I hear everything he doesn't want to say. The burden of caretaking. The fear of an unknown future. The grief of losing his wife one tiny piece at a time. But Dad doesn't complain, he just does what needs doing.

"Alright. I'm just out in the barn, so I'll be there in a minute."

"Thanks, Dad."

I fold my arms and lean against the wall, the ache between my ribs sharper than I've felt in quite a while. Mom's been doing really well, but the reality of living with Parkinson's is that there are good days and bad days, ups and downs, new symptoms and old complaints. The only constant in the disease is how unpredictable it can be.

I hear the garage door open and close, then the faint murmur of voices as Jack and Dad exchange greetings in the kitchen. I watch the hall until my dad comes into view.

"Hey, Dad," I say, giving him a hug.

"Hey, sugarplum," he says, pressing a kiss to my forehead. He releases me and pushes open the door to his room, stepping inside as I turn to make my way back to the kitchen.

Jack's been busy while he waited. The pile of dirty dishes in the sink is nearly gone, and the counters are all clean and bare. I look around, impressed.

"You didn't have to clean up my mess," I say, "but thank you."

"You're welcome," he says, flipping a towel up onto his shoulder. "I figured I may as well be useful while I waited." He glances behind me. "Is your mom going to join us?"

"She's not feeling well at the moment," I say, putting a plate of cookies on the table. "So it will just be the two of us." Jack takes the chair opposite mine as I grab myself a cookie. "Help yourself," I say.

He picks one up and takes a bite. "Oh, wow," he moans, "these are amazing. Is that coconut?"

I nod. "And oats."

"Really?" He chews for a minute, then smiles. "I taste it now."

"I grind up the oats into a flour before mixing them in," I say.

"Ahh, that's why the texture isn't what I was expecting. Wow, Emily, these are seriously amazing."

Warmth seeps into my middle, and not just from the cookies. "Thanks. They're my own recipe." I get up to grab some water glasses and fill a pitcher at the sink. When I come back to the table, Jack is writing in a notebook.

"Before I get too distracted by these cookies," Jack says, "let's get started on a list. What kinds of things do you think we should sell?"

"Should it just be Christmas stuff?" I ask.

"We definitely want a Christmas-y feel to the shop," he says, "but we should also carry some non-holiday items. What did you have in mind?"

"Well, this *is* a Christmas tree farm, so Mom thought having a Christmas tree on display would be a good idea," I say. "We can set a small one up on a table and decorate it with ornaments for sale."

"Great idea," Jack says, taking notes.

"And going along with that, I'd really like to have some of those wooden, vintage-looking signs that say 'Fresh Cut Christmas Trees, $5' or whatever. And maybe some with those little red trucks—you know, the old-fashioned Chevys?—with a Christmas tree in the back."

"Perfect. We'll be sure to get all kinds of Christmas decor, for tabletops and walls," Jack says.

"What do you think about some handcrafted stockings?" I muse. "Something embroidered or made of fur or something—more fancy than you can find at a box store."

Jack writes it down. "That's exactly the kind of stuff I was hoping for—unique handmade items that people can't get anywhere else."

We're silent for a minute while we think of ideas. "A lot of people do baking at Christmas," I say. "Maybe some Christmas-themed baking mixes or kitchen utensils?"

"Hmm," Jack picks up a cookie, looking thoughtful. "Do you think we could turn this recipe into a baking mix? One of those cookie-in-a-jar type things, you know, where you add butter and eggs and mix it up?"

"Probably," I say, "although they wouldn't be exactly the same."

"Pity," he says, "because these are delicious." He shoves the whole thing in his mouth, and I laugh.

"We should have a corner of candy cane inspired items," I say, tapping the paper in front of him to bring us back to the task at hand. "Candles and kitchen towels and socks and stuff. Since it's the Candy Cane Boutique," I say.

"And we'll need some promotional items as well," Jack adds. "T-shirts that say 'Kenworth Christmas Tree Farm' and stuff like that."

We trade ideas back and forth while Jack writes everything down, even if it's something I know won't make the final cut for the boutique. "We're brainstorming," he says. "No idea is a bad idea at this point."

Soon we move on to making a list of non-holiday items to sell in the shop as well. Pine-scented soaps, balsam fir candles and air fresheners, lavender sachets and hand lotions; common gift items one usually finds in a boutique. After an hour, the cookies are gone and the paper is filled—along with our bellies.

"You know what might help," Jack muses, biting the end of the pencil, "is if we took a trip into Seattle and visited an artisan market. We could get some more ideas for the shop, and possibly find some artists and vendors who might be interested in selling their items on commission."

"That's not a bad idea," I say. "Do you want to do that this weekend?"

Jack smiles. "I'm game if you are," he says.

"Oh!" I laugh self-consciously. "Um, sure, I guess I could go with you." My heart gives a happy little trill in my chest.

"Great. I'll pick you up at nine tomorrow morning," Jack says, getting up from the table. "Will Chase want to come with us, do you think?"

"I'll ask him," I say, half-hoping my brother will say no.

"Sounds good," Jack says. "See you tomorrow."

I do *not* spend all evening worrying about what to wear, nor do I toss and turn all night, overthinking Jack's invitation and agonizing over whether or not it's a date. Rather, I casually try on every item of clothing I own (just reorganizing my closet, you know) and spend ~~half the night~~ only a few minutes studying my ceiling.

I get up with the sun, since I'm too keyed up to sleep anymore, and take a long, hot shower to calm my nerves. The smell of bacon and frying potatoes wafts into my room as I'm getting dressed, and my stomach twists painfully—whether from hunger or from nerves, I really couldn't say.

I've managed a few bites of toast and half a cup of coffee when the garage door opens and Jack walks through the mudroom and into the kitchen. His eyes find mine immediately, and he smiles.

"Merry Christmas, Jack," Dad calls. "Come on in."

"Um, Merry Christmas?" He laughs. "You know it's only May, right?"

Dad chuckles. "Not here, son. It's always Christmas for us."

I take my dishes to the sink and scrub them off. "Let me grab my things and then we can go," I say, putting them in the dishwasher.

"Are you coming with us, Chase?" Jack asks.

Chase makes a face. "As tempting as it sounds to wander through overpriced shops smelling of incense and beeswax, I think I'd rather not."

Jack chuckles. "Your loss," he says as I duck out of the kitchen to get my things.

I grab my jacket and purse from my room, then stop to check my appearance in the mirror. Usually I wash my face, throw my dark hair up in a ponytail and call it good, but today I took the time to straighten my hair and pull it half back with a clip. I even put on some lip gloss and mascara, which is more makeup than I ever wear.

"It's not a date," I whisper to myself, "and he's probably not even interested." But my heart twirls inside my chest, hoping that maybe after today, he will be.

I shake off my nerves, don my sneakers, and head back to the kitchen. Jack and Chase are laughing about something when I come in. It might be my imagination, but Jack's smile seems to get a bit brighter when he sees me.

"Ready when you are," I say.

He opens the door for me as we call our goodbyes, heading into the misty morning. The sky is dark and overcast, the ground soggy from the rain overnight.

"Do you have an umbrella?" he asks.

I pat the hobo bag slung over my shoulder. "Never leave home without it," I reply in a singsong voice. He laughs, and we climb into his car.

Jack starts the car and fiddles with some of the dials. "Feel free to adjust whatever you need to be comfortable," he says. I nod, setting my purse down at my feet and buckling my seatbelt.

"You know," he says as we pull out of the long gravel driveway and onto the small mountain road that leads to the highway, "I'm kinda glad Chase didn't want to come."

"You are?" I say, my stomach turning somersaults.

"Yeah." His eyes are on the road, but he glances at me with a sheepish grin. "I've been trying to get up the guts to ask you out for a week now, and while this isn't exactly what I had in mind, I'll take it."

"Really?" My lips pull into a goofy grin, my stomach full of fluttering wings.

"Is that such a surprise?"

"It is to me," I say, looking ahead of us at the road, feeling embarrassed. "I mean, you're *Jackson McKinley,* and I'm just... Emily."

"What do you mean I'm Jackson McKinley?" he asks, bemused. "Why'd you say it like that?"

I let out a breathy laugh. "You know, you were the popular guy. The good-looking athlete that all the girls were wild about."

"I was?"

"Oh, come on, you have to have known that!"

He grins at me. "I kinda knew that, yeah. But..." he looks back at the road, "were *you* wild about me?"

I bend down and dig in my purse, as much to avoid looking at him as to retrieve my sketchbook. "Does it matter?"

I pull my sketchbook onto my lap and flip it open to a blank page. When he still doesn't respond, I glance over at him. He looks thoughtful. "Jack?" I say.

"You're right, it doesn't matter," he says lightly. "High school was a long time ago."

"Yeah. And I didn't really know you at all." He nods, and before I lose my nerve, I add, "but I'm enjoying getting to know you now."

It's his turn to look surprised. "You are?"

I laugh self-consciously, echoing his words. "Is that such a surprise?"

He chuckles. "Touché."

We lapse into silence, and I wonder if he feels as awkward as I do. A quick glance at his face tells me it's not likely. He wears a relaxed smile, leaning back in his seat with one arm gripping the steering wheel. I look away, searching for something to say.

He seems content to let the silence linger, though, so eventually I start sketching. After a few minutes he asks, "What are you drawing?"

I shrug. "Just a generic landscape. Mountains, trees, birds flying overhead."

"Do you ever sketch people?"

"Not usually. I prefer sketching things in nature."

"Things that remind you of home."

It's a statement, not a question, and I glance over at him. He gives me a smile. "That tracks," he says lightly, and a warmth fills my insides. It's nice to feel seen.

Eventually Jack turns on some music, and when I assure him I don't care what we listen to, he settles on a Spotify playlist that includes Ed Sheeran, Coldplay, Billie Eilish, and The Weeknd. I settle more comfortably in my seat, pleasantly surprised to see that we have a similar taste in music.

We don't say much on the drive to Seattle, but as we get nearer to the city, I put my sketchbook away. "Where are we going first?" I ask.

"Pike Place. There's a crafts market there with dozens of artists and vendors. They'll have a good selection of items, and the artists are often right there so we can chat with them."

I watch out the window as the towering trees become towering buildings, their mirrored windows piercing the clouds. Cars and traffic lights multiply, making everything louder, faster, brighter, until suddenly we're swept into the chaos downtown, swallowed by the city's rhythm. Jack finds somewhere to park, and soon we're walking down Pine Street toward the market.

I've been to Pike Place before, of course, but not often. I'd forgotten how much there was to see, not to mention the sheer number of bodies milling around the space. Inwardly I cringe, wishing there weren't so many people.

"You ready for this?" Jack says, a delighted smile on his face.

I don't respond, my eyes trying to take in everything at once. He must see the trepidation on my face, because he takes a step closer.

"Hey, it's alright," his voice says in my ear. "I've got you."

He places a hand gently on the small of my back, and his touch jolts me out of my anxiety-induced stupor. I take a deep breath, looking up at him.

"Thanks," I say. "I just... don't like crowds much."

He frowns. "Sorry. I should have realized there'd be more people here on a Saturday morning. Would you rather come back a different day?"

I can hear the concern in his voice, and it warms me to know that he'd be willing to turn around and go back to the farm if I say the word. But I shake my head.

"No, I'll be okay. I can handle a little discomfort for a few hours."

I give him a small smile, and he searches my face. "Alright," he says at last, "but when you hit your limit just let me know and we'll head out."

I nod, and he takes my hand, pulling me toward the covered stalls with a smile. "Come on—let's see what treasures we can find."

Chapter 9

I barely have time to register the feel of Jack's hand in mine before we're swept along with the crowd toward the colorful booths lining the walls of the main covered market. The first one we come to has all sorts of silver jewelry on display. Cuffs, bangles, earrings, pendants—the polished metal shines like sunlight off an icicle.

"How do you feel about selling jewelry at the boutique?" Jack asks. The noise of the crowd around us ensures that the vendor, sitting at the back of the stall on her phone, can't hear us.

"Hmm. It wouldn't be my first choice," I say, "but maybe?"

Jack drops my hand to pull out a notepad and pen. "We'll plan on no jewelry for now then," he says, making a note. "There will be dozens of jewelry stalls, so just let me know if any of them catch your eye, okay? Otherwise we'll just pass them by."

I nod, and we walk through the crowd to the next booth. I stay as close to Jack as possible, missing the warmth of his hand in mine. He turns and I pause, leaning forward to hear what he is saying.

"Why don't you walk ahead of me?" he says, his breath warm on my neck. "That way if you see anything you'd like to explore a little more, we can stop and take a look."

My eyes must betray my anxiety at being the leader, because he slips his hand back into mine. "I'll be right here."

"Can you keep hold of my hand?" I ask.

He smiles. "Sure. I'll only need both hands when I'm writing something down, and we'll be stopped together whenever that happens."

He squeezes my fingers and gently pulls me ahead of him, leaning in close to whisper, "I'm right here," again. His lips brush ever so slightly against my earlobe, and a burst of heat runs through me. I shiver, feeling my knees tremble, and I can't be certain if it's because of the crowd or because of Jack.

We move forward slowly, glancing at the tables on either side of the wide walkway. We pass stalls selling bags and purses, handcrafted knives with wooden handles, and a booth displaying native artwork. Soon the earthy scent of cedar and moss tickles my nostrils, and we come to a table displaying candles in metal tins, along with bars of soap embedded with pine needles and flowers.

"Wow," I say, picking up a candle and smelling it. The heady scent of balsam fir fills the air, enveloping me in the feeling of the forest. I close my eyes and breathe it in, unconscious of the smile it brings to my face.

"That good?" Jack asks, reaching for a block of soap. He sniffs, and with a look of appreciation nods at me. "These would be perfect."

"I know," I say, and my eyes dart to the woman seated

behind the table. She wears a colorful wrap on her head, under which dark, skinny braids fall past her shoulders. Her smile is warm, and when I catch her eye she stands and comes over to us.

"Like it?" she asks, nodding at the candle still in my hand. "It's one of my most popular scents."

"I do," I say, too quietly for her to hear. I clear my throat. "I do," I say again, louder this time. My mouth goes suddenly dry, my heart pounding in my chest. I look to Jack for help, but he's already leaning over the table with his hand out.

"Jack McKinley," he says, shaking the woman's hand. "Do you make all these yourself?"

"Yes," she says proudly. "Small batches straight from my home."

"Excellent. Are you by chance interested in wholesaling them to an exclusive boutique?"

She looks taken aback. "Um, I don't know. I do pretty well for myself as it is..."

"Commission, then. Here," He pulls out one of my dad's business cards from his wallet and flips it over. Scrawling his name and phone number, he hands it to her. "We're opening a boutique at the Kenworth Christmas Tree Farm, and your merchandise is exactly the kind we're looking for. If you'd like to think about it, my name and number is on the back there— give me a call and we can talk it over."

"Alright," she says, sounding pleased. When she looks over at me, I hand her the candle I've been clutching.

"I'd like this one, please," I say. "And a bar of cedarwood soap."

She wraps the items in tissue paper and places them in a small paper bag with raffia handles. I pull out my wallet and tap my card to the reader she holds out, then take the bag from her. "Thank you," I say, slipping one of her business cards into the bag.

"Good find," Jack says, taking my hand again. Just the feel of his fingers around mine helps calm my racing heart.

"Thank you for handling that," I say. "These will be perfect for the boutique; I hope she agrees to work with us."

"I think we can convince her," he says, giving me a smile.

After that first interaction, we fall into a rhythm. I do the finding, Jack does the talking. We wander through the craft market, and I pause to look at a few stalls in turn: one selling colorful hats, mittens, and scarves made with the softest wool I've ever felt; another with carved wooden figures of bears, moose, trees, and raccoons; and a small booth showcasing all sorts of locally sourced, flavored honey products.

Just as we're coming to the end of one row, my eye catches on some bright, colorful candy wrappers. I move closer to investigate. A large banner reading *Seattle Chocolate is now MAEVE Chocolate!* stretches across the front of the table.

"Hello!" the young salesman standing behind the table greets us. "Have you tried our chocolate before?"

"If it's the same Seattle Chocolate, then yes," I say, picking up a large truffle bar and examining the kaleidoscope of colors on the wrapper.

"For the boutique?" Jack asks me, making a note.

I smile. "For me *and* the boutique," I say. "It's my favorite."

The salesman beams. "It's the very same chocolate, just with a new name and look. The rebrand took place in March, so we're trying to get the word out."

I nod, setting the chocolate bar down. "Did you keep all the same flavors?"

"Many, but not all of them."

"Do you still have Hazelnut Butter Crisp?"

"We do! Only in the truffles for now, but we may decide to bring it back in the bars in the future."

Relief washes through me. "The truffles are my favorite."

"Who do we contact about wholesaling?" Jack asks, as I pay for the package of truffles the man sets in front of me.

"Wholesale at Seattle Chocolate dot com," the man says.

"Great," Jack says. "Thanks."

We take our items and join the crowds once more, milling along the aisles and walkways of the market. Jack passes out as many business cards as I collect, and by the time we finish a couple hours later, our arms are full of treasures. It started raining while we shopped, but I don't have an extra hand to hold the umbrella, so we hurry through the drizzle to the car.

"I wish you would have let me pay for some of this," Jack says as we stash everything in the trunk.

"Business expenses," I say. "It's easier to submit to the accountant when it's all on the same card."

We climb inside and I release a big breath, tipping my head back against the seat. "That was a lot."

"It was," Jacks says, starting the car. "But we made some good contacts and have a lot of great ideas for the boutique."

"That's true," I say. "But still—I feel like crawling under a rock and not talking to another person for a month."

He laughs, and the sound sends a flicker of warmth down my spine. There were so many shared looks and little touches today, each one sending giddy sparks of delight all through me. I wonder if he feels it, too, or if it's just me.

"So, any thoughts about lunch?" he asks.

SHAELA KAY

"I definitely want some lunch," I say. "But preferably somewhere with a drive through. I'm all peopled out."

"Fair enough," he says, backing out of the parking spot. "I know just the place."

He takes us to Dick's Drive-In, leaving me in the blessed silence of the car while he goes in to order. I lean back and close my eyes, the gentle tap of the rain on the car like a lullaby. Ten minutes later, I startle when Jack opens the door.

"Sorry," he says, seeing me jump.

"It's fine," I say, reaching for the paper bags he holds toward me. "Mm, smells good. Thanks."

"Of course."

We eat in relative silence, enjoying the food and the quiet *tap, tap* of the rain on the roof. When we're finished, I take the bags and wrappers out to the trash can and then we head back to the farm. The silence settles between us, comfortable and warm, and I'm glad this time when Jack doesn't turn on any music. I don't even pull out my sketchbook—just revel in the silence and his company. I wish I could bottle up the quiet comfort of this moment forever.

"I think I'd like to find an artist to showcase in the boutique," I say as Jack takes the exit off the highway for Echo Ridge, "but nothing we saw today really felt quite right."

"The wooden sculptures we picked up are pretty amazing," he says.

"They are, but I was thinking two dimensional art. Paint or ink or something."

He glances at me. "Any reason you don't want to showcase your own work?"

His question startles me. "What?"

"Your watercolors and sketches. We could have prints made

up of your drawings. Like that bird you were working on the other day."

"That was just for fun."

"It's *art*, Emily. You're an artist. A good one."

His words feel strange and uncomfortable. I've never felt like an artist—I just like to doodle and draw. I mean, sure, I won a few art competitions in school, but that doesn't mean I'm an artist. And it *certainly* doesn't mean that I'm good enough to sell my work.

I can see by the look on Jack's face that he's ready to argue his point, which isn't something I'm in the mood for. So I give him a vague reply telling him I'll think about it and change the subject.

Twenty minutes later we pull onto the long gravel drive, and the butterflies inside me wake up with a sleepy stretch of their wings. This wasn't *really* a date, but based on our conversation earlier—not to mention all the looks and hand-holding that happened—I *think* it kind of was? Maybe? Ugh. I hate this part about new relationships. Not that I've had many to compare this to. There aren't a lot of guys willing to pursue shy, introverted, farm girls.

But Jack might. I hope he does.

We pull up to the house and Jack pops the trunk. Loading our arms with our boutique treasures, we head into the house.

"We're back," I call from the mudroom, kicking off my shoes so I don't track dirt into the house. Jack does the same, then follows me through the kitchen into the living room. It's empty.

"Hello?" I call. There's no response.

I turn to Jack and shrug. "Everyone must be out," I say.

We go back into the kitchen and set everything down on the

table. "Thanks for today," I say, fiddling with one of the gift bags to give my hands something to do.

"It was a lot of fun," Jack says, gracing me with another one of his dazzling smiles. "I'm glad you could come. And I'm glad that Chase stayed home."

He winks at me, and the spark in my middle turns into a fire. But then he turns and goes into the mudroom, effectively dousing the flames.

"Let me know what your mom thinks of everything," he says, putting on his shoes. "I'll be by on Monday and we can talk about it then, okay?"

"Oh, sure. Yeah, that's a good idea," I say, standing in the doorway to the kitchen.

"Great. I'll see you Monday then." He flashes me another smile and reaches for the handle.

"Um, Jack?"

My voice causes him to look back. "Yeah?"

I fold my arms self-consciously across my chest, my insides swirling like a spring storm. "I was just wondering if, um... you know, are we...?"

My voice trails off and I look at him expectantly, hoping he'll save me from the awkward question I feel compelled to ask.

He lets go of the doorknob and turns to face me, one eyebrow raised. "Are we... what?"

I moan and drop my face into my hand for a moment. I hear him chuckle, and when I raise my head he has both hands on his hips, and a sideways smile even more devastating than his previous one.

I take a deep breath. "I was wondering about what you said this morning. You know, about wanting to ask me out? And then, today..." My voice trails off again, strangled by my embarrassment.

I should have kept my mouth shut.

He takes a step closer. "Today...?

I drop my eyes, unable to look at him a moment longer. "Never mind," I say. He tips his head to the side, studying me. I remember what Sophie said, about him taking off his shirt on purpose to tease me, and I can't help but think he might be doing the same now. That wicked grin looks *far* too innocent to be so naïve.

"I think I know what you're asking," he says, dropping his voice and coming still closer.

"You do?"

"You want to know if we're an item now?"

He's standing right in front of me, and I can't tear my eyes away from his face. "Um. Dating... is the word... I was thinking. But yeah. That," I stammer.

He laughs again, soft and low. "I'm not sure," he says. "What do you think?"

Are you kidding *me?!* "I... don't know," I say, feeling my face burn. "That's why I asked."

He looks at me for a long moment, at the pink flooding my cheeks. He reaches up and strokes his thumb along the blush, then lets his arm drop. His touch leaves a trail of fire on my skin.

"I guess it depends on your definition of dating. Are we counting today as a date?" he asks.

"Um, yes?"

He grins at my uncertainty, and I feel my knees wobble. "Okay. So we've been on one date. But dat*ing* implies more than one." He looks into my eyes and I stare back at his, noticing tiny flecks of green amid the brown. "Would you like to go on another date with me, Emily?"

His eyes dart down to my lips, then back up to my eyes. For a moment I can't breathe, but at last I whisper, "Yes. I... I'd like that."

He smiles, soft and slow, and I watch his mouth, wondering if this is the moment. Will he kiss me, here, now? He lifts his hand again, and this time brushes an errant lock of hair away from my face. "I'd like that, too," he murmurs.

I hang there, suspended in time—wanting, waiting—until he draws in a breath and steps back. "Next weekend?" he says.

"Next weekend," I say automatically, trying not to let him see how much I'm trembling.

"Good. This time, I'll take you somewhere with a lot less people."

I let out a tremulous, breathy laugh. "Thanks, I would appreciate that."

He gives me another long look, and the tension between us starts building again. Abruptly he turns and grabs the handle.

"See you Monday, Em," he says. Flashing me a final smile, he opens the door and steps out of the house.

Chapter 10

Sunday dawns clear and warm, and shortly after breakfast I head outside. At the edge of the front lawn, where the sparse grass turns into earthy humus and the ferns wave a hello to the house, an enormous Douglas Fir stretches nearly a hundred feet in the air. The ground at its base is soft with moss and dry needles, creating the perfect spot to sit and sketch. I settle myself against the trunk, with the house to my right and the enormous expanse of woods to my left, feeling as if I'm balancing on a gossamer thread between worlds.

I don't know how long I've been drawing, but I look up when I hear the screen door slam. Chase steps off the front porch and makes his way toward me, and as he gets closer, I pat the ground. With an indulgent smile, he settles himself cross-legged beside me.

"I was wondering where you'd gone," he says, picking up a long, dry pine needle and breaking it into little pieces.

"It was too beautiful a day to stay indoors," I say, turning back to my sketchbook. Chase watches me for a moment before speaking again.

"How was the trip into Seattle?"

"Good," I say, without looking up. "We found a lot of great ideas and made several contacts with possible vendors."

"That's great. Sorry I didn't come along. I realized after you left that there were bound to be a lot of people. I should have come as a buffer for you."

My heart warms at his words. "Thanks, I appreciate that. There *were* a lot of people, but Jack helped me out." I keep my head down, feeling my face warm at the memory of Jack's hand in mine, and not wanting my brother to ask questions.

"I'm glad," he says. "Jack is a good friend."

A bird calls from somewhere in the forest, and overhead a squirrel chatters back.

"Dad said you met a friend for dinner yesterday," I say without looking up.

"An acquaintance more than a friend. I had a date with a girl I met last week, but it's not going to go anywhere. I probably won't see her again."

"I'm sorry."

He shrugs. "It's fine. We had a nice time, but we don't seem very compatible. There was no spark, you know?"

I nod noncommittally, and I wonder if he suspects about me and Jack—has he been able to see the spark between us? Does he know the attraction we each feel? I chase the thought away, instead concentrating on the fern at the base of a nearby tree that I'm sketching.

As I add more details to the picture, Jack's words from yesterday come back to me. I pause, turning to face my brother. "Can I ask you something?"

"Of course."

"Do you think I'm an artist?"

He gives me a look as if I've sprouted another head. "What kind of question is that? Of course you're an artist."

I sigh. "I mean, like, a *real* artist."

"Em," he says, tapping the edge of my sketchbook, "you *are* a real artist. An amazing one."

"But is my work good enough to sell?" I ask, thinking again of what Jack suggested. *Are there actually people willing to pay for what I do?*

"It is, but that's not what makes you an artist," he says.

"It's not?"

"No. What makes you an artist is your ability to see beauty in everything around you," he says. "Where other people see just trees and grass and sky, you see wonder and possibility, and all the tiny details about life that so many of us miss." He taps the image of the fern again, right where the tightly curled tip begins to uncoil.

I smile at him, and he smiles back. "You really think so?"

"I know so," he says, bumping his arm against mine.

I put my sketchbook down and scoot closer, until I can lean my head on his shoulder. "Thank you," I say quietly.

He puts an arm around me. "You underestimate yourself, Em," he says. "You always have." He sighs. "I know people say you're the 'quiet twin,' and for some reason you think that equates to being 'not enough.' But you *are* enough, Emily. You're amazing. There is no one in this world I would rather have by my side, in any situation, than you."

My eyes prickle at his words, and I scrunch up my nose, blinking before the tears can form and fall. He kisses the top of my head, and we sit in silence for several minutes, listening to the rustle of the wind through the trees and the call of a crow off in the distance.

"I love it here," I say quietly.

"I know. I do, too."

"Do you think Jack's plan will work? Will it be enough to save the farm?"

"Your guess is as good as mine. Only time will tell." After a short pause he adds, "But I trust Jack. He wants to see us succeed as much as we do. Maybe even more, since this is his first real consulting job."

He shifts beside me, and I sit upright so he can get to his feet. "You coming in?" he asks. "Mom and I are going to play Rumikub."

"Sure," I say. "Just let me gather my things and I'll be right there."

He nods and turns away as I tip my head back, looking up into the branches of the massive tree I've been sitting against.

"Thank you for a lovely morning," I say, turning so I can press my palm to its trunk. The bark is hard and rough against my skin, and I move my fingers gently over its surface. Suddenly I hear the familiar rattle of something falling through the canopy. I glance around, waiting, and with a soft *thump* I see a small pinecone land a few feet away, on the grass. I look back up at the massive tree and smile.

"Thanks," I say.

Picking up my sketchbook and the fallen pinecone, I head to the front door.

Chapter 11

M y alarm goes off as usual at six thirty the next morning. I shower and throw on some overalls, then pull my hair back into a ponytail. Dad greets me in the kitchen as I come down the stairs.

"'Merry Christmas, Emmy-girl," he says.

"'Merry Christmas, Dad."

"You going to help me with the mowing today?"

"Sure am," I say, pouring myself a cup of coffee.

"Good. You want to take the big mower to the north fields or work along the incline?"

Before I can answer, the crunch of wheels on the gravel drive cause us both to look around. I frown. "Who could that be?" I ask.

Dad looks out the window, then chuckles. "Jack is putting your brother to shame," he says.

"Jack?" I repeat, incredulous.

I hear his car door shut, and my pulse kicks up a notch. Dad opens the garage door, then holds open the one to the house.

"Good morning, Walter," Jack says, stepping past him.

"'Morning, son. Come on in."

They come through the mudroom together, Jack holding a pink paperboard box. His face lights up when he sees me.

"Good morning, Emily," he says. "Merry Christmas!"

I laugh, surprised. "Merry Christmas to you, too." I lift my brow expectantly. "Is this going to become a regular thing?" I ask.

He shrugs. "I knew you were an early riser, so I thought I'd bring some donuts over for our meeting." He sets the box down on the counter, and Dad opens it up.

"Mm, apple fritters, my favorite," he says, pulling one out.

I laugh lightly. "That's very thoughtful of you. But my mom won't be up for a couple hours yet, and I've got chores to get done before then." I take another sip of coffee, watching him over the rim of my mug.

"Oh. Well, that's okay," he says, rubbing a hand across the back of his neck. "I'm not needed at the store this morning—is there anything I could help with?"

I glance at my dad, who shrugs and takes a bite of his donut. "That depends," I say. "Do you know how to manage a ride-on mower?"

Jack laughs. "Have you seen my parents' lawn? I could drive a mower long before I could drive a car."

I grin. "Great. Have you caffeinated?"

He throws me a mock salute. "Yes ma'am, taking it black as instructed. You'll find I'm alert as a seagull at a picnic."

I laugh, and Dad claps him on the shoulder. "In that case," he says, "we better get you behind a wheel before you run off in search of some French fries."

Jack follows Dad out the door as I add an excessive amount

of creamer to my coffee, trying to cool it as quickly as possible. I down it in three gulps, then hurry after them.

I catch up just as they're opening the wide barn doors. "Jack, you get first pick of the mowers," Dad says.

Looking them over, Jack points to one on the far right. "That one looks similar to the mower I'm used to," he says.

"Great. You take that mower and mow down the grass in the southeast field." Dad points, and Jack nods.

"Here," I say, walking toward him from the supply shelf. I switch on a two way radio and hand it to him. "We use these out in the fields. If you have any questions or run into any issues, just holler."

He nods and clips it to his jeans. "Sure thing, boss," he says. I roll my eyes and give him a playful shove. He tosses me another grin, and I nearly swoon. Smiles like his should come with a warning label.

"Thanks for jumping in to help," I say, as Dad gets his mower started and heads down the road to the southwest field.

"Of course."

"Are you on any time constraint? Do you have other plans today?"

"Nope. Just the meeting with you about vendors. Speaking of," he says, brightening, "The woman with the candles called, and she wants in."

"Really?"

"Really."

"That's great!"

"She said she doesn't have her candles or soaps in any shops because she prefers to sell them herself, but she remembers coming here as a kid to get her Christmas tree and she wants to help us out. She's willing to sell on consignment for now, with the possibility of a wholesale deal in the future."

"That's wonderful," I say. He lifts his hand up for a high-five, which I give him. "Have you heard from anyone else?" I ask.

"Not yet, but I'll be making phone calls after our meeting today."

"Then let's get to work," I say. "The grass won't mow itself."

He laughs, gives me another mock salute, and climbs aboard the mower.

I call a halt over the radio just before ten o'clock. "Jack, let's head back to the house. Dad, I'll be back to finish up after we meet with Mom."

"Roger that," he replies.

"I'll meet you at the barn," Jack answers.

But by the time we put away the mowers and head back to the house, another car is parked in the drive.

"Who's that?" Jack asks.

I grin. "Sophie."

"Sophie Hernadez?" he asks. "I didn't know she was still around."

"Yup. She comes on the first Monday of every month to give Mom a manicure. Oh! That's today." I sigh. "I'm so sorry, Jack, you waited all this time for our meeting, and I completely forgot that Mom has another appointment."

He shrugs. "It's fine. We can chat about it another time— maybe after I make those phone calls today." He bumps me with his shoulder as we walk up to the garage. "At least I got to see you."

My heart does a triple flip and promptly swoons. I, on the other hand, ~~walk calmly~~ trip on the way up to the door.

"Are you okay?" Jack asks, grabbing my arm.

My cheeks burn, but I manage a little laugh. "Yeah, I'm fine. Thanks. Um, do you want to come in and say hi to Sophie?" I ask, changing the subject.

"Sure. So she's a nail tech?"

"More or less," I say with a shrug.

Bemused, he asks, "What's that supposed to mean?"

"She considers it more of a passion than an occupation," I say. "It's not what she does for work."

I open the door and step into the mudroom, with Jack right behind me. After taking off our shoes we walk into the kitchen. Two heads turn in our direction.

"Jackson McKinley," Sophie says with a grin, standing from her place at the table.

"Hey, Sophie. It's been a while." He gives her a brief hug and then steps back.

"You look good," she says, raising an eyebrow at me. "Most definitely still the MVBOC."

I flush and turn away, but not before I see the look of confusion on Jack's face. "What was that?"

"Never mind," Sophie says, sitting back at the table. "I can't chat—I'm working on Kathy's nails and that will *always* take priority."

I busy myself at the sink, inwardly cursing Sophie and wondering if I'll ever be able to look Jack in the face again, when he sidles up beside me.

"Can I help?" he asks, glancing at the dishes in the sink.

"Um, sure. Towels are in the drawer to your right."

I wash a pan and hand it to him. He takes it from me and leans in a bit closer.

"What was that Sophie called me? The MVP-something?"

I sigh. Sophie will be the death of me—if I don't kill her first.

I shrug, not looking at him. "It was just a nickname we had for you in high school."

"We?"

I wince. "*She*. She had for you," I say, but the warmth in my neck gives me away and he grins.

"Uh-huh. So, what does it mean?"

I don't answer at first, desperately trying to think of something, *anything*, that will satisfy his curiosity without killing me with mortification. I hand him another dish.

"Um—"

But Mom's voice interrupts. "Emily, can you bring me the magazine on the counter in my bathroom, please? There's something I want to show Sophie."

"Sure," I say, drying my hands quickly. I throw Jack a sheepish smile as I hurry from the room, and he narrows his eyes at me.

I take my time getting the magazine, still trying to think about what to say to Jack, and when I finally return to the kitchen, he's nowhere in sight. I set the magazine down on the table next to my mom.

"Where did Jack go?" I ask. Sophie glances at me with a sly grin, but Mom is the one who answers.

"He got a phone call and said he had to go," she says, watching Sophie shape and buff her nails.

A mixture of relief and regret washes through me. "Oh, okay." I stand there for a moment, gathering my thoughts. "Guess I should get back to work then," I say, moving into the mudroom.

"Hang on, Em," Sophie calls. "Kathy, we're going to let that dry for a sec before I do the next coat, okay? Don't touch anything, I'll be right back."

Sophie comes to stand beside me while I put my shoes back on.

"Well well well," she says, "*somebody* seemed really helpful in the kitchen back there." She waggles her eyebrows, and I groan.

"Please, Sophie, don't embarrass me. Speaking of," I smack her leg, since I'm still crouched down, tying my shoes, "why did you say that to Jack? He's going to plague me now until he finds out what it means."

As if to prove my point, my phone buzzes in my pocket. I pull it out and see a text message from Jack.

JACK

Sorry, I got a call and had to run. It's about a job. But I'm not letting you off the hook—what was that about a high school nickname?

I groan. "You see?" I turn my phone to face her, and she squints at the screen.

"You gave him your number?" she says, crossing her arms and giving me a smug smile.

"No! I—" I huff. "He works for us now, so Chase gave him my number."

"But you text him?"

"Well, yeah, but—"

Her grin widens, and I make an exasperated sound—half laugh, half growl. "Sophie, it's really not that big a deal."

"Who said it's a big deal? You're the one looking guilty."

"I do not!"

She laughs, and as I get to my feet she embraces me lightly. "Calm down, *chiquita*. I'm only teasing you. I'm sure nothing's happened."

She pulls away, and though I try to keep my face impassive, her eyes narrow. "*Did* something happen?"

I think of our trip to Seattle—what he said about wanting to ask me out, the feeling of his hand in mine—and though I don't respond, she gives a little laugh.

"I know that look," she says. "You're falling for him, aren't you?"

My eyes dart to the open door leading into the kitchen. "Maybe?" I sigh. "I don't know. It's all just... kinda new."

"How new? What's happened?"

"Nothing has *happened*," I say, not wanting to tell Sophie about Seattle. "But... it feels like something *could* happen, you know?"

She squeals. "Has he asked you out yet?"

My cheeks warm, and I smile, nodding. She squeals again.

"Sophie, please, be quiet!" I say, though I can't help but laugh at her excitement. She was always more exuberant than me.

"Okay, okay, I'll stop," she says, grinning like a nutcracker. "But I expect a full report after your date, okay?"

I roll my eyes, trying not to smile. "I've got to get back to work, and you need to finish my mom's nails."

"Yes, yes, back to work," she says. "But when is your date?"

"Bye, Sophie," I call, heading out the garage door.

She yells something at me in Spanish, but the door shuts before I catch it all. Relieved, I pull my phone out of my pocket and see that Jack has sent me another text.

JACK

If you're free, I'd like to take you out Saturday afternoon. I'll pick you up at 2pm.

We'll be outside, so prepare for the weather.

I smile, a flutter of excitement landing in my stomach. Before I can respond, he sends another message.

JACK

BTW, I expect to hear all about that nickname when I pick you up.

Chapter 12

You know how time seems to slow down in the week leading up to Christmas? The anticipation, the excitement, the wonder—all combine to steal the rhythm of the clock until rather than a march, each second drifts by like a snowflake, soft and slow.

That's how the week feels.

But Saturday finally arrives, and too full of nervous energy, I take my sketchbook out on the porch to wait for Jack's arrival. The anticipation proves even too much for my pencil, however, because by the time Jack pulls up I've barely made a mark on the page.

I stand as he gets out of the car, excitement pulling the corners of my mouth up into a grin.

"Hey Emily," he says, walking over.

"Hey Jack."

"You ready to go?"

"Ready as I can be, without knowing what we're doing," I say.

He chuckles. "You'll see."

I hold my arms out, letting him inspect me. "Well, am I dressed appropriately? All you said was that we were going to be outside."

He looks down at what I'm wearing—jeans and sneakers, with a long-sleeved flannel shirt open over a simple white t-shirt. His eyes don't linger overlong, but when he looks back at my face there's a fervor in his eyes that wasn't there before.

"You look fantastic," he says, and it fills my insides with warmth.

He opens the car door for me and I climb inside. "Now, before we get going, there's something I need to ask you," he says.

I look over at him, curious. "Sure."

"What was it that Sophie called me the other day?"

I groan. "You're never going to let that go, are you?" He chuckles, shaking his head. "If I tell you," I say, "will you give me a hint about where we're going?"

He answers without hesitation. "Gladly."

I sigh again. "Fine. She called you the MVBOC."

"MVBOC?"

"Yep."

"What does it mean?"

I shrug innocently. "You only said I had to tell you what Sophie called you, not what it meant." Laughing at his indignant look, I elbow him playfully. "Your turn. Give me a hint."

He thinks about it for a moment. "We're not leaving town."

That significantly lessens the possibilities, and I frown. "Are we going bowling?"

"Outside, remember?"

"Oh, that's right. Hmm." I glance behind us at the back seat but nothing is there. "It's past lunchtime, so I doubt we're going on a picnic."

"Correct."

"Will we be hiking?"

He considers for a moment. "Not exactly," he says, "although we will be moving around outside."

"Will we be alone?"

He looks over at me, hiding a smile. "Do you *want* to be alone?"

I'd be lying if I said I didn't fantasize about being alone with Jack, and how occupied our lips would be, but he *definitely* doesn't need to know that. "Um. I guess it depends?" I say.

He laughs. "On what?"

On what we'd be doing if we were alone. On if you want to be alone with me. On whatever this is between us.

"Never mind," I say, then lapse into silence. The playful question provokes a deeper response in myself than I expected, and I chew on my thoughts as we drive.

He glances at me a couple times, and after a few minutes he says, "We won't be alone, but we won't be with a crowd of strangers."

I nod, and the quiet settles around us again.

We drive through town and out the other side, heading up the road to The Point. I wrack my brain, trying to think of what he could have planned for us when we suddenly turn off the road onto a gravel drive. I frown, trying to figure out where we are. After a minute I see a plywood sign reading "Johnson Adventure Outfitters" posted in front of a small dirt parking lot.

"The Johnsons'?" I ask. "Are we using the shooting range?"

He gives me a sly look. "You'll see."

I frown, trying to remember all the different rentals the

Johnson family provides. It's not the season for snow sports, and it's too chilly to go out on the lake—we're not dressed for it, either. And then it dawns on me.

"Paintballing?" I gasp.

He grins. "Paintballing."

He parks the car and we get out, making our way to the rental office built into the side of the house. My heart is doing jumping jacks and I can't stop the grin that stretches across my face as we walk. Mr. Johnson comes out to greet us.

"Hi, Mr. Johnson," Jack says, shaking his hand.

"Jackson, good to see you. Emily, how're you doing?"

"I'm good, thanks Mr. Johnson."

He indicates the large pole building behind the house, which has one of the bay doors open. "I've got everything ready for you in there," he says. "You'll have the range and the course to yourselves for now, but I've got a large group coming in at four."

"No problem," Jack says. "Are the girls going to play with us?"

"Courtney and McKenna said they will—I'll round them up and send them out."

"Great, thanks."

Mr. Johnson leads us into the building. After Jack and I sign a waiver, Mr. Johnson shows us to the table where he laid out all the equipment. "Coveralls are hanging there," he points, "and you can use the lifejackets as padded armor underneath, if you'd like." He indicates the row of lifejackets hanging on the far wall next to the paddleboards.

"Padded armor?" I say quietly, giving Jack a questioning look.

"Thanks, Mr. Johnson," Jack says as the man waves and

heads back toward the house. He turns to me. "I asked for the softest paintballs he had, but sometimes they can still sting a bit. You can buy specially padded suits for paintballing, but it looks like the Johnsons just use regular coveralls," he says, glancing at the lineup along the wall. "Pretty ingenious, actually, to offer life jackets to wear underneath. That's equipment they already have. But it might make it more difficult to move around in."

I pick up one of the pink paintballs from the container on the table and roll it between my fingers. The fluid inside gives a little, but the plastic-like membrane surrounding it is still pretty stiff.

"How much does it hurt?" I ask.

He shrugs. "It depends. We can try it without the life-jackets first, and if it's too uncomfortable we can come back and put them on. Maybe put your jacket on first as an extra layer?"

"All right," I say.

Jack pulls on a sweatshirt and I zip up my jacket before stepping into the coveralls. Thankfully I'd braided my hair this morning, so there's no ponytail to make the googles fit funny. Jack hands me a pair of gloves.

"Here," he says, "you're going to want these."

"So are there rules or anything?" I ask, taking the gloves and pulling them on.

"No face shots if you can help it," he says, "and I'd prefer you watch your aim below the belt as well." He smirks, and I snicker.

"Noted," I say.

We hear voices outside and turn to see two teenage girls walking toward the shop. One looks to be about fourteen or fifteen, and the other a few years younger. They both smile as they come inside.

"Hi guys," the older one with blonde hair greets us. "I'm McKenna and this is Courtney. Our dad said you were looking for a few more players?"

"Yes, please," Jack says. "Emily here has never played before, which gives me an unfair advantage."

"Oh, you're going to love it!" Courtney says, looking at me. "We'll play us three against him."

"Hey now, I don't think she needs *quite* that much help," Jack says. I give him an amused look.

"You afraid to get beaten by a trio of girls?" I tease.

McKenna and Courtney both give him smug looks, and he holds his hands up in a sign of surrender. "Easy there," he says with a laugh. "If that's what you want, I'm game."

The girls start suiting up while Jack helps me with the gun and ammunition. "We're going to shoot some targets to get warmed up," he calls to them. "We'll meet you in the field in twenty minutes."

It doesn't take long to get the hang of shooting the paintball gun, so after a few rounds we head over to the field. The Johnsons' property spans nearly thirty acres, most of which is still heavily wooded. But six acres have been thinned and enclosed with a netted orange safety fence to mark the play area. Huge trees, mostly pine and red cedar, still stand throughout the playing field, along with several outcroppings of stone and rock. Rusted-out cars and trucks are scattered throughout the area like war-torn relics. Their doors and windshields are missing, which makes them perfect for ducking behind or firing through. I take it all in, impressed.

"Looks like fun," I say.

"Here's hoping," Jack says, grinning at me.

Courtney and McKenna join us, decked out in camouflage gear far more sophisticated than what we're wearing. Jack gives them an appraising look.

"I was already regretting agreeing to three-on-one, but now I'm *really* regretting it," he says.

McKenna laughs, and Courtney looks smug. "Owner perks," she says, propping her gun over her shoulder like a nonchalant soldier. I laugh, liking her already.

"Here," McKenna passes us each a small plastic whistle. "Dad forgot to set these out this morning. If you get hurt and need some help, blow the whistle."

"But *only* if you genuinely need help," her sister adds. "No crying wolf. And if you get tired and want to end the game, blow three quick blasts to let everyone know."

We nod, and I tuck the whistle into the slim pocket along my right thigh. Jack does the same.

"So, any rules you two want to consider?" McKenna asks, looking between us.

Jack shrugs. "I don't think so." He looks at me. "Any questions or concerns from you, Em?"

I laugh lightly. "I have so many concerns it's not even funny. But I'm sure it will be fine. Let's give it a go."

"Alright then," McKenna says, looking back at Jack. "We'll give you a thirty second head start. Go!"

Flashing me a grin, he turns and takes off into the field, veering to the left and disappearing from view a few moments later. I look at my new teammates.

"Any words of advice?" I ask.

Courtney cocks her gun. "Don't get hit," she says.

"Time!" McKenna yells. She nods at us and takes off into the field, followed closely by her sister.

I start out going left, like Jack did when he ran off. But after a minute I hear the pop of a gun and a cry of delight over to my right. I recognize Jack's shout of laughter and turn in that direction.

The weather is perfect. Patches of sun and shade from the clouds moving across the sky create an ever-shifting pattern of light, making it more difficult to track movement. I pause, listening. A light breeze blows across my face, bringing with it the scent of damp earth and pine sap. I breathe it in, letting it ground me.

Suddenly a paintball whizzes past my shoulder, and I instinctively duck. Jack steps out from behind a tree, grinning at me. He has a blue splatter on his arm from a previous hit.

"You really need to work on your stealth," he says. "I heard your shoes crunching from a mile away."

I lift my gun and take a shot at him, but he ducks behind the tree again.

"I *meant* for you to hear me," I lie. "I wanted to draw you out of hiding."

"Is that so?"

A flash of movement behind him catches my eye, and he sees the surprise flit across my face. He whirls around right as I hear another *pop!*, and the shot catches him right in the chest.

McKenna crows, but before she can dodge away Jack fires, hitting her in the leg before he takes off at a run. I sprint after him, trying to keep him in sight.

As soon as he slows to a jog, I duck behind an empty oil

drum before he hears or sees me. Trying to catch my breath, I listen for the sound of his footsteps, but I hear nothing. I set my gun down and peek around the barrel, looking to where I last saw him.

There's no one there.

I lean on my hands and stretch myself out further, scanning the trees for any sign of him, but he's nowhere in sight.

"Looking for me?"

His voice startles me and I yelp, falling forward. Quickly I roll onto my back, but my gun is too far away and I can't reach it. He laughs, crouching down beside me.

"You keep sneaking up on me," I say, my heart pounding in my ears.

He grins. "You need to pay better attention."

"Did you know I was following you?"

"Of course." He reaches a hand out to help me up, and I take it.

"Thanks."

He picks up my gun and hands it to me as well. "Just like that?" I ask, narrowing my eyes at him.

He shrugs. "Sure."

"Why?"

Leaning in close, he says, "I like being chased by you."

Before I can respond, he flashes me a smile and takes off through the trees again.

Chapter 13

I t's the most fun I've had in a very long time. The first time I
got hit with a paintball it was a bit of a shock, but more
surprise than pain. It triggered my competitiveness, however,
which made for a far more interesting experience. Eventually
Jack and I decide to team up against the sisters, who are much
better and far more ruthless than we had imagined. He says it's
because they have better gear. I say it's because they're actually
better.

We're tired and sweaty by the time we take off all the gear
and gather our things. Waving to the girls, we head back to
the car.

"Want to grab something to eat?" he asks, opening my door
for me.

Before I can answer, his phone rings. Glancing at the
screen, his eyes light up. "Sorry Em, do you mind if I take this
call?"

"Not at all."

"Thanks."

He turns around. "This is Jackson McKinley," he says,

starting to walk away. I shut the door and watch him through the window, wondering who's on the phone. Whoever it is, he seems to be very excited to hear from them.

He stands with one hand on his hip, the other holding the phone to his ear, and I'm struck again by how ~~hot~~ handsome he is. Even in rumpled clothes with mussed-up hair, it's impossible not to find him attractive. I wonder if he finds me attractive as well.

After a minute Jack ends the call. "Sorry about that," he says, opening his door and climbing into the car. "That was a company I'd sent my resume to a few weeks ago." He starts the engine. "So, lunch? Or ice cream?"

"*Always* ice cream," I say.

We drive back down the gravel road, making our way toward the only ice cream shop in town (because Dairy Queen doesn't count, and I'll fight anyone who says otherwise). As we drive, Jack reaches over and takes my hand. Tingles race up my arm as he does, settling in my chest like a purring cat.

PineCones Ice Cream Parlor is a cute little shop with about a dozen flavors of old-fashioned, slow-churned ice cream. Most of them are standard favorites that are always available, but the owner, Marjorie Grover, always makes a couple seasonal flavors as well.

"Welcome in," she calls as we come through the door. A handful of customers sit around the tables, talking quietly and eating their ice cream. Jack leads me to the display counter and looks down.

"Do you get the same flavor ice cream every time?" he asks, looking at me. "Or do you like to try different ones?"

"It depends," I say. "I usually pick my favorite, but sometimes the seasonal flavor sounds enticing, or I'm in the mood for something different. How about you?"

"I like to try different flavors," he says. "I don't think I've ever picked the same flavor ice cream twice in a row in my life."

"So you don't have a favorite?"

"Oh no, I definitely have a favorite," he says, smiling at me. "But if I never try anything else, how will I know if it's *still* my favorite?"

I laugh, but his logic kind of makes sense. Marjorie finishes ringing up a man with two small children and then turns to us. "What'll it be today?"

Jack looks to me and indicates that I should go first. "I'll have two scoops of pralines and cream on a waffle cone, please."

"And I'll have the same," Jack says, surprising me.

She hands us our cones and Jack promptly passes his off to me so he can pay. Instead of sitting down at a table, we take our cones outside and settle on a bench. I take a bite of ice cream, the sweet, buttery crunch bursting with flavor in my mouth. I savor it, letting the cream sit on my tongue as it melts, then biting into the toffee-crusted pecan bits left behind. It's pure heaven.

"So is this your favorite flavor?" Jack asks, taking a bite of his cone.

"Yes. I figured I already tried something new today, so I deserve something deliciously familiar." A drip of melting ice cream sneaks down the side of my cone, and I lick it up.

"Fair enough," he chuckles.

"And you?" I ask, taking another bite. "I was surprised that you ordered the same as me."

"Would you believe me if I told you this was my favorite flavor as well?"

"Not for a minute," I say, and he laughs.

"Good, because it's not." He winks. "It just sounded good when you asked for it, and I don't think I've tried it before. It's nice."

I stare at him. "You've never had pralines and cream ice cream before?"

"Not that I remember."

I shake my head. "City boys," I mutter, and he laughs again, loud and long. The sound fills my stomach with butterflies.

We roll the windows down on the drive back to the farm. Jack holds my hand again as he drives, singing along to Justin Beiber and encouraging me to do the same. I just smile and shake my head, enjoying the carefree, happy moment. My heart sighs, feeling perfectly content.

Too soon we pull down the long gravel road leading to my house. My head comes out of the clouds slowly, not wanting to feel the pull of gravity and reality waiting for me below. Jack gets out of the car to walk me to the door, taking my hand as soon as he's beside me. Anticipation churns in my stomach, filling me up with bubbles that never seem to pop.

"Do you want to come in?" I ask when we get to the door.

"I'd like to, but I promised my mother I'd be home for dinner tonight, and I'll need to clean myself up. My sister is bringing her boyfriend to meet the family."

"Oh, nice. I hope you like him."

"I do too," he says. "Jenny seems pretty smitten."

He looks at me when he says it, and the bubbling in my stomach overflows. "Thanks for a great afternoon," I say, looking down at my hand in his.

"I'm glad you came," he says, his voice softer. "I haven't been paintballing in years—I'd forgotten how much fun it could be."

I look up, surprised. "Years? You looked and sounded like you did it far more often than that."

He smiles. "Nah. But I thought you might enjoy it, after what you said about missing out on your brother's birthday party." His thumb traces small circles on the back of my hand, and my heart trembles.

"You remembered," I murmur.

He nods, his eyes searching my face, and I wonder if he sees how hard I'm falling, if he knows my heart is at stake. Could his be as well?

Suddenly his look turns playful. "Would the fact that I remembered something significant earn me the privilege of knowing what MVBOC means?"

I can't help but laugh, even as my cheeks flood with color. "Ahh, Jack!" I groan, covering my face. "You're killing me!"

"Come on, is it really that bad?" he cajoles.

"Yes. It's horrifyingly embarrassing."

"Okay, now I *have* to know what it means." He reaches up, gently prying my hands away from my face, but I keep my head down, too mortified to look at him.

"Please?" he says.

I release a defeated sigh, leaning my forehead against his collarbone. "Most valuable body on campus," I mumble, wishing I could disappear.

"Most valuable... what?"

"Please don't make me say it again," I moan.

He laughs, rubbing his hands up and down my arms, sending tingles all through me. "Alright, I won't. I think I caught what you said."

His tone is amused, and a peek up at him. He meets my eye, letting his hands brush down the length of my arms until he takes my hands in his. Without breaking my gaze, he lifts my right hand and presses his lips to the back of it. Heat floods my body, tearing through my limbs like a forest fire, and I suck in a breath.

"I had a great time with you today," he says, lowering our hands. He twines our fingers together, inching closer.

"Me, too," I manage to say, feeling lightheaded.

"Would it be all right if I ask you out again?"

A puff of nervous laughter escapes as I open my mouth to answer. "Another date with the MVBOC? Yes, please."

He grins. "Good. It might be a while before we get the chance, though—my parents are leaving town, so I'll need to help at the store. And I don't want to plan a date too far in advance in case I'm gone when the time comes."

I frown. "Gone? You mean for good?"

"Not yet, no. But I've been applying for jobs all over the country, and if anyone wants an in-person interview, I might have to travel."

I think of the phone call he took after paintballing, and how excited he sounded about it. "Do you have any interviews lined up at the moment?"

"Only online for now," he says, "but yes, I have an interview on Monday. It's with a company in Baltimore. That's who called earlier."

Baltimore. *Maryland.*

Clear across the country.

Chapter 14

The rest of the month passes in a blur. A depressing, practically Jack-less blur. I mean, sure, he's still around. Occasionally. When he isn't helping at his family's hardware store or searching for jobs, that is. He and Chase paint the exterior of the shop-turned-boutique, but I'm too busy mowing the fields, ordering fertilizer, and prepping the pots and seeds for planting to help. And when my daily chores are done, all my time and energy goes into planning the big Christmas in July event with Mom. I'm lucky if I have time to swallow some dinner before passing out in the evening, let alone make time to spend with my crush who may or may not feel the same and may or may not be moving away.

Jack has an online interview with the company in Baltimore, and about a week later they fly him out in person. I feel sick and annoyed about the whole thing, convinced that if they spent that kind of money on him, he was a sure pick for the position. But he hears from them at the end of the month that they decided to go with another candidate, and I ~~shout with joy~~ commiserate with him about it.

"Sorry, man," Chase says. "That sucks."

"It's fine," Jack says, taking a swig of his soda. "There will be other jobs. I actually have an interview in Seattle next week."

It's rare when Chase and Jack come in for lunch at the same time I do, since we're each working on our separate projects. I confess to lingering in the kitchen a bit longer than usual, hoping to see them arrive, and I'm glad I did.

I offer Jack a smile. "Seattle is a lot closer than Baltimore," I say, infusing my tone with cheer.

He looks over at me, and his eyes soften. The sight gives me both a quiet thrill and a sudden ache. *Don't get too attached,* I remind myself.

I'm afraid the warning might be too late.

After our near-perfect first date ended with the bombshell of his interview in Baltimore, we decided to wait to have our next date until after he heard about the job. So his news today, while disappointing on one front, is quite exciting on another. His look tells me he's thinking the same thing.

"Well, we know we'll have to give you up sometime," Chase says around a mouthful of sandwich. I shoot him a frown but he just shrugs at me.

"That's true," Jack says. "But I'm glad I'll be here for the big summer event. I just wish I could have been more help."

"How many business consultants do you know would be out there painting their client's business, hmm?" I ask, lifting an eyebrow at him.

He smiles. "Fair enough. How are the other preparations coming?"

"Good. Mom and I are almost finished decorating the interior of the boutique, and the last shipment of soil and planters for the Adopt-A-Tree project will be here any day."

"Excellent."

"We've got flyers and ads all over town, on the radio, and in the Seattle Times," Chase adds. "I sent some info over to North Bend and the surrounding communities as well."

"What other things do you have lined up for the weekend?" Jack asks before taking another bite of his lunch.

I tick them off on my fingers. "Sophie will have a pop-up stand selling frozen hot chocolate and PineCones' Peppermint Ice cream, Dad and I will be giving tours and explaining the Adopt-A-Tree program, Mom is going to help Rebekah in the boutique, and Chase is supposed to line up a Summer Fun Santa for pictures." I give my brother a look. "Which I would like an update on, if you don't mind."

"Relax, Em," Chase says. "It's all taken care of."

"You only tell me to relax when it's something I most definitely should *not* be relaxed about," I say, folding my arms across my chest. "You haven't even told me who you've hired."

"Sophie said her cousin Manuel would do it for fifty bucks," Chase shrugs.

"What! No, Chase, absolutely not. We've tried him as a temp before, remember? Half the time he was a no-show."

"Sophie seems to think he'll be great."

"Yeah, well, Sophie tends to turn a blind eye to her family's offenses," I mumble, putting away the lunch meat and lettuce left on the counter.

"It will be fine, Em." I hear the tone in his voice and turn to catch him rolling his eyes at Jack. I glare at my brother.

"Have you even *talked* to him, Chase? Please tell me that you've at least spoken to him."

Chase downs the last of his soda and gets up from his seat. He pointedly ignores me while rinsing his dishes and putting them in the dishwasher. Finally, when he goes into the mudroom to put his shoes back on, I hear his voice.

"We've still got two weeks before the event, Em," he says. "How hard can it be to throw on a Hawaiian shirt, Santa hat and beard, and pass out candy canes to kids?"

I grind my teeth together, following him into the mudroom so I can glare more effectively. "You know it's not that simple, Chase."

"Em, I've got this, okay? Seriously, it's the one thing you said you'd let me handle, so just let me handle it. Come on, Jack."

Chase storms out the door, and Jack gives me a helpless look. "I'll try to talk to him, if you want," he says.

I sigh, rubbing my forehead. "No, I don't want you getting dragged into this mess. Chase is right—I should just let it go and leave it to him."

Jack smiles. "Try not to stress about it, okay? I'm sure it will be fine."

Turns out, it most definitely was *not* fine.

The second Saturday in July dawns as bright as the star over Bethlehem. The forecast calls for record high temps, and by nine-thirty the first two cars pull into the parking lot. We only finished decorating the night before, and I've been more than a little stressed out all week, afraid we wouldn't get everything pulled together in time.

The large wooden sign posted by the parking lot has been freshly painted, its dark green letters announcing the entrance to the *Kenworth Christmas Tree Farm* with pride. All the decorations that we pull out in December—the herd of reindeer,

Frosty the Snowman, and various garden gnome "elves"—have been set up and decked out with sunglasses and cheap floral leis. The speakers positioned around the farm play a steel drum rendition of *Jingle Bells*, and everywhere you look, strings of lights await the setting of the sun to twinkle like fallen stars on the beach.

Looking around at it all, a thrill of excitement and nerves runs through me. It's been a lot of work, and a lot is hinging on this weekend. Jack reminded us that the success of the event must be measured over the course of three to five years. "The first year is never the best," he warned us. "But it will be a good indication of whether it will grow to be profitable or not."

A few families are milling around the area, and I wave at a little girl as I pass by. Next to the beachfront backdrop set up for pictures with Santa is the booth where Sophie will be selling drinks and treats, and I make my way over to her.

"Hey, Soph," I say. "Do you have everything you need?"

"I think so," she answers. "But when will Marjorie be bringing the ice cream?"

"I told her to have it here no later than eleven o'clock. Do you want me to call her and find out?"

"Nah, it's fine. I just couldn't remember." She gives me an appraising look. "You okay?"

I blow out my breath. "Yes? I think? I'm just nervous. We've put a lot of work—and money—into this event, and if it doesn't do well we might be sunk," I say, rubbing my forehead.

"Hey, it's going to be all right, okay? Have some fun with it. You *love* Christmas, so try to relax and enjoy your hard work." She gives me a genuine smile before her look turns sneaky. "And if you're lucky, maybe the MVBOC will kiss you under the mistletoe, hm?"

SHAELA KAY

My cheeks warm. "There isn't any mistletoe," I say, suddenly wishing I would have thought to hang some somewhere. Like over Jack's head.

"And whose fault would that be, hm?" she says, giving me a look. I swat her arm and she laughs, waving to me as I go in search of my brother. He's standing near the entrance to the parking lot, giving instructions to a couple as they pass.

"Hey Chase," I ask, "when is Santa supposed to be here?"

He sighs. "I have it handled, Em, you don't need to worry about it."

"I'm not worried," I lie. "I'm just... trying to gauge the timing for everything."

"He'll *be here*, Em. Relax." A car pulls into the lot, and Chase turns from me to smile and wave at them. The driver rolls down the window, and Chase hands him a flyer listing all the activities available. The car pulls away, and Chase looks back at me.

"Where's Dad?" he asks.

"I think he's up in one of the greenhouses."

"And Mom?"

"Helping in the boutique," I say. "Actually, I should check that Rebekah has everything in hand there."

"You can't be everywhere doing everything, Em," Chase calls as I walk away.

I ignore him and head up the hill. I'm still worried about the arrival of Santa, but as I hurry toward the woodshop-turned-boutique I can't help but smile. The darling little shop is hardly recognizable with its red siding and stark white trim. The roof and corners are all lined with Christmas lights that will be turned on at sunset, but for now its doors and windows are thrown wide open to the warm summer air.

Chase and I went back and forth, trying to decide if I

140

should be the one to run the boutique during events and on the weekends, but in the end we agreed that we should hire someone part-time. Shannon, Mom's home health aide, knew a college student looking for work and introduced us to Rebekah. Her schedule is flexible, and she loves Christmas *almost* as much as I do, which made her the perfect choice.

"Hey Mom, hey Rebekah," I call, stepping inside. "Is everything ready to go?"

"As ready as it can be," Rebekah replies. She gives me a reassuring smile.

Mom sits near the double doors next to a small counter where we have the new till set up. She reaches a trembling hand toward me, and I hurry to her side. She pats me gently on the arm.

"Stop fussing, sugarplum," she says. "You and the boys have put together a fabulous event for this weekend. There's so much for people to see and do!"

"Which equates to so much that can go wrong," I sigh. She presses her lips together in what is supposed to be a stern line, but the slight tic of her head counters the severity of her look. I take a deep breath and turn back to Rebekah.

"If you have any trouble at all, will you let me know right away?"

"Of course. But seriously, Emily, your mom is right. This is brilliant. My younger siblings can't wait to come this afternoon with my dad. It's going to be a huge success, I'm sure of it."

"Thanks." I bend down to kiss Mom on the cheek. "I'm going to make sure Dad has everything ready for the tours. Shannon will be here soon, okay?"

She nods and pats my hand, then I head out the double doors and up the hill toward the greenhouses. But instead of taking the road, I veer off into the field, reaching out an arm and letting my fingers brush against the trees as I pass. The sharp pricks and minuscule scratches serve to center me, and I pause, leaning in close to a tree and taking in a warm, slow breath. The spicy scent of fir fills my nostrils, chasing away the anxiety that has filled my belly all week. I close my eyes and breathe in again.

Don't worry, the tree seems to whisper. *We're here. We've got you.*

I smile to myself, letting my body relax. Giving the tree a loving little pat, I cut through the field to the nearest greenhouse. I don't see Dad when I peek inside, but I find him in the next house over, talking to Jack. He sees me come in the door and gives a wave, causing Jack to turn. Jack's smile lights up like the star atop a Christmas tree, and suddenly Sophie's teasing comment about the mistletoe sounds delightfully appealing.

"Hey sugarplum, what's up?" Dad says.

"People are starting to arrive," I say. "Do we have everything ready for the tours?"

"Ready as ever," he says. "Are you taking the first or am I?"

"I was planning on it," I say. "You'll take the next, at noon."

"How can I help?" Jack asks.

I prop my hands on my hips. "I already assigned you a task," I say.

"Not really. You just said to keep myself available in case anyone needs anything."

I laugh. "Exactly. We need you to be a runner, since the rest of us will be tied up with our various duties."

"But what if no one needs anything? I feel a bit useless just standing around."

"Then don't stand around. Talk to people. Ask what they think about everything. Try to feel things out."

His eyes brighten. "Ahh, market research! Perfect."

My phone buzzes in my pocket, and I pull it out. Chase's charming smile looks up at me from the screen, and I swipe to answer it. "Hey Chase, what's up?"

For a moment the only thing I hear is some woman yelling in the background. But then Chase's voice comes through the phone.

"Em? We have a problem."

Chapter 15

B y the time Jack and I get down to the parking lot, Chase is trying to disperse the small crowd that has paused to watch the show. The *show* being an irate Sophie, yelling (and probably cursing) at her cousin in rapid-fire Spanish. My eyes dart between them, searching for the cause of concern. He's dressed appropriately, in a Hawaiian shirt, cargo shorts, Santa hat, and white beard. But suddenly he tips sideways and stumbles, then starts giggling.

Oh, no.

I walk up to Sophie and try to calm her down, but at the sight of me she launches into an angry diatribe, gesturing wildly at her cousin.

"Manuel is here, did you see?" she says, folding her arms across her chest. "But if you couldn't already tell, he's stupid drunk." She spits the word out of her mouth, as if she's eaten something particularly nasty. "The good-for-nothing *pedo* can't even manage a simple entertainment gig without bringing shame to himself and the family." She glares at him, but he doesn't seem to notice.

I frown. "How did he even get here if he's so wasted?" I ask.

She scoffs. "My *other* cousin, Ernesto, brought him, the—" She spouts off in Spanish, and I flinch at her tone. "But *he* didn't stick around, just dropped him off and high-tailed it out of here, the coward. But my Tia Maria is going to hear *all* about it, believe me."

She glares at the Santa-man, now sitting in the gravel looking around at everything. He slurs a bit in Spanish but doesn't seem bothered at all by the angry woman standing over him. I look helplessly at Jack.

"What do we do?" I ask. "Chase was supposed to—"

Chase. White-hot anger courses through me, and I whip my head around, looking for my brother. He's still trying to keep curious onlookers away from us, but as he glances back he catches my eye. With a grimace he turns and comes toward us.

"I know what you're going to say, Em," he says, holding up his hands as if shielding himself from the anger I can feel rolling off me. "And you were right. Okay? I said it. You were right. I should never have trusted Sophie."

She turns and shouts at him in Spanish, and he immediately steps back. "Manuel!" he cries. "I mean Manuel. I trust Sophie. It's Manuel's fault."

"No, this is *your* fault," I say, my anger making my head buzz. I look around at the world we've created. Couples and families wander around the property, some stopping to take a picture of the herd of Hawaiian reindeer, others waiting at Sophie's drink stand, watching us.

I throw my hands out in frustration. "What are we going to do?" Hot tears leak from the corner of my eyes and I brush them angrily aside.

"I'll figure something out," Chase says. "Don't worry about it, okay?"

He flinches as I glare at him. "I meant, I'm sorry. I'm sorry I didn't take it more seriously, and I'm going to fix this."

Jack steps into my line of sight, ducking his head so he can look into my eyes. "Emily? It's going to be okay. We're all here. You're not alone in this—it's just step two."

Anger still clouds my vision, but his words confuse me. "Step two? What are you talking about?"

He gives me a half-hearted smile. "It's something my mom has had taped to her fridge for as long as I can remember. It's a sticky note that says, 'When planning an event, follow three simple steps: Step one: it's good to have a plan. Step two: things will never go according to plan. Step three: things will be okay.' See? This is just step two. All that's left is step three. Everything will be okay."

It sounds ridiculous, but somehow when Jack says it, I believe him. I take a deep breath and nod, forcing myself to calm down. It would be easier if I could escape into the trees—I always feel more grounded in the forest—but for now, deep breaths will have to do. Jack gives me an encouraging smile, and I turn to face Sophie, whose angry brows are still pointed at her cousin in disgust.

"I'm going to let Jack and Chase handle Manuel," I say, "so we can get back to work." I glance at the drink stand again, where several people are still lined up. "Guests are waiting for drinks and ice cream," I say, as calmly as I can. "Do you think you can go back to your booth while they sort this out?"

She glances at the crowd and huffs. "Fine. But don't give this *maldito* any special treatment. Lock him up until tonight if you like, but don't let him wander off or he'll make an even bigger mess."

"We'll handle it, Sophie, I promise," Jack says. He gives her a reassuring nod and she finally turns away, heading back to her stand.

Chase helps Manuel up off the ground, letting him lean on his shoulder as they stagger away from us. I press my lips together, the anger simmering in my gut starting to boil over again.

"Hey, look at me," Jack says, putting his hands on my shoulders. "It's just step two."

"But look at it!" I say, indicating the photo op staging area nearby. Not only is there a beachfront backdrop, but Sophie and I amassed a huge collection of fun props for people to wear to have their picture taken with Santa. Giant sunglasses, floral leis, oversized Hawaiian shirts to put on over their clothing— even an old surfboard that we painted a Christmas tree on. "How can we offer pictures with Santa *without* Santa?"

Jack looks at everything we had prepared, then turns back to me.

"People can still take pictures with the setup," he says. "Santa just won't be in the shot with them. We can put up a sign that says, *'Gone on vacation, be back Christmas Eve. Love, Santa'* or something. It will still be fun for the guests. It won't go to waste."

I look up into his cinnamon-colored eyes and sigh. "Alright," I say. "You win. I won't let it ruin my day."

His face splits into a grin. "There's the Christmas cheer I was hoping for," he says, and I almost laugh. He looks around until he locates Chase, struggling up the road with Manuel. "I'm going to help your brother clean up his mess a bit," he says. His eyes search mine with genuine concern. "Are you going to be all right?"

I rub my forehead with one hand. "Yeah, I'll be fine. Thanks, Jack."

"Alright. And remember, it's just step two. Things will be okay." He leans down and kisses me on the cheek.

Before my face can register my surprise he's gone, sprinting up the hill toward my brother.

With the cause of the commotion gone the crowd disperses, and I sneak away to the seed orchard, stepping into the little grove of trees until I'm mostly out of sight. The dry pine needles crunch under my feet, and I plop down on top of them. Tipping my head back, I look up past the tops of the trees to the cerulean sky, closing my eyes and breathing deeply.

"I can't believe he messed up the one thing I gave him to do," I grumble to the trees.

They sway in commiseration.

"I just wanted everything to be perfect today. This could make or break us, you know?"

The trees hold me in silent sympathy, shielding me from scrutiny and allowing me the dignity to cry in private. After a minute I wipe my eyes, then press my palms to the ground. I focus on the feel of the dry, brittle needles beneath my hands, letting the stress and tension of the last twenty minutes fade away.

When I'm sure that the color has faded from my cheeks and I'm no longer in danger of crying, I get up from the ground and make my way to the greenhouses. A quick glance at my watch tells me the first tour is about to start, and I hurry inside.

"There you are, Emmy-girl," Dad says when I walk up beside him. "I was about to start without you. Is everything okay?"

There isn't time to fill him in, so I just shake my head. "No, but it will be. I'll explain later."

"Do you want me to take this one?"

I glance at the small group of people milling around the greenhouse. "I think I can manage. But thanks." I give him a hug and then turn to our waiting guests.

"Merry Christmas, everyone! Welcome to the Kenworth Christmas Tree Farm," I say in my cheeriest voice. "Who's ready to start the tour?"

I'm a bit out of practice, but soon enough my mind pulls up the words and explanations I used to give when we did the school tours. I take them to the seed orchard and explain how we harvest the cones each year, then up past the grow beds where I tell them about planting. They follow me down through one of the fields as I explain how we fertilize and shear each tree by hand, then back up to the greenhouses for some hands-on learning. Dad has two folding tables placed end to end, with an empty seed starting tray in the middle of each table.

"Alright everyone, it's time to get your hands dirty!" A couple of the kids cheer at my words, and I smile. This was always my favorite part when we were giving tours. "Go ahead and fill an empty cell in the tray with soil. Mr. Kenworth will be coming around to hand you a seed and help you plant it correctly. While he's doing that, I'd like to share with you an exciting new program we're offering here at the tree farm."

I swallow, suddenly nervous, since this is a script I'm not used to saying out loud. "As you all just learned, there's a whole lot that goes into growing Christmas trees," I say. Several people nod their heads. "It's something that our family has done for generations, and we love it. But with the rising costs of labor and supplies, it's getting more difficult to maintain the same quantity and quality of trees that we're used to."

I pause for breath, and Dad gives me an encouraging smile. "Which is why we're starting a sponsorship program. For a minimal fee, you will be able to adopt a tree on our family farm and watch it grow from a tiny seedling into a fully mature Christmas tree."

I think about the Christmas tree that always stands in our front window, with golden lights twinkling in the dark and silvery baubles hanging on the branches. A lump forms in my throat, and I swallow, doing my best to smile through the sudden emotion I feel.

"Your donation will be used to help cover the costs of fertilizer, pest control, and the labor needed to help the tree thrive as it grows. Sponsors will receive semiannual updates, complete with photos and interesting facts about your tree's current stage of development, as well as a coupon that can be used toward the purchase of a fresh cut Christmas tree in December."

The adults in the group are nodding at each other and exchanging impressed comments, and Dad and I share an excited glance. I pick up the forms and a new mobile card reader, and as he helps the children plant their seeds, I walk around the table, asking each adult if they would like to sponsor a tree.

All but one say yes.

As our guests call their goodbyes and make their way out of the greenhouse, Dad turns to me with an exultant smile.

"You did wonderful, Emmy-girl," he says, drawing me into a firm embrace. I squeeze him back, tears pricking my eyes.

"Let's hope this works," I say.

He chuckles. "I've always had hope, Emmy-girl, but remember what Jack said—only time will tell."

I smile at him. "I remember. But I've got a good feeling about this."

Dad lifts his brow, giving me a twinkling smile. "Kind of like the good feeling I have about Jack?"

I flush, surprised that he's noticed, but he just laughs again. "Go on, see if you can find him and tell him what a triumph you were."

"What a triumph *we* were."

He waves me off. "Sure, sure. You tell him I said hi, and I'll see you back up here at noon."

The success of our first sponsorship tour carries me down the hill like one of the ten lords a-leaping, but the sight that greets me at the bottom brings me up short. Dozens of people mill around the parking lot and through the nearby trees. Many are holding disposable cups of frozen hot chocolate, while others carry cones of ice cream. I look around in awe, amazed that so many people have come to a Christmas tree farm in the middle of summer. A gaggle of children darts past me, each with a piece of paper in hand, looking for a garden-gnome-turned-Christmas-elf that they can check off on the scavenger hunt

SHAELA KAY

(one of Dad's brilliant ideas). A quick glance up toward the Candy Cane Boutique tells me there are even more customers up there, and a long line of families wait patiently for their turn to take a photo with Surfer Santa.

I jerk my head back, convinced I'm not seeing correctly. But Santa is there, holding the surfboard and posing with a group of children while a woman takes their photo.

But... how? Who?

I walk closer, and it's clear by the color of the man's shins that it's not Manuel. But he's wearing the same shirt, the same cargo shorts, and I'm pretty sure the Santa hat and beard are the same as well. Chase, maybe? But then Santa looks at me, and even under the fake beard there's no mistaking those smiling brown eyes, the color of warm gingerbread.

Jack is underneath the Santa suit.

I watch him interacting with the kids, throwing his voice deeper and making it more animated as he asks them what they want to do on their summer vacation. He coos at the babies and bounces toddlers on his hip, and when a trio of teenagers comes up, he gives them all high fives and they pose with their hands making peace and hang ten signs.

It takes ten minutes for the line to disperse and for Santa—Jack—to address me.

"Aloha, miss!" he calls, and a laugh bursts out of me. Jack laughs, too (his regular laugh, not his Santa laugh) and I step closer so we can talk in normal voices.

"For someone who claims not to like Christmas very much, you look remarkably comfortable behind that beard," I tease.

"Don't be fooled," he says, pulling it away from his face a bit. "It's the delirium of heat stroke that you're seeing, not comfort."

152

I chuckle. "So are you going to tell me or do I have to ask?"

"Ask what?"

I raise my brow and gesture to his person.

"Oh. Well, Chase and I had a talk while we were helping Manuel up the hill to your brother's car. He was planning to take him back to Sophie's house, since he didn't know where Manuel lived and we knew he wouldn't be able to tell us." Jack makes a face, and I nod.

"That sounds like a reasonable assessment," I say.

"But then I thought, why not borrow his costume and play Santa ourselves? He looked to be about the same size as Chase and I, only a little shorter."

I look at him, dumbfounded. "You can't be serious. You stripped him down and took his clothes?"

Jack laughs, loud and long, then suddenly switches to a more jolly *ho, ho, ho!* when he catches some children looking our way. He waves at them, and when they turn away from us, Jack looks back at me. His eyes are sparkling with mischief.

"We didn't have to," he says. "Have you ever asked a drunk guy to take off his clothes? He's usually more than happy to do so."

Jack laughs at my shocked look. "There's no way that actually happened," I manage to choke out.

"It actually happened," Jack says with a grin. "It was getting him to put on some old clothes belonging to Chase that was the problem."

I burst out laughing, and a moment later Sophie comes up beside me, one hand propped on her hip.

"I'm wondering what Santa could possibly be saying to make Emily laugh so hard," she says. "Care to let me in on the joke?"

Jack shakes his head. "Private joke, sorry Sophie."

She pouts. "*Psh!* Then keep it down, everyone is staring."

Jack and I compose ourselves, and Sophie clears her throat. "So. Did you take care of that *baracho* cousin of mine?" she asks, lifting a perfectly shaped eyebrow at Jack.

"We did," Jack says, sobering. "Chase took him back to your place."

"*Que!* Why did he do that! I don't want him at my house!"

"Sorry, we didn't know where—"

But Sophie isn't listening. She's pulled out her phone and dialed her mother. "*Mamá, necesito que vaya usted a mi casa...*" She walks away, chattering angrily in Spanish, and I grimace at Jack.

"I wouldn't want to be Manuel when he comes to his senses," I say.

"Me neither."

I look into his laughing eyes and smile. "Thanks for doing this, Jack. It really means a lot to me."

"Of course. I told you it was just step two—you just had to hold on for step three: everything will be okay."

He winks at me, and a swirl of desire grips my heart. Before I can talk myself out of it, I stretch up on my toes a plant a quick kiss high on his cheek, above the faux white beard. His eyes register first surprise, then pleasure.

"I should get back to the greenhouses," I say, feeling suddenly shy. "We'll talk later, okay?"

He opens his mouth to reply, but before he can get a word out, he's set upon by a little girl desperate to tell Santa her summer wish. Giving me an apologetic glance, he turns and addresses her in his deeper, jollier voice.

I watch him for a moment, letting the sweet tendrils of new romance curl into the cracked places of my heart. Every day it feels more and more possible that we're going to save the farm, and every day I find myself falling harder and harder for Jack.

Chapter 16

Our Christmas In July event is a huge success. Hundreds of people come on Saturday, and nearly as many on Sunday. It's the perfect introduction to our Adopt-A-Tree program, as well as the grand opening of the Candy Cane Boutique. We all work hard on both days, and when the last car drives away on Sunday night we're exhausted.

"I want to go to bed for a week," Chase groans as we head up the hill in the twilight.

"Too bad we'll have to take everything down tomorrow," I say. Chase whimpers like a child, and Dad chuckles.

"No rest for the weary, son," he says, clapping a hand on his shoulder.

"I thought it was 'no rest for the wicked?'" Jack says.

I grin. "In my brother's case, that's essentially the same thing."

We all laugh, and Chase shoves me playfully away from him. I stumble a bit, falling against Jack, who steadies me. The touch of his hand on my bare arm sends electricity zinging through me, and I glance up at his face. He pulled the Santa beard down and is wearing it around his neck like a tie, the faux white hair glowing faintly in the dim light. It's hard to see many details of his face in the growing darkness, but his look is warm. I want so badly to kiss him.

The thought is enough to shock me into stepping away from him, glancing at the faces of my Dad and brother, reminding myself that they're here, walking with us, and I shouldn't be thinking about kissing Jack in front of them. My dad surprised me this weekend, though. He must see or suspect the attraction between us, but judging from his comment in the greenhouse yesterday, I think he approves.

Chase, on the other hand, is a wild card. I know he wants me to be happy, but I'm not sure how he feels about Jack. They're friends, sure, but he's also technically employed by us. Not to mention he's almost certainly leaving sometime this summer. How would Chase feel if he knew Jack and I want to be more than just friends?

Mom has been up at the house with her health aide, Shannon, for several hours already, and Rebekah locked up the boutique before dark. Sophie, too, packed up her booth and took off an hour ago, so it's just the four of us climbing the hill toward the house. Dad breaks off from the group, heading toward the barn and the main electrical switch to turn off all the outdoor lights.

"Chase, why don't you come with me, I want to talk to you about something," he says, not stopping to wait for an answer.

Chase sighs but turns to follow, leaving Jack and I to finish the walk to the house alone. I wonder idly if my dad *actually* has something he wants to talk to Chase about, or if he was just being sneaky and trying to give Jack and I some time alone. The thought makes me smile.

Suddenly Jack's hand is in mine, warm and rough from all the work he's been doing here on the farm. He gives my fingers a little squeeze, and it awakens the butterflies sleeping in my belly.

"We haven't had any time to ourselves in quite a while," he says, "what with preparing for the event and all."

"And thinking you might be moving to Baltimore," I add, pointedly. He grimaces.

"Yeah, I've got to be honest, I'm kinda relieved that one fell through. Baltimore is just..."

"So far away," I say quietly. He squeezes my hand again.

"I hear it's a great city, though," he says, his voice rising a bit. "The national aquarium is there, and some amazing art exhibits and museums. I would have loved to go and see the sights. And it's only an hour from D.C., which has even *more* amazing attractions. There's so much to see and do. So much more *life* than there is here."

His words sting a little, but they're not unexpected. I know how much he loves the city. "There's so many *people*, though. And not nearly enough trees, I'd bet."

He laughs quietly beside me. "Not as many Christmas trees, that's for sure."

We walk through the open garage to the mudroom door, but as I reach for the handle he suddenly tugs my other hand, still held in his own. He pulls me toward him, and for one wild moment I think—I *hope*—he's going to kiss me. But he doesn't. Instead, he wraps his arms around me, completely enveloping me in his arms. "You were incredible," he murmurs into my ear, his hot breath making me shiver. "There were a lot of people and a lot of strangers here this weekend, but you managed everything so well. Chase mentioned something about it, too. We're both really proud of you."

I wrap my arms tightly around him as well, not wanting him to let go of me. "I think it's because this is my home, my happy place. I'm comfortable here, so even though I had to interact with a lot of people and strangers, I felt more relaxed than I do in crowds and cities."

He doesn't reply, and instead of overthinking his silence I let myself rest against him. But the polyester fibers of the beard are scratchy against my face, so I lean back, reaching for the beard to pull it over his head. As soon as he feels me let go he releases me, but that's not what I wanted.

"No," I say quickly. "I just wanted to get this beard out of the way."

I take it in both hands, and as I start to bring it up over his ears he ducks his head, as if to make it easier, bringing his face inches from mine. My breath hitches as I stare into his eyes, my body motionless, the beard hanging limply in my hands.

He brings his arms back around me, slowly pulling me close until my body is pressed against his. I drop my arms, and with them the beard. It dangles, forgotten, at my side as we stare at each other. His eyes dart down to my mouth and back again, and I lick my lips, drawing his gaze once more. All it would take is for either of us to lean in, just a little, and our lips would touch.

But a moment later he lifts his chin, and instead presses a gentle kiss to my forehead. I close my eyes, feeling the warmth in my body cool beneath his tender touch. It's not the kiss I wanted, but oh, how my heart still thrums.

The sound of approaching voices breaks the quiet stillness, and the moment drifts away like snow in the wind. He releases me, and slowly I turn, opening the door to the house and stepping into the mudroom. I hand him the beard and he takes it from me.

"I'm going to change back into my clothes," Jack says, moving past me into the house. I kick off my shoes and place them in a cubby, then walk through the kitchen to sit down at the table. A moment later Dad and Chase come through the door.

"Oh good, you haven't turned in just yet," Dad says when he sees me. "I was telling Chase I think we ought to barbecue tomorrow, since we kind of skipped over the Fourth of July, what with the preparations and all."

"I think that's a great idea," I say. "I'll pick up a watermelon from the store, and we can make some potato salad, too."

"Sounds like a plan," Dad says.

"I'm going up to bed," Chase mumbles, his foot on the bottom stair. "See you all tomorrow."

We call our goodnights just as Jack comes down the stairs, passing my brother on the landing.

"You still here, Jack?" Dad says, leaning on the counter in the kitchen.

"Just had to get out of the Santa suit," he says with a smile.

"We're going to have a barbecue tomorrow and celebrate a late Independence Day," Dad says. "Care to join us?"

"Sounds like fun," Jack says. "I'd love to."

"Great," Dad replies. "Bring your folks, and your sister, too. We'll make a family affair of it."

Jack nods. "I'll let them know they're invited, thanks." He lifts a hand in half a wave. "I better get going. See you all tomorrow, then."

"See you, son," Dad says, moving toward the stairs. "Merry Christmas."

"Bye, Jack," I call, getting up from the table to follow my dad.

"'Night, Emily," Jack says. Then, taking a step toward me, he lowers his voice. "See you in my dreams," he says, just loud enough for me to hear.

His words send a cascade of longing crashing through me, but with nothing more than a wink, he turns and leaves the house.

That night I dream about Jack. When I wake up in the morning, I think about texting him to tell him so, but it feels too intimate. And he hasn't even kissed me, for goodness sake. I wonder about that for a moment, trying to decide what the reason for the lack of lip service could be. I'm sure he likes me, and I know I haven't mistaken the flirting and chemistry between us. Maybe he's just shy? Of all people, *I* could certainly understand that. Although I wouldn't mind at all if Real-Life Jack took a few lessons from Dream Jack. Dream Jack was a really, *really* good kisser.

Chase sleeps in longer than any of us, and by the time he comes downstairs and into the kitchen it's almost lunchtime.

"Good morning, sleepyhead," I say, slicing a watermelon and cutting it up into bite-size chunks. "Nice to know you're still alive."

He groans. "Sorry. I was up texting Marilee *way* too late."

"Who's Marilee?"

He loads the coffeemaker and presses start. "She's a girl I met on a dating app."

I stare at him. "Since when have you been on dating apps?"

He shrugs. "I dunno. A while. How else are you supposed to meet anyone in this tiny little town?"

He pulls a mug from the cupboard and I go back to cutting up the watermelon. I can't tell if I'm just surprised or genuinely upset by the news that my brother is on *dating* apps.

"So what's she like?" I ask.

"Hmm?"

"This girl. Marilee. What's she like?"

He pours himself a cup of coffee and takes the creamer out of the fridge. "We've been chatting for a few weeks, and she seems nice, I like her. She's an editor for a company in Tulsa."

"Like a magazine editor?"

"No, a technical editor. She edits professional papers, training manuals, that sort of thing."

"Huh. That's kind of cool."

He takes a sip of his coffee, nodding. "Yeah. And we have a lot in common."

"Except for living on the same side of the country, you mean," I tease.

"That's not as big a deal as you seem to think," he says. "It's a lot easier to date long distance these days. And people travel all the time."

"Are you saying you're going to move to Tulsa?"

He rolls his eyes. "We haven't even met in person, Em. Don't get all weird on me."

I let him drink his coffee in silence for a few minutes while I finish the watermelon. I put the lid on the big plastic bowl and pop it in the fridge. Grabbing some red potatoes, I start washing them at the sink.

"You know, you should try it sometime," Chase says suddenly.

"Try what?"

"A dating app."

"Why on earth would I want to do that?" The thought makes me shudder.

"To meet people, Em. You can't stay holed up here on the farm forever."

"Why not?"

"You'll never meet anyone that way."

"You don't know that," I say, thinking of Jack.

"Sure I do. You haven't had a date in years. Do you want to end up all alone?"

I set the potatoes on the counter next to the cutting board and grab another bowl from the cupboard. "Jack took me paintballing last month," I say, feeling defensive. He barks a laugh.

"That's different; you guys are just friends," he says, getting up from his seat to put his mug in the sink. "Besides, Jack is on the dating apps, too."

I freeze.

Jack is on dating apps? Is that why he hasn't kissed me? My body feels hot and cold all at once. I feel like a fool. Of course he'd be on dating apps—why wouldn't he be? A good-looking, charismatic guy like Jack probably has a dozen matches he talks and flirts with online. I pick up the knife and stab a potato, slicing it with more force than necessary.

Chase watches me for a moment, then turns to go back upstairs. "I'm going to shower," he says.

"Dad wants you to help take down the decorations before dinner tonight," I call.

He mumbles something in response but continues up the stairs. I cut another potato into small cubes, mulling over what Chase said.

Jack sent a group text this morning, letting us know that his parents would be coming tonight but not his sister, who had other plans. I wonder if there's any chance I'll have an opportunity to get Jack alone long enough to ask him about what Chase said, but I don't think it likely. We still haven't even had a chance to revisit the possibility of *actually* dating since things have been so busy. I might just have to text him about it.

I finish cutting the potatoes and put them on the stove to boil. Fetching my sketchbook, I set a timer and sit down at the table where I can keep an eye on the pot. Opening my book to a blank page, I start to draw.

Most of the time I like to draw something I can see. A view from the porch, a bird sitting on a nearby branch, the tree growing just outside my bedroom window—natural elements that remind me of home and the forest I love so much. It's always harder for me to pull something out of my imagination and draw it, like so many illustrators and cartoonists do. But today there's an image that I can't get out of my mind, so I decide to do my best putting it to paper.

After fifteen minutes the timer for the potatoes goes off and I get up to drain and rinse them. I hear my dad come in through the mudroom door and take off his boots before stepping into the kitchen.

"Chase up yet?" he asks.

"He came down for coffee but went back upstairs to shower," I say.

He grunts, shaking his head. "Don't know how that man is going to survive in this world if he can't get himself up in the morning," he says.

"It was a long weekend, and apparently he stayed up late chatting with a girl he met online." I rinse the potatoes and put them in a bowl, then grab the celery from the fridge.

"Huh. I wonder if that's the girl he mentioned to me last week."

"Chase said something to you about her? I just heard about her today."

Dad shrugs, moving toward the living room. "Just in passing. Didn't think much of it."

"Well, he said he really likes her, so maybe we'll get a chance to meet her sometime." I start dicing the celery, adding the pieces to the bowl of potatoes.

"Is this what that is, then? Chase and that girl?"

"Is what that?" I call over my shoulder, looking for the jar of pickles in the fridge.

"This sketch you're working on."

My body stills, and slowly I turn my head. Dad is standing next to the table, looking down at my open sketchbook. I pull out the pickles and set them on the counter, my insides trembling.

"I'm not sure, actually," I say, trying to sound as nonchalant as possible as I open the jar. "Just an idea I had."

"You don't normally draw people," Dad says, looking up at me. "I figured it must be someone particular for you to take the time to sketch them."

I meet his gaze but look quickly away, lifting a shoulder. "Like I said, just an idea I had. Trying something new to stretch my skills, you know?"

I can tell by the twinkle in his eye that he doesn't believe me, but he *hmms* as if he does. "Looks good," he says, turning away. "I'd love to see it when you're done."

He walks out of the kitchen whistling to himself, leaving me flustered and embarrassed, my hands covered in pickle juice.

Chapter 17

Jack and his parents arrive shortly after six o'clock. Mom greets them from her seat at the picnic table outside while Dad calls a hello from the grill. The smoky sweet smell of barbecued ribs saturates the air, smelling of summer. I sit next to Mom and wave when Jack smiles at me, and he and his parents come over to join us.

Dinner is delicious. Dad's a master on the grill, and my potato salad gets several compliments, as does Mrs. McKinley's pasta salad. Our parents talk and laugh and catch up on life, while Chase and Jack argue about whether the American League or the National League is going to win the All Star game next week. Every once in a while I catch a questioning glance from Jack, but I just smile and try to join whatever conversation our parents are having.

When the last rib has been eaten and the watermelon is gone I get up from the table. "I'm going to stretch my legs a bit," I say, bending down to kiss my mother on the cheek. Dad gives me a smile.

"Don't wander too far, we won't wait on you for dessert."

The others chuckle and I give him a wave of acknowledgment, making my way toward one of the little paths at the edge of the lawn.

I head off into the woods, but I only make it a few steps before the sound of someone behind me causes me to turn. Jack jogs up beside me, a grin stretching from ear to ear.

"Mind if I join you?" he asks.

"Not at all," I say. "Although the path isn't wide enough for two—let's go back and walk along the tree line instead."

We backtrack the few yards to the edge of the grass and turn to walk the perimeter of the yard. As soon as we're side by side, Jack takes my hand.

"You've been quiet tonight," he says.

I don't respond. He watches me for a moment, then pulls me to a stop.

"Hey, is something wrong? You seem distant." He frowns. "What did I miss?"

I look up into his concerned eyes and immediately regret it. His look is so intense, so searching, that the question burning in my mind bubbles to the surface without any thought.

"Why haven't you kissed me yet?" I blurt.

He blinks at me. "What?"

I look down, not wanting him to see the uncertainty in my eyes. "Why haven't you kissed me yet?" I say again, softer this time.

At first he doesn't respond, but then in a great huff he blows out his breath, and I look up at him in surprise. He drops my hand and glances away, running his fingers through his hair. "It's not because I don't want to," he says, then looks back at me, laughing humorlessly. "Believe me, I want to."

His eyes burn into mine, and I feel myself catch fire.

"But Chase is my friend," he continues, "and I know how protective he is of you; of your whole family. I don't want him to get the wrong idea, you know?"

"The wrong idea?"

"Sure."

"What do you mean?"

He tosses his hands in the air. "I don't know, that I'm messing around? That this is just some fling?" He lets out his breath in a half-growl. "I know that I'm going to be moving away," he says, his voice suddenly defeated, "whenever I can find a job. But Emily," he steps closer, his eyes piercing mine. Gently he rubs a hand up and down my arm, then reaches his other hand up to cup my face. "I care about you. I really do. And I don't want to mess this up. Whatever 'this' is."

His words seep into my soul, washing away the seeds of doubt planted this morning by Chase's words. I lean my head into Jack's palm.

"Thank you for telling me," I say. "It's good to know that the reason you haven't kissed me isn't because you don't want to."

He laughs softly. "It's definitely not that, trust me."

I smile. "I'm glad. And I'm glad to know that it's not because you're secretly flirting with a dozen girls online, either."

The look on his face makes me laugh, filling me with warmth. "Where did *that* come from?" he asks.

"Chase."

He frowns, suddenly serious. "Chase told you I was talking with girls online?"

"Oh, no, not really. He just mentioned to me that you were on dating apps, after he told me about Marilee."

"Is that the girl he's been talking with, who lives in Oklahoma?"

I nod.

"No wonder you wouldn't talk to me at dinner," he says, then sighs. "Chase knows I've been on dating apps before. But I hid my accounts or deactivated them shortly after you and I started working together."

"You did?"

"I did." He grins. "After the paint incident, I knew I wasn't interested in anyone else."

His words send a giddy spiral of delight all through me. "So it really has been just about Chase?"

"Yeah. I mean, you have to admit, the situation is a bit complicated."

"It is," I say. "But Jack, my brother doesn't get to decide how I spend my time or who I spend it with. I know you'll probably be moving away," I sigh and look down as I say the words, "but that doesn't mean we can't make the most of the time we have together."

He tips my chin up and searches my face. I see the same hunger in his eyes that I feel deep down in my soul. "Are you sure?" he asks.

"Yes."

"You know I can't stay."

The words slice at my heart, but I force myself to nod. "I know."

His eyes caress my face, coming to rest on my mouth. Rubbing his thumb gently across my lips, he leans down, and my eyes flutter closed.

His kiss is gentle, soft as a snowfall, and the fire burning inside me spreads outward into my fingers and toes. Slowly he pulls me closer, and I relax against him. His lips move against mine, still soft, still slow, until I melt into a puddle in his arms.

Too soon he pulls away, and he chuckles when I follow, reaching for him with my lips. I kiss him again and then draw back, looking up into his face.

"There," I say. "Was that so hard?"

"Kissing you isn't the problem," he says, dipping his head to brush his lips against mine. "It's forcing myself to stop that I'm afraid of."

He kisses me again, and again, as the air cools and the crickets come out to sing. After several minutes he takes my hand and we start walking once more.

"So are we going to tell Chase?" I ask, wondering if I look as giddy as I feel.

He shrugs. "What do you think? He's your brother; you know him better than I do."

I consider as we walk along the edge of the woods, listening to the sound of the forest at twilight. "He thinks we're just friends," I say, "and you're right that he's protective. Maybe if we ease him into it? Let him see that we're interested in one another?"

He looks at me sideways. "If he hasn't picked up on that already, he might be a lost cause."

I laugh. "Yeah, I know. Even my dad has figured it out."

"He has?"

"Yeah."

"Do you think he minds?"

I shake my head. "No. I'm pretty sure he approves, actually."

"Well that's a bit of a relief, I guess."

We walk in silence for a few more minutes, following the line of trees as it dips and turns around the property. The indigo sky fades to purple, bringing with it a handful of stars that wink and flash overhead like tiny Christmas lights.

We cut across the eastern field, pausing every so often to kiss each other. As we get closer to the house, I turn to look at him.

"Why don't you mention something to Chase," I say, "the next time it's just the two of you together?"

"You want *me* to tell your brother I've been pining after his sister all summer?" He grimaces. "As long as I'm not within swinging distance, we can try that."

I smile. "I think he'll be reasonable. This morning he was trying to convince me that *I* should try some dating apps."

Jack groans. "I swear, your brother is as blind as a bat."

That draws a laugh from me, which Jack effectively stops by placing his mouth over mine. I linger in his kiss, savoring the warmth of his lips, not wanting the night to end.

"Guess we better get back to our families," he murmurs, not breaking the kiss.

"Mhmm."

He chuckles, pulling away slightly, then presses his lips ever so softly to the edge of my cheekbone. "If I have a black eye the next time you see me, blame your brother," he says.

"If he gives you a black eye, I'll give him one."

Jack laughs again, the sound thrilling me clear down to my toes. It's intoxicating, and I want to fall into it, fall into *him*, over and over again.

"Just... don't wait too long to talk to him, okay?" I ask as we come within sight of the house. I don't see or hear any sign of our families, which means they probably moved inside as it got darker.

"Why not?"

I pull him to a stop, then slide my hands up around his neck, pulling his lips down to meet mine. The ease with which

I'm able to do so gives me a thrill of delight, confirming to me that he's as eager to keep kissing me as I am to kiss him.

"Because I don't want to have to wait another month for a night like this," I say.

His breathy laugh is warm against my cheek. "Trust me," he says, "you won't have to."

Chapter 18

With the celebration done and summer in full swing, our lives once again return to the chores on the farm. We decide to keep the Candy Cane Boutique open just on the weekends for now, and Rebekah is happy to handle it when I'm not available. Chase and Jack take charge of the mowing, since it's something that allows them a bit of flexibility to keep the business running smoothly in the office. It's a never-ending job, however, because by the time they've finished mowing all the fields throughout the week, it's time to start them all over again the next.

Dad and I work with a couple of temps to get all the trees fertilized and sprayed for bugs. At the same time, we make a preliminary inventory of the trees that will be ready for harvest in the fall, making note of the various heights and fullness within each variety. Our Colorado Spruce for the year are looking really good, and I'm excited to see how they sell in the coming season.

"Jack said we need to increase our price for our wholesale buyers," Dad tells me one afternoon.

"Why? We've been charging Tim and Jesse the same price for years," I say, tagging a tree with an orange landscape ribbon.

"That's just it. Jack compared our prices to other small farms with similar trees, and he said we've been charging less than half the cost."

I blink. "Less than *half?*" He nods and walks along the row to the next tree. "Wow," I say, following him. "That's a huge amount, considering how many trees we wholesale."

"Yep." Dad holds up the measuring pole, then hands me a blue ribbon. "Could be part of the reason we've been bleeding funds." He sighs, shaking his head.

I reach out and touch his arm. "It's not your fault, Dad. You've had a lot on your mind and on your plate these last few years."

He forces a smile. "I'm just glad Jack is here. He'll set us right."

I couldn't agree more.

On Wednesday afternoon I'm in the house reading to Mom when I get a text from Jack.

JACK

Incoming storm, consider yourself warned

I frown. Chase and Jack finished the mowing yesterday and decided to spend today putting together a budget for the Winter Wonderland event, so they should be in the office. How does Jack know there's a storm coming? The sun is out, and—

The back door bangs open and Chase marches into the room. When his eyes land on me, they narrow.

Oh. *That* kind of storm.

I'm surprised—and relieved—to see Jack walk up behind him. A quick assessment tells me that he appears to be in one piece, without either a black eye *or* a noticeable limp, which I take to be a good sign. His face is calm, but there's a tightness around his eyes that isn't usually there. He gives me the tiniest smile.

"Chase, is something wrong?" Mom asks. "Why did you barge in here like that?"

"Sorry, Mom," he says, his voice strained. "But I need to talk to Emily for a minute."

I mark the place in the book and get up from the couch. "Sure. Jack, would you sit here with my mom until I get back?"

"I'd like to talk to *both* of you, actually," Chase says, his eyes darting between us.

His possessive anger lights a fire of my own, and I glare at him.

"You don't need Jack. I'm sure you've already said what you need to say to him, and now you and I can have a little chat." I keep my voice light, but my look is withering.

Mom sits up, her head ticcing slightly back and forth as she tries to look at each of us in turn. "What's happened?" she asks. "Chase?"

Chase jerks his chin at me. "I think Emily should answer that question, actually."

I take a deep breath, trying to calm the swell of anger that keeps rippling through me. Bending down, I squeeze Mom's hand. "It's fine, Mom. I think Chase is just a little surprised at something he discovered in the office."

She looks back at him. "Not mice, I hope."

Jack chokes on a laugh, which eases the tension enough to

give my brother and I chance to reset. I watch Chase carefully, relieved when his shoulders relax just a fraction.

"No mice, Kathy," Jack says, coming over to the couch, "but I'd be happy to sit with you while Chase and Emily talk. Would you like me to keep reading?"

I thank him and head out to the front porch, my brother hot on my heels. He closes the door a bit harder than necessary, but he doesn't slam it. I take a few steps down onto the lawn and turn, crossing my arms.

"Judging from everything that just happened in there," I say, "I gather that Jack told you we're dating."

He scowls. "He did. And even though he's already answered my question, I'm going to ask you the same one."

I raise an eyebrow at him.

"Why on earth do you seem to think that's a good idea? Emily! The man is actively looking for a job *somewhere else*. He has known *all along*—and been perfectly clear, I might add— that he is *only here* until he finds permanent work. Why are you dating him? You have no future together!"

"You don't know that," I retort, and he laughs.

"Emily, I know enough about Jack to know he'll never be happy in a podunk little town like Echo Ridge—he couldn't wait to get out of here, remember? He's got big dreams and big plans, and he loves the city the way you love the forest." His look softens, and his voice follows. "And I know *you* like I know my left hand. You love it here. The woods. The rain. The trees. You wouldn't be happy anywhere else, either. It would kill you to leave the farm."

I don't answer, and not only because his words ring a little too true for comfort.

He sighs. "Look, I know he's an attractive guy, but that doesn't mean—"

"Is *that* why you think I want to date him?" I ask, incredulous. "Wow. It's nice to know you have such a high opinion of me, Chase."

He flinches, but then his look hardens. "Listen, you don't know—"

"No, *you* listen, Chase," I say, and when he tries to keep talking I hold up my hand, glaring at him. "You might be my brother—you might even be my *older* brother, if only by a few minutes—but you do *not* have the right to dictate how I live my life."

"Emily—"

"You do *not* get to choose who I do and don't like, or for what reason. You do *not* get to decide how I spend my time or who I spend it with. And you *certainly* do not get a say in *any* of my romantic relationships."

We stand there glaring at each other for several long moments—Chase standing on the porch, his hands on his hips, and me standing a few yards away on the lawn, my arms folded across my chest, just as defiant. It reminds me of one of the rare fights we got into as kids, when we were about seven or eight. I don't recall what the argument was about, but I remember that we ended up in a shouting match, one of us on either side of the room, yelling as loudly as we could to drown out the other. The irony, of course, is that in yelling at each other, neither of us heard what the other was saying, nor that we were essentially saying the same thing.

I unfold my arms, and the movement seems to thaw the air between us. Chase sits down on the steps and drops his head into his hands, and after a moment I sigh and go sit beside him, close enough that our shoulders touch. He takes a deep breath, and I rub his back, right between his shoulder blades.

"Thank you for loving me," I say, my voice more calm than it was only a few moments ago.

He laughs humorlessly. "Some way to show my love," he says. "First I lecture you about getting online to find someone to date, then yell at you for finding someone to date."

I allow myself a chuckle—more for his sake than my own, to let him know I understand. "Yeah, that's a bit of a contradiction. You might want to work on that."

He laughs again, just a puff of air while he shakes his head. Finally he turns to look at me.

"You know I'm just worried about you, right? I don't want to see you get hurt."

"I know."

"Because you know he's most likely going to land a job and be gone in another month or two, right?"

"I do."

"But you want to date him anyway?" He makes a face. "Can you help me understand? Because right now, none of it makes sense to me."

I draw a slow breath and look out at the woods, noticing the ferns nodding in the light breeze and the flash of movement as a squirrel darts up a tree.

"Do you remember," I say, "when you had a crush on Olivia James back in eighth grade, and for weeks you agonized over asking her out, only to have *her* finally ask you over to watch a movie with her family, and you realized she liked you, too?"

He frowns. "Yeah... but what does that have to do with anything?"

I look back at the trees. "I've never known what that feels like."

"What what feels like?"

"To have someone *like me back*. To have someone *see* me. I've never had that before, Chase."

His brow furrows, thinking. "What about Colin Daniels in tenth grade? Didn't you go to Homecoming with him?"

"I did, at your insistence," I say. "But I didn't actually *like* him. I've never had a crush on someone who had a crush on me, too. And the boys that did like me? Well, you know how *that* always went," I say, tucking my knees up to my chest. "We'd go on one or two dates until I begged you to tell them that I just wanted to be friends, because I was too scared to tell them myself."

A ghost of a smile crosses his face. "I remember doing that. I *hated* doing that."

"But you did it for me. Because you love me." I bump him gently with my shoulder, and he bumps me back. "I know it might be reckless. I know I could get hurt. But Chase, if I don't see where this goes with Jack—whatever *this* is," I say, thinking of Jack's words, "I'm going to wonder about and regret it for the rest of my life."

Chase is silent for a long moment, and then without a word he puts an arm around my shoulder, pulling me to him.

"I understand, Em," he says, "and I'm sorry I wasn't more supportive. Thank you for explaining it to me."

"So you won't freak out about us dating anymore?"

He sighs. "Yeah, yeah, I'll stop freaking out. Just... don't get all lovey-dovey on me, okay? We all still have to work together, you know."

"I know," I say, and then I sigh. "Until Jack finds a job, anyway."

My brother lifts an eyebrow at me. "You sure about this? That doesn't sound like you're sure about this."

I laugh lightly and get to my feet, offering him my hand so he can do the same. "I'm not sure about anything," I say. "But I'm sure about Jack. And that's enough for now."

Chapter 19

J ack and I decide not to push Chase too hard, too soon, but he still manages to grumble whenever he sees us together. Which isn't very often, actually, because life keeps us all busy in different ways. Chase and I have chores around the farm, and Jack takes off on a vacation with his family the last week of July. When he gets back we go out for coffee.

"I got an offer for an interview with a company in California," he says.

We're sitting at a little table in *The Jitterbug* with Sophie, who promptly took her break when we arrived, in order to have coffee with us.

"What part?" she asks. "I have family all over down there."

"San Diego."

"How do you feel about the job?" I ask, taking a sip of my iced gingerbread latte.

"All right, I guess. The pay isn't great, but there's a lot of room for growth with the company."

"And San Diego is fantastic," Sophie says. She looks at me. "We can go down and visit Disneyland with him!"

Jack looks at me and grins. "Disneyland sounds great!" he says with mock excitement. "All those people!"

I laugh, and Sophie rolls her eyes. "Fine, fine, I'll go by myself. But maybe I can crash on your couch, eh, Jack?" She makes a kissy face at him, and I gasp.

"Sophie!" I say, shock coloring my laugh.

"Sorry Soph, but you're not really my type," Jack says. He leans over and kisses my cheek, earning himself a muttered retort in Spanish from Sophie, and a quick kiss on the lips from me.

We finish our coffee and stand up to go, when both of their phones go off at the same time. Mine pings a short while later.

"It's from Chase," Jack says, pulling out his phone. "Said he's planning a big bonfire tomorrow night and he wants us there."

"Who is he inviting?" I ask.

"Us, of course," Sophie says, looking at her screen. "As well as Matt, Jack's sister Jenny, and anyone we want to bring along. There's also a number I don't recognize. Looks like a 918 area code?"

"It's Marilee," I say, looking at my own phone. "Chase just texted me."

Sophie looks over my shoulder. "Who's Marilee?"

"A girl he met online. I guess she's coming to visit."

"The one from Oklahoma?" Jack asks. I meet his gaze and nod. "Wow."

"I didn't think they were that serious," I say, my eyes skimming his text.

"They might not be," Jack says. "She might just be coming to visit so they can meet in person."

Sophie lifts one perfectly penciled brow. "No girl flies

halfway across the country for a guy she doesn't see a future with," she says. "Ah, *amor*." She sighs dreamily, then goes back around the counter, tying her apron back on.

"I know that look," I say. "Are you and Matt on again, then?"

"*Psh!* He wishes," she says, waving a hand dismissively in the air. "I told him we were through for good last time. Or at least until I start to miss him," she adds, almost as an afterthought.

"Chase must be done meeting with the accountant," Jack says to me. "Want to head back and talk to him about the bonfire?"

I nod, and Sophie blows me a kiss. "Thanks for coming to visit!" she calls. "See you tomorrow night." We wave and head out to Jack's car.

We find Chase still in the office when we get back to the house. "What's this about Marilee coming to visit?" I ask, leaning against the doorframe.

"She has a conference in Seattle, and wanted to come out and say hi," he says.

"Will she be staying here?"

"Nah, she's staying at a hotel in Bellevue. But since she's coming out for the evening, I thought it might be fun to have a bonfire. She liked the idea when I mentioned it to her, so that's why I texted everyone."

Jack stands beside me in the doorway. "How long have you been talking with her?" he asks.

Chase lifts a shoulder. "More than a month. She's nice, I like her. And we have a lot in common. So I guess now we get to find out if we have any chemistry."

"That's great, Chase," I say. "How can I help?"

"I'm going to mow some of the grass down and set the wood

tomorrow afternoon," Chase says, "but will you take the water tank out before dark, and gather some blankets and camp chairs?"

"Sure thing."

"Thanks. And I'd really appreciate it if you'll make an effort to get to know Marilee when she comes. She obviously won't know anyone there except me."

I nod. "Of course."

"I'm covering for my dad at the store tomorrow," Jack says. "But I'll pick up Jenny and come out after we close."

"Great," Chase replies. "If we're not here when you arrive, Dad can take you out there."

About a quarter mile off the westernmost access road of the farm is a large meadow. It sits on part of the forty-five acres my dad bought twenty years ago, which he intended to use to expand the farm. He hasn't, of course, but the land hasn't lain useless. In the center of the clearing sits the fire pit—a wide, shallow bowl dug carefully into the earth, ringed with large rocks dug up from the fields. A rough circle of logs and stumps provide some seating, but we usually bring out a handful of camp chairs as well. We haven't had a fire out in the meadow since last year, so it's a bit overgrown, but nothing a quick pass with the weedwhacker can't fix.

Chase and I are waiting in the front room the next night when we hear the crunch of gravel from an approaching car.

"That might be Marilee," Chase says, jumping up. I follow him outside, but it's only Sophie and her on-again, off-again boyfriend Matt. Another man I recognize but don't know well is also with them. Sophie and Matt get out of the car, bickering like an old married couple, but when Sophie spits something at him in Spanish, he just laughs and grabs her around the waist, kissing her cheek. Sophie makes a show of trying to push him away, but I can tell she's hiding a grin.

"Hey guys, glad you could make it," Chase says.

"Thanks for the invite," Matt says. "This is my roommate, Aiden."

Aiden lifts a hand in greeting, and we all turn as another car pulls up to the house. It's Jack, his sister Jenny, and a girl I assume to be Jenny's friend. Jenny's a few years younger than us, but it looks like she was happy to accept Chase's invitation to the bonfire. She waves when she sees me.

"Hi Emily," she calls.

"Hey, Jenny," I say. "Who's your friend?"

"This is Madison—she goes to beauty school with me."

"Hi Madison, glad you could join us."

Madison, who has raven hair and a sparkling stud in her nose, smiles at me. "Thanks."

Chase checks his phone for a message from Marilee, but at half past eight I offer to take everyone else out to the clearing. "I'll take the camp chairs and blankets while you stay here to wait for her—we'll get the fire going and you guys can join us when she gets here."

He sighs. "Alright, yeah, that's a good idea."

I give him an encouraging smile. "She probably just got stuck in traffic. Or maybe her conference ran late today."

He nods, distracted, and I motion to Jack to help me. He grabs the camp chairs from the garage and helps me load things up in the pickup. "Anything else?" he asks.

"That should be everything—I've already got the blankets."

With the gear loaded, everyone climbs into the back of the pickup except Jack—he gets into the cab next to me.

"Feels strange to be the one riding shotgun instead of driving," he says.

I grin at him in the fading light. "I feel that way every time I climb into your car."

He laughs as I turn the key, and the engine roars to life.

The sun has already dipped below the tree line, leaving a periwinkle expanse of sky overhead, the edges just barely tinged gold. The ride is a bit bumpy once we leave the road and drive through the sparse trees to the meadow, and I go as carefully as I can. Parking the truck in the grass, everyone spills out, grabbing chairs and blankets and a small cooler filled with drinks.

The crickets are out in abundance tonight, and soon the crackle of the fire adds to their chorus. The wood—which never fully dries out here—smokes a bit, but it pops and snaps cheerfully as the flames lick up the logs. Aiden brings out a guitar, and soon Jenny and Madison are singing along as he strums the chords to a familiar tune.

Jack brings me a drink as I settle onto a log, an old quilt draped across my knees. He sits down beside me.

"Thanks," I say, taking the drink.

"Think she's going to stand him up?" he asks.

"I hope not. He seemed really excited about her coming."

Jack pokes at the fire with a stick. "Yeah, he'll be a bear for days if she doesn't show."

I lean my head against his shoulder, and together we watch the flames. The dusky sky fades from blue to purple as tiny sparks pop and fly from the fire. Light conversations drift around the group, interspersed with shouts of laughter and playful banter.

Ten minutes later I hear the sound of a four wheeler getting close. I lift my head as Chase pulls into the clearing, a young woman holding on behind him.

"Hey, look who finally made it!" Sophie calls.

The woman—who I assume to be Marilee—climbs off the back of the four wheeler and looks around. Chase hops off as well, and together they walk toward us.

"Hey everyone, this is Marilee," Chase says, indicating the woman standing beside him. She's slightly taller than he is, with dark hair pulled back in a ponytail and long, painted nails. She waves, an easy smile on her crimson lips. She looks oddly out of place.

A chorus of hellos greet her, and Chase leads her over to the empty camp chair beside my log.

"Hi Marilee," I say, "I'm Chase's sister Emily."

Her face lights up. "Oh, you're Emily! I've heard so much about you."

"All good things, I hope," I say, eyeing my brother as he sits on an upturned log beside her chair.

"Yes, yes, all good things," he says. "I wasn't about to risk giving you cause to lay my faults at her feet."

She laughs—a light, airy sound—and appraises him. "What, like not being a Dallas Cowboys fan?"

He shrugs good-naturedly and leans back, watching the fire. "I prefer baseball to football," he says calmly.

Marilee glances around the clearing. "Is this part of the tree farm?" she asks me.

"We own the land," I say, "but we haven't developed it yet."

"We drove past a lot of trees on the way here," Marilee says. "I had no idea there would be so many!"

I laugh lightly. "We're actually a pretty small establishment."

Her eyes widen. "Really? Wow. I'd never have guessed that."

"Does your family use fresh cut trees?" I ask politely.

"Oh, no, I'm actually Jewish," she says. "I've never had a Christmas tree. But they're pretty—I always like to see the decorated one that my office puts up every year."

I try to hide my shock—*never had a Christmas tree!*—behind another polite question. "You're an editor, right?" I ask.

"I am," she says brightly. "But not a fun editor—I don't work for a magazine or a publishing house, unfortunately. The company I work for is usually contracted to edit training manuals and government forms and the like."

"Sounds exciting," Jack says wryly.

"It's pretty dry reading, I'll admit," she says. "But I don't mind. I like my work. Finding typos and fixing grammatical errors is kind of like searching for buried treasure. I always get a little thrill when I come across an error that I can fix."

"So what's your take on the oxford comma?" I ask.

"I am one hundred percent Team Oxford Comma," she says boldly. "You'll have to pry them out of my cold, dead, and lifeless hands."

I grin, liking her already. "Same."

"What about you?" Marilee asks, turning to Chase on her other side. "Are you Team Oxford Comma?"

He laughs in a self-deprecating way. "If I knew what that was, I'd probably have an opinion on it."

"Chase doesn't read much," I say.

"I do so," he retorts, but I roll my eyes.

"Sports Illustrated doesn't count. And neither does Quick-Books," I say when he opens his mouth. Jack chuckles beside me.

"Do you like to read?" Marilee asks, turning to face me again.

I nod. "I love to read, though I haven't as much time for it as I'd like."

"What sort of books?"

I shrug. "Novels mostly. I'm not picky about the genre, as long as it has a happily ever after."

She laughs. "No psychological thrillers for you, then."

I shudder. "No, thank you."

"I don't mind thrillers," Jack says, pulling the quilt from my lap and unfolding it once so it can cover both of us. "But I prefer histories and biographies myself."

Marilee brightens. "I love history as well, especially histories of other countries and cultures. I find it fascinating, learning how people around the world used to live."

Jack nods, and I snuggle up beside him. Chase gets up from his seat. "Would you like a drink?" he asks Marilee.

"No thanks," she says with a smile.

He smiles back at her, then moves away to get himself a drink from the cooler. I watch him go, wondering what he's thinking.

"Chase said you were in Seattle for a conference," Jack asks. "When do you go back home to Oklahoma?"

"I go back on Sunday, but Tulsa isn't really home," she says. "Oh?"

"I only moved there for work, and I've only been there a couple years. Home is actually New York, and I'd love to get back there someday."

I nod, understanding the desire for home. But New York is about as far away from Echo Ridge as you can get without leaving the country—has Chase thought about that?

"You're from New York?" Jack asks, and she nods. "Who's your team, the Yankees or the Mets?"

"Yankees," she says without hesitation. "I can't stand the Mets."

"What about the Mets?" Chase asks, coming back to his seat. We all look over at him. Jack grins.

"Marilee was just telling us how she feels about the Mets," he says.

Chase lights up. "They're great, aren't they? So much better than the Yankees."

I laugh, and so does Jack, who shakes his head. Chase looks between us in confusion, while Marilee looks bemused.

"I happen to love the Yankees," she says. "I was actually hoping to catch a game between them and the Mariners while I was here, but the timing didn't work out."

"Oh! Uh, sorry about that," Chase says. He shoots Jack a dirty look. "I misunderstood. But I'm sure we agree about the White Sox."

She lifts an eyebrow. "Are you?"

"Sure—no one likes the White Sox." He laughs nervously. "Do you?"

She watches him for a moment, amused. "I don't, no."

Relief washes over Chase's face, and then he grins. "Well, there you go."

They start chatting about the various teams in Major League Baseball, and I turn to Jack. "What do you think?" I say, keeping my voice low, so only he will hear me.

He glances at Chase and Marilee on my other side, then

looks back at me. "She seems nice, but I think your brother may have exaggerated how much they have in common."

I make a face. "I agree. So far it seems the only thing might be an enjoyment of baseball."

"But not the same teams," Jack says.

"They agree about the White Sox, apparently."

Jack chuckles. "Everyone agrees about the White Sox, Em. No one likes them."

I straighten in my seat. "I beg your pardon. *I* happen to like them very much."

He blinks. "You do?"

Grinning, I pull up my pant leg to reveal my sneakers and the tops of my white crew socks. "Sure—they're my favorite kind."

He laughs, then pulls me close, pressing a kiss to my temple. "Emily Kenworth," he says, "that was the lamest joke I have ever heard."

I elbow him playfully in the side. "It made you laugh, though. *And* you kissed me. Seems like a pretty successful joke to me."

Chapter 20

W e stay out far too late, but it's been nice to escape the stress of the farm to hang out with some familiar faces. We talk and laugh and roast s'mores, but at last the fire burns low and a sleepy silence settles over everyone. Sophie has fallen asleep with her head on Matt's shoulder, tucked under a blanket against his side. I smile knowingly at him, and he winks at me. Jenny and her friend Madison laid out a blanket nearby and are gazing up at the stars. Aiden put his guitar away a while ago and is staring into the fire like the rest of us. Finally Jack gets up and stretches.

"I think it's time I head out," he says. "Jenny?"

His sister sits up, acknowledging him, and she and Madison fold up the blanket. Everyone else begins to stir, gathering their things and folding up the chairs. Chase walks over to my truck and turns the headlights on, then grabs the hose from the back of the water tank trailer and sprays down the fire. It coughs and sputters, sending a cloud of steam and smoke into the air. Marilee stands and smiles at me.

"This was fun," she says.

"I'm glad you came out," I reply. "It was really nice to meet you."

"Same." She glances at Chase, still focused on getting the fire out. "You're quite different from your brother."

I laugh. "You sound surprised."

"I am. I thought twins were usually very similar."

"Not in my experience," I say, folding up the blanket that Jack and I had across our laps. "We're close in our own way, but no more alike than any other pair of siblings you might come across."

She looks thoughtful. "Well, it was nice to meet you, and to meet Chase in person. He's not quite what I expected, but he seems like a really nice guy."

Uh-oh. That doesn't sound promising. "Maybe we'll see you again sometime?" I venture.

She smiles softly. "Maybe. If you ever find yourself in Tulsa, look me up, okay?"

I smile. "Okay."

Everyone helps load up the truck, and when the fire is completely out Chase comes to stand next to Marilee. "Ready to go?" he asks.

"Yup." She turns to wave at everyone. "It was nice to meet you all," she says.

A chorus of "you too" and "see ya" greet her words, and she climbs onto the back of the four wheeler with Chase. He lifts a hand to me and heads off into the dark, back toward the farm.

"Well?" Jack asks, coming up beside me.

I shrug. "Seems like a dead end to me," I say, and he nods.

"Me too. Let's hope Chase figures the same."

Chase does *not* figure the same.

"Isn't Marilee great?" he asks me at breakfast the next morning.

"She's nice," I say, measuring my words, "but... different than what I expected."

"What do you mean?"

"Well, you told me you have a lot in common, but that doesn't seem to be the case, based on our conversation last night."

He rolls his eyes. "That's just one conversation. She and I have been talking for weeks."

I lift an eyebrow at him. "So, what all do you have in common? Besides an affinity for baseball."

He picks up his coffee cup. "You can't put me on the spot like that, but trust me, there's a lot." He turns, moving toward the office and the work ahead of him. I sigh, hoping she lets him down easy.

The summer is drawing to a close, and there's a lot to prep and do as we head into the busiest season of all. Dad and I trade off spending time with Mom, who is getting less stable on her feet and more and more confused. Dad worries about her, but there's not much else we can do. "Just the natural progression of the disease," the doctor tells him.

We spend hours each day measuring and tagging trees for the coming harvest, counting and recounting so we can estimate how many man hours we'll need when the time comes. Chase and a couple guys we hire repair some of the big dips and ruts in the access roads, knowing that if we don't, the coming rain, snow, and freezing temps will make them impassable until spring.

On her good days, Mom keeps us all smiling, singing Christmas carols around the house and reminiscing about past holiday seasons. On weekends I take her down to the boutique with me, and she shuffles around the small space, rearranging candles and chatting with the guests. Sometimes she gets confused, thinking that the customers are stealing her personal belongings and not buying items we have for sale, and I often have to call on Dad to come get her. It tears at my heart to see her like that, and I wish there was more we could do for her.

Jack and I steal as many moments together as we can, but they are few and far between. I console myself with texting him every night, staying up far too late having the kind of conversations I've never had with anyone else.

JACK

I just finished a great book

EMILY

What book?

JACK

Killing Lincoln by Bill O'Reilly

EMILY

Oh I've heard of that! What did you like about it?

JACK

It's a historical biography, but it reads more like a novel. It was really fun.

EMILY

Good narrative nonfiction is hard to find

JACK

What are you reading these days?

EMILY

I'm rereading Emily Wilde's Encyclopaedia of Faerie. It's one of my favorites.

JACK

Sounds like fun. What's it about?

EMILY

It's an urban fantasy about a scholar of dryadology who's trying to compile a book about all the different fae in the world.

JACK

Wow. That sounds really cool!

EMILY

It is. I'll let you borrow it when I'm finished.

JACK

Sweet. Thanks.

EMILY

Have you ever wanted to write a book?

JACK

Nah. I'd have no idea what to write about. You?

EMILY

I think it'd be fun to try, but I don't know that I'd actually be able to. What's something you've always wanted to do?

JACK

Skydiving

EMILY

OMG are you serious?? 😳

JACK

Sure, it would be fun

EMILY

> Jumping out of a perfectly good airplane is the craziest idea of fun I've ever heard

JACK

What about you? What's something you've always wanted to do?

EMILY

> Well, I would say paintballing, but thanks to you I can cross that one off my list 😊

One morning early in September I'm out pruning trees when my hand trimmers break. Annoyed, I finish the tree as best I can, then head back to the barn for another pair. When I can't find any, I call up Dad on my phone. He's in the house with Mom today, so he doesn't have a radio.

"Hey Dad," I say when he answers, "do you know where all the hand pruners are? I just broke the only pair I can find."

"I'm not sure, sugarplum. Have you checked in the barn and the lower shed?"

"I checked the barn but not the shed. I'll take my truck down there and look, and if I can't find any I'll head into town for another couple pairs."

"Sounds good."

Grabbing my keys and wallet from the house, I fire up my truck. It's sweltering inside, so I crank down the window to let the cool breeze in before taking off down the hill. I don't find any hand pruners in the shed either, so off to Ace I go.

I'm not sure if Jack is working at the store this morning, but luck seems to be with me because he's behind the first till when I come through the automatic doors. My heart soars at the sight of him.

"Hey beautiful," he says. "What brings you in today?"

"Broken tools," I say. "I need some new hand pruners."

"Let me show you where they are." He comes out from behind the counter, and I laugh in amusement.

"I know where they are," I say.

"No, you don't," he says confidently. "Let me show you."

Smiling indulgently, I follow him toward the back corner of the store, then frown as we cut through the aisle of fasteners and turn left at the dowels, finding ourselves in the *actual* corner of the store. I look around, confused.

"This isn't where the pruning tools are," I say.

He turns to face me, cupping my face with his hands. "No, but this is where the broken security camera is so I can kiss you guilt-free."

He presses his mouth to mine, effectively ending the laugh that bubbles up at his words. He doesn't kiss me long, but long enough for my heart to grow wings and flutter right up to the ceiling. I sigh happily.

"I have another interview in California," he says, and my heart plummets back to earth.

"Why'd you have to ruin a perfectly good kiss with news like that?" I say, turning to walk up the aisle toward the garden tools. He chuckles.

"Sorry. But is there ever a good time for news like that?"

"I guess not." I clear my throat, smoothing my forehead and forcing a smile. "I'm sorry. That's great about the interview! I hope it goes well."

He groans. "Come on, Em, you know I need the work. I can't stay here forever."

I know this, but it still stings every time he brings it up. Why *can't* he stay here forever? He could work at his parent's store until the economy recovers and he finds a good job in

Seattle. Is that too much to ask? Doesn't he *want* to stay with me?

I can't ask him that, of course, so instead I continue to the gardening supplies and look through the pruning shears. He stands beside me, hands shoved into his pockets, waiting.

Finally I select a couple pairs and turn to face him. "I do want you to find a good job—one that you'll love, in a place you'll be happy. I just... don't want to say goodbye."

His look softens. "No one's saying goodbye just yet," he says. "It's just an interview."

I sigh, and we turn to go back to the checkstand. "I know. But eventually it will end with a job offer and then you'll leave."

He walks around the counter to the till, punching in the code to log back in. "Let's not think about that just now," he says, ringing up my purchase. "What are you doing Friday?"

"I was going to go foraging, but—" I pause, my face lighting up. "Actually, do you want to come with me?"

"Foraging?" He frowns. "Like, for mushrooms?"

"No, for cones," I say, pulling out my business credit card.

"I thought you had the seed orchard for that?"

"We get most of our seeds from there, yes. But we save those for the Christmas trees, whereas we like to harvest wild seeds for people to plant during the tours."

"Oh, that's cool, I didn't know that."

"Yeah, the seeds from the orchard are special. Those trees have been carefully curated for the specific qualities we want in our Christmas trees," I say, "so it's best not to just give them away. And occasionally a sapling will grow from a wild seed that we end up wanting to propagate for the farm as well."

He hands me my receipt and I smile up at him. "So what do

you say? Feel like hiking through the woods collecting cones with me on Friday?"

He grins. "I can't think of anything I'd like to do more."

Summer lingers, sultry and warm, climbing like a cat into the lap of September. The nights are cooling off, but the days still leave me hot and sweaty, dreaming of the coming Christmas season and the promise of snow.

I get up with the sun on Friday morning to prune a few more trees before Jack and I head out to forage. By ten o'clock I'm standing at the kitchen sink filling a water bottle, when I hear the door from the garage open. "Jack?" I call. "Is that you?"

The answer comes a moment later, when Jack slides his arms around my waist from behind, leaning down to brush his lips against the edge of my collarbone. I close my eyes, shivering in delight.

"Did you miss me?" he murmurs in my ear.

In response, I turn in his arms, reaching up to pull his mouth down to mine. His lips are gentle but sure, and the molten rush of desire spills into my blood like warm honey.

"Ugh, please stop," Chase's voice calls from over Jack's shoulder. "You have no idea how uncomfortable this whole situation still is for me."

Jack and I break apart, and I see my brother walking through the kitchen on his way to the living room. I scowl after him, but Jack just smiles, going to sit on a stool at the counter.

"Chase, are you coming with us?" I call.

"I'll get him," Jack says, getting up from his seat.

"Thanks."

I put the lid on the water bottle and pack it in one of the backpacks on the counter. Right now there are just two, but if Chase decides to come with us I'll have to get a third.

I grab some snacks from the pantry and have both packs ready to go by the time Jack returns. "He's not coming," he says. "Apparently we're too nauseating for him at the moment."

I roll my eyes. "He's one to talk. In high school he didn't have any qualms about making out with Kelly Stratford in the back seat while I drove us home."

Jack chuckles. "I'm not surprised. I think it just bothers him to see us together when he and Marilee live so far apart."

"Are they still talking? I thought she would have called things off by now."

"They're not exclusive, but yeah, I think so," Jack says. "He was just talking about her the other day and a conversation they had about libraries."

I blink. "Libraries?"

Jack lifts his hands, laughing. "I was just as confused as you are, but that's all he said." He looks at the two packs on the counter. "Are these for us?"

"Yup. Water and snacks, but mostly empty so there's lots of room for cones."

"Will we fill them up?"

"Hopefully. I always try to gather as many as I can."

He grabs the packs and follows me into the mudroom, where I lace up my boots. Taking one of the bags from Jack, I grin up at him. "Ready?" I ask.

"Hang on," he says, before leaning down to kiss me on the cheek. "Okay, now I'm ready."

We walk through the garage toward the barn, where I stop

to collect a retractable cone-cutter, then cut behind the greenhouses to a trailhead leading south from our property. The day is already warm, but only a few steps into the forest and the air cools significantly.

We follow the soft ribbon of dirt and dried needles into the wilderness. Towering firs and ancient cedars line the path, their massive trunks blanketed in thick moss. The trail winds through the trees, sometimes lost to view beneath a sea of ferns, only to emerge again on the other side of a fallen log. We cross a small stream—just a trickle, given the time of year—leading down the mountain to a murky pond. The chatter of birds and squirrels drops off as we walk nearby, starting up again the moment we pass. Sunlight slants through the gaps between trees, catching on spiderwebs and turning dust motes into floating gold. It's absolute paradise.

We hike in silence for thirty minutes before I call a halt, stopping beside a half-fallen tree to take a drink, then look around. It's not a full clearing, but the trees are thinner here, where larger patches of light can get through. Several young saplings sprout up amid the giants, their tender green needles reaching heavenward. Suddenly I gasp, pointing excitedly.

"See that tree, off the path a bit?" Jack nods. "That's a Noble, and they're hard to find around here. Let's check it out."

We pick our way through the undergrowth, watching for poison hemlock and trying not to squash too many ferns. When we get to the tree, I glance up, grinning like a kid on Christmas morning.

"Perfect," I say, setting down my pack. I pluck a cone from the top of a lower branch. "They're at just the right stage for harvesting."

"That's a pinecone?" Jack asks, taking the long, fat cylinder I hand him.

"Not a pinecone—a *fircone*. This is a Noble fir," I say indicating the tree.

He looks up, appraising the tall, straight trunk and long, bluish branches. "And they grow sticking straight up, like that?"

I laugh. "Yes. I called them candle-cones when I was a kid for that very reason. They do grow naturally around here, but they're not as easy to find as cedar and other fir trees. I was actually expecting to gather Douglas cones today."

I pluck another cone from the tree, opening my pack and dropping it inside. "Try not to collect the damaged ones," I say. "We'll let those fully mature and reseed the forest. But gather any of the full cones that you can reach."

Jack opens his pack and starts pulling cones from the tree while I extend my cone cutter and start reaching for the higher branches. We work in companionable silence for a time, until both our packs are bursting with the soft, dark brown cones. I prop my fists on my hips, considering.

"These are a lot bigger than Douglas cones," I muse, looking down at the open bags.

"Should we head back to the farm, empty our bags, and come back for more?" Jack asks.

I bite my lip, considering. "No, I think it's fine. We'll get thousands of seeds from this lot as it is. So the question is actually whether we should head back to the farm and call it a day, or stay out and enjoy the afternoon together?"

He crouches down, zipping up the packs. Swinging one up onto his shoulder, he asks, "Didn't you pack some snacks?"

"Yes."

"Then let's keep going. I'd forgotten how much I loved hiking in these woods—I'd rather not go back just yet."

Grabbing my own pack, I indicate the trail we left. "Lead on then, soldier. Let's hike until that wanderlust is satisfied."

Chapter 21

We make our way back to the trail and continue south, following the path as it curls around towering evergreens, their branches scattering the sunlight into dappled mosaics on the forest floor. The air is cool but calm. Squirrels race up tree trunks while Jays call from the canopy. And in the distance, the tops of the trees sway with a silent breeze, carrying with it the whisper of fall.

The quiet rhythm of our footsteps matches pace with my heart, which thrums in my chest like the ten drummers drumming. Jack walks ahead of me, setting a steady pace, pausing only now and then to glance back at me. Every time our eyes meet I feel of jolt of something electric, tugging at my insides, pulling me toward him in an inevitable collision course.

The path winds along the edge of a ridge, and we pause to take in the view. The world opens wide and still before us, the forest stretching out like a deep green ocean—waves of fir, cedar, and hemlock rolling to the horizon, broken only by the craggy ridges of the Cascade Range.

I take a deep breath, letting the air fill my lungs and elongate my soul. "I could never leave this place," I murmur. "Who would ever want to?"

The moment I say the words, I realize how it must sound, and I glance at Jack. He's looking out at the view and not at me, but I see his jaw tighten, pulling his mouth into a hard line.

But his smile returns when he looks back at me. "Let's follow the trail around the ridge a bit and see if there's a spot to have a picnic," he says.

I nod, and we begin walking again.

Within ten minutes the path has pulled us back into the dense forest, skirting a small river and leveling out nicely. We pass a patch of blackberry bushes, the dark, plump berries just begging to be picked. Jack pulls off a handful and pops them in his mouth.

"Mmm," he says. "Makes me think of my mom's blackberry pie."

I sit down on a clear patch of earth, the ground springy with moss and ferns. Opening my pack, I pull out my water bottle and take a long drink. Jack sits down beside me, doing the same.

"Pretty spot," he says.

I nod, looking around. "It is."

"Worthy of a picnic?" he asks.

"I think so," I respond, pulling out some snacks.

Within moments we're munching on crackers and trail mix, supplemented with blackberries from the obliging bushes. I see a red huckleberry bush with a few berries still clinging to the branches on the other side of the creek, and take off my boots and socks to wade across and collect some. Jack does the same, and we practice tossing them in the air to one another, trying to catch them in our open mouths. The berries bounce off our noses and foreheads, and twice we nearly slip into the water. My stomach hurts from laughing so much.

After we've eaten, Jack lays down on the forest floor beside me, tucks his hands beneath his head, and closes his eyes. I watch him for a while, admiring his long, dark lashes and the defined muscles of his arms and chest. When his breathing slows, I quietly retrieve my sketchbook and pencil from my pack. Ensuring that his eyes are indeed closed, I open to the unfinished picture of him and me.

I've filled in the details of the trees, but I've been saving the people for last, worried that I won't be able to do them justice. But spending the day out here, in the forest that I love so much, with the man I am quite certainly falling in love with, feels serendipitous, lending me the confidence I've been lacking to complete the image. Putting my pencil to paper, I start to draw.

Birdsong filters through the air as I work, adding shadows here and leaving space for highlights there, squinting at the subjects as I define their edges. After fifteen minutes I pause, scrutinizing my work, pleased with the result.

"Is that us?"

Jack's voice startles me, and I clutch the book to my chest, hiding the picture from view. "Jack! You scared me. I thought you were asleep."

He's propped up on an elbow looking at me, his eyes intent on my face. "What was that drawing you were working on?" he asks.

"Nothing," I say, my cheeks warming as I try to think of a way to close my sketchbook without exposing the page.

He sits all the way up, his shoulder brushing mine. "Please, Emily? May I see it?" He reaches for, but does not grab my sketchbook. I stare at him, my heart pounding a staccato in my chest. His eyes hold mine, begging me to let him in.

I close my eyes in surrender, willing myself to be brave. "Alright," I say, opening my eyes and holding the sketchbook out to him.

He takes it gently from my hands, and I watch his face, anxious for his reaction. Despite all the times I've kissed him, this feels so much more intimate, so much more personal a thing to share, and I tremble inside, waiting for his response.

He turns the book slowly in his hands until the image is upright, studying it. I try to see it through his eyes: a young woman, with her dark braid hanging down between her shoulder blades, looking up at the man she walks beside. He stands half a head taller than her, looking down into her eyes with what can only be described as adoration. Their hands are entwined between them as they walk along the path, enclosed in a wooded world that is only their own.

He stares at it for a long time. Finally he lifts his head, and my heart skitters at the look he gives me. Without a word, he sets the sketchbook down, cups my face in his hands, and kisses me.

His lips are soft, tentative at first, but the kiss quickly grows deeper. I lean into him, my fingers curling into the fabric of his shirt, pulling him closer as the kiss grows more urgent, less guarded, like we're finally saying what neither of us can seem to find the words for.

Without breaking the kiss, Jack pulls me toward him until I'm sitting sideways on his lap. I slide my arms up his chest and around his neck. My lips part, ever so slightly, and he deepens the kiss, one hand tangling into my hair, the other curving around my waist, holding me close.

I pull back, catching my breath, and his lips move from my mouth to my jawline, tracing kisses down my neck until his lips brush my collarbone. I shiver, my fingers curling into fists, clutching at him. I feel the steady, thunderous rhythm of our hearts beating in our chests, until his mouth finds mine again and the world tilts, letting me fall.

Time slows as the kiss stretches on. It changes in rhythm— sometimes urgent, often soft, always burning. Every meeting of our lips, every brush of our fingers, is a wordless confession. A surrender. A plea.

Slowly, gently, the passion between us burns low. He pulls away, but my lips linger on his, desperate and wanting. A low chuckle sounds in his throat, and he presses his mouth to mine with aching tenderness.

"Emily," he says, my name like a prayer on his lips.

My eyes flutter open, and the depth of raw emotion I see in his eyes causes my breath to catch.

"It's us, isn't it?" he asks, his voice husky.

"Yes," I whisper.

He wraps his arms around me, pulling me closer. Turning his head, he presses the side of his face to the top of my chest.

"I can hear your heart," he murmurs. "It sounds as fast as a hummingbird's wings."

I hold him there, not wanting to let go. Something in this moment feels so tenuous, so fragile, as if it might snap with the least bit of resistance. He pulls his arms even tighter around me, and we hold each like that for a long while, until my heart ceases striving to escape my chest.

Slowly my arms release him, the heat of desire giving way to the warmth of affection. He pulls away slowly, looking up at me as if I'm the most beautiful thing he's ever seen.

"Emily," he murmurs, his eyes searching mine. "I wish..."

I place a finger gently against his mouth, and he stops. When I'm sure he won't speak, I press my lips softly to his.

"You don't have to say anything," I say.

"Thank you," he says.

I smile.

He shifts, and I move to sit beside him once more. "I meant, thank you for showing me the sketch," he says.

"Oh," I duck my head. "You're welcome."

"May I look through the rest of the book?"

I nod, feeling safer than I've ever felt before. He flips through the pages slowly, pausing to examine some sketches more closely, his lips curving into a smile or parting in wonder by turn. When he comes to the image of the squirrel Mr. Tumnus, half-colored with paint, he taps it with his finger.

"This one might be my favorite," he says.

"Really?"

"Well, besides the one of us," he grins. I blush, pleased.

"Thanks."

He hands the book back to me, and I tuck it back into my pack. "Are you ready to head back, then?" I ask.

"Not quite," he says, pulling me toward him again. I laugh, until his mouth finds mine and I fall into his kisses once more.

Chapter 22

The hike back to the farm is just as beautiful but takes twice as long as the hike out. The reason being, of course, that Jack keeps stopping to "look at the view." Which is actually code for *kiss Emily senseless.*

"I swear," I say, laughing as I pull away again, "if we keep stopping like this, we're gonna have to camp out here tonight."

"Oh dear," he says, kissing the edge of my jaw, "stuck in the woods with only you and the stars? What a nightmare."

I swat his arm and start walking again. He laughs, catching my hand and pulling me back so he can press a kiss to my cheek.

"So what are we going to do with all these cones?" he asks as we start along the trail again.

"We need to dry them out so we can harvest the seeds," I say.

"And how do we do that?"

I wipe my forehead, feeling a piece of twig caught in my hair. "We'll place them in paper bags and leave them somewhere warm to open," I say, pulling out the twig. I hold it up, glaring at him, but he merely grins, a lopsided smirk that floods my body with heat.

As we get closer to the farm, my phone suddenly pings in my bag, buzzing with an alert. Then another. And another. I stop, pulling off my pack and digging around for my phone.

"What's up?" Jack asks, coming to a standstill behind me.

"I don't know," I say. "My phone just started going crazy.

"We probably just got back into range," he says.

I finally extricate my phone and see half a dozen missed calls from Chase, all only a minute or two apart. Frowning, I tap to call him, but after four rings it goes to voicemail.

"That's odd," I say, looking back at the screen.

"He tried to call me, too," Jack says, putting his phone to his ear. I watch him, feeling suddenly anxious, but after a moment he shakes his head.

"Nothing."

"Let's hurry back," I say, "in case something's wrong."

We pick up the pace a bit, and a few minutes later my phone rings. I pull it from my pocket, still moving down the trail.

"Chase?" I say. "What's going on? Is everything okay?"

At first I hear nothing, then the staticky sound of muffled speech. I stop in the middle of the trail. "Chase?"

"Been... you di... Mom... al..."

"Chase, you're breaking up. Can you hear me?"

More staticky, inaudible sounds follow, and a knife of worry slides its point between my ribs. The line goes dead, and I look up at Jack.

"Something's wrong," I say.

"What did Chase say?" Jack asks.

"I don't know, he kept breaking up."

I start to run down the trail, my pack bouncing against my back. I hear Jack running behind me but I don't turn around, knowing he'll be able to keep up.

I estimate that we're less than a mile from the house, but the trail is still unpredictable in spots, and the last thing I want is to trip and twist an ankle. I run as fast as I comfortably can, holding the straps of my pack tight to try and stop it bouncing around so much.

Fifteen minutes later I see the house through the trees, and I force my legs into another burst of speed. I break through the treeline and head straight for the house, taking in the state of the farm as I run. There's no sign of anyone anywhere—Dad's truck and my own are still next to the house, but Chase's car is gone.

I slow to a stop by the closed garage door, which is a sure sign that no one is home. But where would they all be? I lean against my knees, gulping air, and just as Jack comes up beside me, my phone rings again.

"Chase?" I gasp.

"Em! Can you hear me?"

"Yes, what's going—"

"Mom fell. She hit her head and we had to call an ambulance. Dad and I are following them to the hospital right now," he says.

My knees buckle and I sit hard on the ground. Jack rushes over to me.

"Is she okay?" I ask, still breathless from my run.

"I don't know," he says, and I can hear the worry in his voice. "She hit her head pretty hard. There was a lot of blood..."

I squeeze my eyes shut, my stomach turning. "Okay. I'll be there as soon as I can."

Jack doesn't even hesitate. The moment I hang up the phone with Chase, his arms are around me.

"What do you need?" he asks.

Not *what happened?* or *what did Chase say?* He saw me falling apart and immediately wanted to know how he could help me. My heart swoons at his gallantry, but ever the practical one, my brain calls the troops to attention.

"Get me to the hospital," I say, trying to stand.

In one swift, fluid motion he picks me up from the ground, carrying me to his car. Pulling the door open, he sets me in the passenger seat.

"Do you need anything from the house?" he asks.

"No, nothing."

He nods, shutting my door and racing around to the driver's side. Before I can even buckle my seatbelt, he's got the car in drive and we're racing down the hill.

I cry the whole way to the hospital. Jack glances at me occasionally, worry etched across his features. Eventually my sobs lessen, leaving me feeling wrung out like a rag. Jack reaches over and takes my hand, and I squeeze it tight, grateful he's here.

The sun is low on the horizon when we pull into the hospital parking lot. We slide into the first spot we see and rush across the asphalt to the emergency room doors. The waiting room is empty save for Chase and Dad, who both stand when they see us.

"Where's Mom? Is she going to be okay?" I ask.

Dad takes me in his arms, holding me tight. "They're stitching her up right now and doing a thorough assessment. We'll be able to see her soon."

As if on cue, a woman in scrubs comes into the waiting room. "Mr. Kenworth?" she calls.

We all turn.

"Yes, that's me," Dad says, hurrying over.

"The doctor would like you present for the next part. The rest of you will have to wait here for now."

Dad looks back at us. "I'll let you know how it's going when I can," he says, then turns to follow the nurse into the back.

I watch them go, the knife of worry now firmly lodged in my chest. I turn toward Chase and he reaches for me, holding me close as the tears begin again.

When my sobs subside, I pull away, wiping my eyes. "What happened?" I ask, sitting down on one of the hard waiting room chairs.

Chase sits beside me, blowing out his breath. "She and Dad were in the front room, but then Dad went into the kitchen to start dinner. I guess she needed something or didn't want to wait for him, so she got up and followed him to the kitchen—without her walker."

I close my eyes, shaking my head.

"I was in the office when I heard a crash, and then Dad yelling," Chase says, running a hand through his hair. It's all standing on end, and I wonder how many times he's done that since it happened. "I came running down the hall and saw Mom on the floor by the table, not moving. There was a chair on its side and Dad was beside her, yelling. Her head was covered in blood..."

I put a hand to my mouth, and Jack takes my other hand, squeezing it tight.

"The paramedics said the cut on her head wasn't deep, but

head wounds bleed a lot, so it looked worse than it was. But they're pretty sure she's got a concussion."

Both my phone and Chase's alert at the same time, and I pull it from my pocket. "Dad says they got her wound bandaged up and are doing a cognitive evaluation now," I say to Jack, since Chase is reading the message on his phone as well.

"That must be why they wanted Dad," Chase says. "To find out what symptoms are new and what's been around with her Parkinson's."

We settle in to wait—Chase paces back and forth along the front windows, while Jack and I sit beside one another, watching the doors that Dad and the nurse went through. Jack holds my hand, occasionally rubbing my arm, and whenever I glance at his face, he gives me an encouraging smile. He doesn't speak, and for that I'm glad. There aren't really words for this, anyway.

The emergency room isn't busy. No one comes in all afternoon except a woman with a crying child, complaining of a possible broken arm. They get taken back almost immediately, and we're left alone again. After about an hour Chase gets a phone call. "Hey, Marilee," he says, "thanks for calling." He walks out of the waiting room, telling her about what happened. I watch him go.

"I still don't think that's a good idea," I say, nodding at the outside doors where he disappeared. Jack follows my gaze.

"Nothing we can do about it, I'm afraid."

While Chase is outside talking to Marilee, another nurse comes out to the waiting room. Jack and I get to our feet. "Mrs. Kenworth's children?" she asks.

"I'm her daughter," I say. "My brother is outside."

"You can come back now," she says.

Jack squeezes my hand, and I look up at him. "Go," he says. "I'll let Chase know."

"Thank you," I say, then turn back to the nurse, who leads me through the doors.

The emergency room smells sharp, like antiseptic and anxiety, and my stomach turns over as I follow the nurse down the hall. She leads me to a room with a sliding glass door that's half-closed.

"Right in here," she says, giving me a warm smile.

"Thank you."

I ease the door open a bit more and sneak around the drawn curtain. Dad is sitting in a chair, but he gets up when I come in.

"Emily," he says, embracing me. "Where's Chase?"

"He's on the phone," I say. "Jack is going to send him back as soon as he can."

Dad nods, and I look at Mom lying on the bed. Her head is bandaged and she's attached to all sorts of monitors. Her eyes are half-open, watching me.

"Hi, Mom," I say softly, not wanting to startle her.

Her eyes find mine, but where there should be recognition, there's just emptiness. She hesitates, and confusion clouds her face. "Walter?" she asks.

"I'm right here, sweetheart," he says, moving to her side and taking her hand. He looks at me. "The doctor says she has a concussion. Her symptoms are pretty severe, but they're likely exacerbated because of her Parkinson's. They want to keep her for observation for a few days. Just in case."

I look down at Mom. *Just in case.* I hate how vague that is. She looks so frail, in her yellow hospital gown and bandaged head, with bruises blooming on her arms and cheek.

We hear the door slide open, and a moment later the curtain is pulled back. I turn, expecting to see Chase, but instead it's a dark-haired man in navy scrubs. He looks too put-together for this space, and the contrast between his appearance and that of my mom's makes hers look all the worse.

"Good evening," he says with a smile. I'm sure he means it to be reassuring, but it's a bit too formal to feel genuine. "I'm Dr. Bakshi." He steps closer to the bed, tucking his hands behind him as he talks. "How are you feeling, Kathy?"

Mom turns to look at him, trying to focus. "Walter?"

"Is it normal for her to be so disoriented?" I ask. "She didn't recognize me when I came in."

"Very normal," the doctor assures me. "Your mom is experiencing a moderate-to-severe concussion from her fall, which is essentially a mild traumatic brain injury. In severe cases, the brain hits the inside of the skull with enough force to disrupt normal function for a prolonged period of time. The damage caused by the impact can affect memory, balance, speech, even personality for a while."

Mom sighs, then closes her eyes, looking exhausted. "Is she going to be okay?" I ask, lowering my voice.

"I believe so." Dr. Bakshi gives me another clinical smile. "It's not uncommon for patients to have headaches, confusion, mood swings, or trouble concentrating in the days—or sometimes weeks—afterward, but most recover fully in a month or two. In Kathy's case, her Parkinson's disease already affects a great deal of her motor and cognitive abilities, so it's hard to determine if the symptoms she's experiencing are caused by the concussion or by Parkinson's."

"And that's why she needs to stay? For observation?" I ask.

"Correct. We want to make sure she doesn't develop an infection from her head wound, and we'll be watching for signs of hemorrhagic stroke. A CT scan should show us if there's any bleeding in the brain."

I look at Dad, my eyes widening. He looks down, shaking his head.

"When will she be able to get the CT scan?" I ask.

"I've already put in the orders," Dr. Bakshi says, "so as soon as the imaging department is ready they'll be coming to get her. In the meantime, we'll continue to monitor her closely, until we get her admitted and settled upstairs." He smiles at Dad, looking between us. "Do you have any other questions?"

I have so many. But I shake my head.

Dad clears his throat. "Thanks, Doctor. Appreciate you."

Dr. Bakshi gives us one more composed smile and heads out, leaving the door cracked behind him.

I sit down in the chair vacated by Dad, my head spinning. A moment later I hear the door slide open again, and Chase comes in.

"Dad. Mom," he says, moving to the bed. "How is she?" he asks.

"She's doing all right, considering the circumstances," Dad says.

"Where's Jack?" I ask.

"In the waiting room," Chase says.

I stand up and touch Dad's arm, who turns to look at me.

"I'm going to go talk to Jack while you fill Chase in on everything, okay?"

"Sure thing," he says.

"I'll be back," I add.

He nods, and as I slide the heavy door open he starts to tell Chase everything the doctor said.

The walk back to the waiting room feels infinitely shorter than the walk to Mom's room. Jack looks up from his phone when he hears the doors open, and stands as soon as he sees me.

"How's your mom?" he asks.

I blow out my breath. "Okay, I guess."

I tell him what the doctor said, and what we hope to learn from the CT scan. He rubs my arm, embracing me when I get choked up during my explanation.

"I'm right here, Emily," he says, holding me tight.

I let him comfort me, grateful for his strength, but eventually I step back.

"Would you like me to take you home so you can rest?" he asks. "You look exhausted."

But I shake my head, looking up at him with shining eyes. "I don't want to leave her. What if something happens while I'm gone?"

He nods. "I understand. Would you like me to stay with you?"

My heart overflows at his offer, and so do my eyes. He pulls me into his arms once more, and I hug him back, not wanting to let him go. But eventually I do.

"Thank you, but I'll be okay. Chase and Dad are here. You go home and get some rest."

"Alright," he says. "But call me if you need anything, okay?"

"I will."

Jack presses a long, soft kiss to my forehead, cradling my face with his hand. "I'll have my phone with me all night," he says, looking into my eyes. I nod to let him know I understand, and then he leaves.

Chapter 23

Mom is in the ICU for two days, and then on the medical floor for another three. Chase, Dad and I take turns sitting with her, while the others stay at the farm to oversee the fall chores. Jack has to go to California for a couple days for his second interview with TechNova, but before he leaves, he and Chase install a ramp up to the front door, since Mom will be in a wheelchair now. When we initially mentioned it, she got really upset—which wasn't surprising, considering how vehemently she thought she didn't need a walker. But Dad's not willing to let her take another tumble, so the wheelchair is a must. By her fifth day in the hospital she's mentally almost back to where she was before the fall, and with no further complications the doctor feels comfortable sending her home. Chase, Dad, and I are all there for her discharge.

"Her brain needs time to rest and heal," the doctor says. "No screens, no driving—or in her case, riding in a car; no strenuous activity whatsoever. Lots of sleep, hydration, and a very slow return to normal." He looks at Dad. "Do you have a ramp for her wheelchair?"

"We got it installed a few days ago," Chase says. The doctor nods.

"Good. Now, I've sent a referral for in-home physical therapy—they should be calling you in a day or two; I'd like her to begin that as soon as possible. And she'll need to see the neurologist in a couple weeks for a follow-up and to reevaluate how she's doing."

Dad nods and thanks the doctor, who smiles at us and leaves the room. Chase helps Mom into her wheelchair while I accept the discharge paperwork from the nurse, and then Dad wheels Mom out the door, with Chase and I following. The hallways still smell like antiseptic cleaner, but it doesn't make me nauseous this time.

As we pull up to the house, we see a large banner that says "Merry Christmas Kathy!" attached to the side of the new ramp. Jack and Sophie are standing on the front porch, smiling and waving as we park. My heart skitters at the sight of Jack, who only just arrived home from California.

"We weren't expecting a welcome committee," Dad says, getting out of the car. Chase goes inside to get Mom's wheelchair, while Sophie comes down to give me a hug.

"How are you holding up?" she asks, pulling back to look me in the eye. I give her a tired smile.

"Better, now that she's home," I say.

Chase brings her wheelchair down the ramp, and he and Dad help her get into it. Dad starts pushing her into the house, while I fall into step with Sophie.

"I brought a double batch of tamales for everyone, and there's a pan of enchiladas in the freezer as well," she says.

"Oh Sophie, that's so thoughtful. Thank you so much."

"Don't I get a thank you?" Jack says as we arrive on the porch. "I built the ramp and made the sign."

"*We* built the ramp," Chase corrects.

"And we *both* made the sign," Sophie says, propping a hand on her hip.

I smile, stepping forward to embrace Jack. He wraps his arms around me, burying his face in my hair, holding me close. "I've missed you," he murmurs.

"I've missed you, too," I say. "Any news on the job?"

He pulls back with a sigh. "Not yet. This interview didn't go as well as I hoped it would, though. I don't think I got it."

"I'm sorry."

He shrugs it off, reaching up to trace my cheek and jaw with his thumb. "It's all right." His look softens. "Just means we get more time together."

Life settles into a new routine. Dad now spends all of his time with Mom, leaving me and Chase to manage everything about the farm. Jack is a godsend—I don't know what we would do without him. Actually, I do: we'd crash and burn so hard that even Rudolph couldn't guide us out of the wreckage. But thankfully we *do* have Jack, so no magical reindeer are needed.

On Tuesdays and Fridays, the physical therapist comes to the house to work with Mom. She has been showing slow but steady improvement, and the therapist is encouraged by what he sees. And a week before Halloween, the neurologist confirms that she is nearly fully recovered from her concussion. We celebrate by going to PineCones and eating far more ice cream than is good for us.

The first week of November settles in like a damp sigh. Mornings are cloaked in a soft, persistent fog that clings to the trees and colors the world a muted gray. The air smells like wet earth and woodsmoke, and it rains more often than not—sometimes as a gentle mist, sometimes in steady sheets that drum against the roof and ripple puddles in the mud.

Jack didn't get the job in California, and I can tell he's getting frustrated and depressed about his prospects. He joins the temp workers we hire to cut, bale, and load the trees that our wholesale buyers have ordered. I was nervous when Dad told me he called both Tim and Jesse to let them know about the price increase, but after asking a few questions and getting some clarity, they each agreed to the new invoices. "We've been buying and selling your trees for nearly thirty years," Tim told him. "We don't want anyone else's."

His loyalty offers some much-needed relief.

Chase has been working on advertising our You-Cut trees, and I've been making sure the harvesting goes off without a hitch. Tim and Jesse each like to have their tree lots set up the week before Thanksgiving, which gives us only a couple weeks to fill their orders. In addition to the wholesale harvest, we're prepping for the You-Cut season *and* trying to plan the Winter Wonderland event for the first weekend in December. There's a tension in the air I'm not used to feeling at this time of year, and it makes me anxious.

"We need a tree," I say to Dad one evening, after he's settled Mom into bed. "Do you have one already picked out?"

Dad sighs, rubbing his face. "I don't, Emmy-girl. I haven't even thought about it, to be honest." He sinks into a chair, leaning his head against his hand.

I sit beside him and put my hand on his arm. "I know that

was something we liked to do as a family," I say softly. "But I can get Jack or Chase to help me cut a tree and bring it in. I know there's a lot going on right now, and it would be difficult with Mom's wheelchair."

"If you don't think Chase will mind, I'll gladly take you up on that," he says. "I'm sure your mother would appreciate it, too." He pats my hand, and I lean over to kiss his cheek.

"Consider it done," I say.

Heading upstairs, I stop by Chase's room. He looks up when I knock on the half-open door.

"Hey Em, what's up?"

"Dad asked if we wouldn't mind picking out a tree for the house."

He stares at me. "Without them?"

I come in and sit on the end of his bed. "Yeah. Dad doesn't really have it in him this year."

We sit in silence for a long moment, until finally he sighs. "Yeah, I guess we could do that. When?"

I shrug. "The sooner the better, I think. I know we're all stressed and anxious—about Mom, about the harvest. But I think it will help everyone to do something a bit more normal and fun, and it will cheer up the house. We're sadly lacking in Christmas spirit this year."

"That's true. So, tomorrow?"

I nod. "Do you mind if I ask Jack to help us?"

Chase groans. "I do *not* want to play chaperone to my sister and her boyfriend," he says, rolling his eyes. I reach out and smack his knee.

"You are so melodramatic," I say. "You know it's not like that."

He grumbles but doesn't object again, which I take to mean

it's fine. "How's Marilee?" I ask. "Is she still coming for Thanksgiving?"

"I think so," he says, though he sounds less confident than I would expect. "She's been busy at work, so we haven't had as much time to talk as usual, but she hasn't told me otherwise."

A little stab of sympathy pricks my heart, wishing he could see what the rest of us can. "Do you think she's ignoring you?" I ask, as gently as I can.

"What? No!" he says, immediately defensive. "She's just busy. You of all people should understand that."

"Of course I understand being busy. I just wonder if maybe she's using work as an excuse to drift away, if—"

But Chase gets up from the bed, cutting me off. "You told me to keep my nose out of you and Jack's relationship, and I'll kindly ask you to do the same about mine," he says.

I sigh and get up. "Fine. Just be careful, okay?"

He folds his arms across his chest, and I move past him into the hallway. As soon as I clear the door he shuts it behind me.

As I walk down the hall to my room, I send a message to Jack.

EMILY

My dad asked me and Chase to pick out our Christmas tree. Want to help?

I change into my pajamas and brush my teeth, and by the time I finish flossing he's sent a reply.

JACK

Sure! When do you need me?

My heart squeezes in my chest. *I always need you,* I want to reply.

EMILY

Tomorrow would be great, anytime after lunch.

JACK

I'll be there 🙂

Chapter 24

November is one of the most unpleasant months in the Cascade Mountain Range. Days are short and subdued, the sun rarely more than a pale suggestion behind thick clouds. It's the season of muddy boots, dense fog, and flannel layers, when the whole world seems to be holding its breath, awaiting the arrival of winter.

Jack arrives shortly after lunch, and Chase runs to fetch a small chainsaw from the barn. Even with hats and scarves, the cold hits the moment we step outside—sharp and damp, laced with the smell of evergreen. I zip my coat up to my chin and rub my mittened hands together in glee.

"This is one of my absolute favorite days of the year," I announce to Jack, who walks beside me.

"That's only because you never remember the part where your hands go numb and someone inevitably gets poked in the face with a tree branch," Jack says.

I jerk to a stop. "How do you know that?"

He laughs. "My family didn't always get a fresh tree," he

says, "but we had enough over the years, even I remember that part of it."

I giggle. "It's usually Chase," I say, "who ends up getting poked."

We wait by the barn until my brother emerges, then the three of us troop through the mist to the western field. The air is thick with fog and everything is damp, even the air. I suck in a breath, and it fills up my lungs like a sponge.

The ground is a patchwork of soggy grass and muddy puddles as we walk. "Do you always get the same variety of tree each year?" Jack asks.

"Usually," I reply. "Noble firs are our favorite, but they're also very popular. Some years we have a surplus of extra-tall Douglas fir or Colorado spruce, so we'll pick one of those and leave the Nobles for purchase."

"Have you ever cut down a 'wild' tree?"

I grin, sharing a glance with Chase, who laughs. "We did, once," he says.

"We were nine or ten," I say, "and it was Chase's turn to make the final call on the tree."

"We hiked into the woods for a good while," Chase says, picking up the tale, "before we found it. But we finally did. It was perfect."

"Oh yeah?" Jack says.

Chase continues. "It had long, full branches..."

"Spindly," I say, in an aside to Jack.

"...lush, green needles..."

"It was practically dead," I add.

"...and it was the perfect height—not too tall, not too short."

I raise an eyebrow. "For a skyscraper, maybe."

Jack laughs.

"I stand by that tree," Chase says, huffing. "We just needed... higher ceilings."

By now we've arrived at the stand of Noble firs taller than Bigfoot and begin circling each specimen.

"This one's nice," I say, pointing at a 10-foot fir with a nearly perfect shape.

Jack grins. "Will it fit in your living room?"

I roll my eyes. "Yes, it will. We've had a twelve-footer before and it fit quite easily, if that tells you anything about the monstrosity Chase picked out."

Jack looks to Chase, who shrugs innocently.

I nestle my face between the branches of the tree, ignoring the tiny pricks and scratches from the sharp, stubby needles. Closing my eyes, I take a deep breath, my lips pulling into a smile even before I exhale.

"Are you ready, my darling?" I whisper.

I imagine the tree reaching out in my mind, clamoring with joy that her year has finally arrived. *Yes!* she cries. *Yes, yes, yes!*

"Yup," I say, reaching inside and patting the trunk affectionately. "This is definitely the one."

"All right," Chase sighs, kneeling dramatically beside the tree and looking up at us, "but if I get poked in the eye, I'm not helping with the decorations."

The chainsaw makes quick work of the trunk. When guests come to the farm to cut down their own trees, we supply them with quaint but sharp little hand saws, since that's part of the experience. But one of the perks of being the owners is that we can use a chainsaw. Which means that in less than a minute, the tree is down.

Jack and I drag the fir to the nearest access road while Chase takes the chainsaw back up to the barn.

"Race you to the truck?" I ask.

Before Jack can respond, I take off running. "Hey!" I hear him call, but I just laugh, sprinting up the hill.

The world rushes past in a blur of cold air and icy puddles. My boots slip a little in the mud, but I don't stop. I can hear his footsteps behind me, gaining fast, his laughter chasing mine through the fog. The cold air stings my cheeks, my breath coming in sharp gasps, leaving clouds of vapor that melt into the mist.

My truck comes into view through the fog, and I run into its side just a second before Jack does.

"I win!" I yell, breathless.

He leans against the door, panting, his eyes sparkling. "Barely."

"Still counts."

"You cheated—you took off before I was ready. Before I even agreed to race!"

I grin, chest heaving. "You ran after me, didn't you?"

He chuckles and steps closer, wrapping his arms around me. "You're ridiculous," he says.

"And fast," I counter.

"And beautiful."

His lips find mine gently, as if everything he's ever wanted lives right here in this moment. I sigh against his kiss, feeling the same.

He opens the door of my truck for me and I climb inside. "I'll tell Chase we're going to drive down and pick up the tree," he says.

By the time we get the tree into the house, Dad has Ella Fitzgerald playing on the stereo and hot wassail simmering on the stove. He's wheeled Mom into the living room so she can watch, and when I see her I run to give her a hug and a kiss.

"Merry Christmas, Mom!" I say. "Just wait till you see the tree we picked out, she's gorgeous!"

She smiles in a vacant sort of way, turning her head to watch as Jack and Dad help to wrestle it through the front door.

Chase comes in through the mudroom, carrying the old tree stand we've used my entire life.

"Figured we'd need this," he says.

"Thanks, Chase," I say, smiling at him.

Jack helps me bring in all the storage tubs full of decorations from the garage, stealing a few kisses in the process, and soon we have them open, looking through their contents to try and find what we need.

"Alright, who put the lights away like this?" Chase asks, holding up a tangled mess of cords.

He looks at me, but I hold up my palms in self defense. "Don't look at me. I know better than to tempt the gods of Christmas Future with that sort of mischief."

Dad lifts a hand, a look of chagrin on his face. "I think that might be my fault," he says.

Chase snorts. "You're the only person here who could commit such an awful sin and be forgiven for it," he says.

"Well, you and Mom," I add, giving her a fond smile.

She's sitting in her wheelchair, happily humming along to the music while playing with a spare bit of tinseled garland. I sigh, wishing she was more lucid today.

Chase drops the lights on the couch. "Alright, Jack, you're officially promoted to Untangler-in-Chief."

Jack salutes him. "Yes, sir."

While Jack wrestles with the lights, Chase and I start unboxing the ornaments. Golden stars and multi-colored baubles fill one box, while another holds all the hand-made ornaments from our childhood: sleds made of popsicle sticks, the infamous glitter pinecones from kindergarten (somehow still shedding tiny flecks of silver), and a miniature clay snowman with three eyes and no arms.

"Remember this guy?" I ask, holding it up like a piece of ancient treasure.

Chase chuckles. "Frosty the Abomination. I made him the year I had the flu over Christmas."

"The craftsmanship really reflects the fever dreams," Jack adds from the couch, still buried in lights.

Laughing, I hang Frosty the Abomination right up front.

"You know you're going to end up moving that to the back later, right?" Chase says.

"I know," I reply. "But he deserves his moment."

He chuckles, shaking his head.

Eventually, Jack conquers the lights with only minimal swearing, and we circle the tree together, stringing them around awkward branches and ducking under each other's arms. At one point, Jack manages to trip over the power cord, accidentally yanking the strand halfway off the tree and knocking the whole thing askew.

Dad and Chase set the tree to rights while Jack untangles himself and restrings the lights. We take a short break to enjoy some wassail, and when we get back to work I bring the step stool from the kitchen. Dad hands me ornaments, which I hang on the higher branches, and slowly, slowly the tree transforms from a bare green skeleton into a riot of color, lights, and memories.

When the last ornament is hung, we all step back to admire our handiwork. The tree leans slightly to the left, the floor is covered in fallen needles, and somehow there's a candy cane hanging from the ceiling fan.

"Well, what do we think?" Dad asks.

I frown. "It's crooked."

"Forget it," Chase says, tossing himself dramatically onto the couch. "The tree is festive and nobody got electrocuted. I'm calling that a win."

Jack wraps an arm around my shoulders. "It looks great."

I lean into him, sighing. "You're only saying that so I don't ask you to fix it."

He laughs, kissing me on top of the head. As we start putting things away, Chase's phone rings. He fishes it out of his pocket from his position on the couch, his face instantly lighting up when he sees the screen.

"Hey Marilee, how's it going?" He sits up, beaming at me. I force myself to smile back at him.

"I'm excited to see you in a couple weeks—do you have your flight information yet?" he asks.

I watch him from the corner or my eye, seeing the brightness fade from his face, his look shifting from one of excitement to confusion.

"What do you mean you're not coming?" he says.

I suck in a breath, glancing at Jack, who's looking away but most definitely following the conversation. He grimaces, shaking his head.

Chase is on his feet now, quickly moving across the room. "No, Marilee, please don't say that..."

He's up the stairs now, his voice a nondescript murmur until his door shuts, cutting it off completely.

The room is silent. Jack and I share knowing looks, my heart aching for my brother and the pain he must be feeling. Finally Dad clears his throat, reaching for the step stool. "We better start cleaning up," he says.

Chapter 25

A fter we get the Christmas boxes put away, Jack heads home. "Let me know if you need anything else," he says, getting into his car. "I have a feeling Chase might not be much use for a little while."

My brother doesn't leave his room for the rest of the day. I knock on his door a few hours later to let him know dinner is ready, but he doesn't respond.

"Let him work things out on his own," Dad tells me. "We'll see him tomorrow."

But I'll be honest, I didn't expect to see Chase much the following day, either. Imagine my surprise when I come downstairs just before eight the next morning to find him in the kitchen, drinking coffee.

I freeze halfway through the door. "Chase?"

He looks up. "Hey, Em."

"You look terrible."

He snorts. "Yeah, well, I feel terrible."

I get a mug from the cupboard and pour myself a cup. "I'm surprised you're up so early."

"Couldn't sleep," he says.

I take the seat beside him at the counter. "Want to talk about it?" I ask.

"Not particularly," he says.

I nod. "Okay."

We sip our drinks in silence for several minutes. Chase stares blankly at the wall, and I count the number of grunts and huffs he makes, hearing in them the anger and hurt he must be feeling.

After thirteen such noises he gets up from his seat. "I'm going to get to work," he says.

Without another word, he heads into the mudroom, pulls on his boots, coat, and gloves, and marches out the door.

The next several days follow the same pattern. Chase is up early every day, working to get everything ready for the season. I've never seen him so focused before, pushing himself to cut and bale more trees than anyone else. I appreciate his help, but after the fifth day I follow him into the mudroom, demanding answers.

"Talk to me, Chase," I say, folding my arms across my chest.

"No."

"I know you're hurting."

"Yeah, well, who cares," he says, bending down to lace up his boots.

"I care."

He scoffs. "All you care about is Jack and this stupid tree farm."

I rear back, the shock of his words like a punch to my ribs. "Stupid tree farm? This is our *home*, Chase. Our livelihood. Without this *stupid tree farm*, how would we put food on the table? How would we pay for Mom's medical needs?

Where would we live, Chase? How would our family survive?"

His hands still, and he closes his eyes. I watch the play of emotions across his face—anger, frustration, fear... pain. I reach out and place my hand gently on his shoulder.

"I'm sorry about what happened with Marilee," I say, and he stiffens. "But you're not alone in this, Chase. We can—"

He stands abruptly, grabs his coat, and storms out the door. My shoulders drop.

So much for being a voice of support.

"I've never seen him take a breakup this hard before," I say to Jack the following Saturday. It's been more than a week since the phone call, and Thanksgiving is just five days away. With the wholesale trees finally delivered, we've been sorting the hand saws for our You-Cut guests, swapping out the blades for fresh ones and ensuring the handles are in good shape. Chase has been quiet and broody all morning, and when we finish the first box of saws he offers to take them down the hill to the lower shed. I consider pointing out that we can take *all* the saws down in the truck later, but I can tell he wants the time alone, so I say nothing.

Jack looks down the hill at Chase's retreating figure, the box of bow saws balanced up on one shoulder. "I don't think it's just about Marilee," he says.

"You don't?"

"No. I mean sure, that's part of it—probably a big part of it. But think about everything else he's had weighing on his shoulders. He had to postpone going to medical school *and* give up the money set aside for that purpose, he's been working his butt off trying to salvage the finances of the family business, he kept strong for you and your dad when your mom fell, and now the woman he's been talking to for weeks and was starting to think might actually like him, dumps him before the busiest, most stressful time of year."

I stare at him, then turn and look to where Chase has disappeared behind the trees. "Wow. I guess I hadn't considered all of that, all at once. That *is* quite the load."

"Yeah." Jack grabs another saw. "I mean, he's been a bit of a jerk about the whole thing, but all things considered, I guess I don't really blame him."

"Me neither," I say, opening another package of new saw blades. "But I hope he pulls himself together soon. I hate to see him so miserable."

He nods, and we continue working. After several minutes, his phone rings. He pulls it out of his pocket. "Jack McKinley," he says, getting to his feet.

I continue working, assuming he'll rejoin me in a moment, but he strides off down the hill. I can hear him talking to whoever's on the other end of the line, but I can't make out the words. He doesn't come back.

Curious, but not worried, I keep working. The day is warmer than usual, and I've unzipped my jacket while I work. Unscrewing a rusted bolt, I pull out an old, dull blade and drop it into the box with the others before fitting the saw with a new one. Fifteen minutes later, the sound of voices causes me to look up. Jack and Chase are coming up the hill, and from the sound of it, they're arguing. I crane my neck, watching for them. As they come into view over the rise, it's clear that Chase is upset about something. I watch as Jack pulls him to a stop, trying to reason with him. But Chase's voice grows louder. He jabs a finger into Jack's chest, then turns and points up the hill toward me.

They see me watching them and freeze.

But only for a moment. When they start up the hill again, Jack says something to Chase, but my brother only shakes his head, scowling. As they get closer, I can see that Jack's brow is furrowed, making two little dents between his eyes. He walks half a step behind Chase, his eyes glued to my brother's back, as if waiting for him to do something. But Chase marches straight up the hill, and instead of coming toward the barn where we've been working, he heads for the house, stomping into the garage and through the mudroom door without a backward glance.

Jack walks up to me, still frowning.

"What was that all about?" I ask.

"Chase and I had an argument."

I huff a laugh. "I can see that. How come?"

He sighs. "Let's just say that your brother and I have very different views on relationships," he says.

"Oh."

Jack is quiet as we get back to work, and I wonder what he's thinking. He doesn't look angry, but whatever passed between him and Chase clearly has him thinking deep thoughts.

We finish the rest of the handsaws and take them down to the shed near the entrance, where they'll be handed out to the families coming to cut their tree for the season. We officially open in less than a week, and I'm restless with anticipation.

"What are your plans for Thanksgiving?" I ask, locking up the shed.

"Not much. Watching football, eating turkey. Just a quiet day with the fam. You guys?"

I sigh. "I have no idea. Usually Dad makes the turkey and Chase and I cobble together the side dishes. But with everything going on this year, we haven't discussed it. I don't think we've bought a turkey yet, and the thought of doing even more work at this point makes me want to cry."

"So don't," Jack says, taking my hand as we walk back up the hill. "Go out to eat somewhere, or order pizza."

"Huh. That's not a bad idea. I'll have to run it past my family and see what they think."

We walk in silence the rest of the way, and when we get to the house Jack stops.

"I think I'm going to head out," he says. "Call you later?"

I nod, and he kisses me on the cheek before heading to his car.

On Monday evening I finally broach the subject of Thanksgiving dinner with my family.

"Hey Dad," I ask, chasing a meatball around my plate, "have you already bought the turkey for Thursday?"

He sighs. "To be honest, Emily, I haven't. Guess we'll have to find a fresh one at this point."

"The turkey for Thanksgiving?" Mom asks.

"Yes," I say, "Thanksgiving is on Thursday."

"Oh, that's right," she says. Dad smiles at her and pats her hand.

"I was actually thinking," I say, crumpling my napkin with my hand, "maybe we shouldn't have turkey this year," I say carefully.

Chase looks up. "Not have turkey?"

"Yeah. Maybe instead of having a traditional meal, we can just... order takeout and relax."

Dad takes a bite of spaghetti, considering. "Your mom

mentioned that once, when it got to be too hard for her to make the meal. I certainly wouldn't complain," he says.

"I wouldn't mind," Mom says.

But Chase scowls. "Are you suggesting that we give up Thanksgiving dinner entirely? No turkey or stuffing or pie or anything?"

I lift an eyebrow at him. "Would you like to make it?" I challenge. "Because Dad certainly has enough on his plate, and I for one am so exhausted from the harvest and prepping for opening I would *much* rather have a day off to relax, than have another day of hard work, just for a fancy meal."

Chase grumbles under his breath, but doesn't actually reply. We eat in silence for a few more minutes.

"I think it's a great idea, Emily," Mom says.

"Agreed," Dad says.

I look at my brother, but his head is down, eating. I look back at Dad, who shrugs. "Anyone opposed to Chinese?" I ask.

Dad and Mom shake their heads and Chase doesn't reply, which I take as silent consent. "I'll get something ordered for us, then," I say.

Chase suddenly drops his fork onto his plate with a clatter, pushing his chair back from the table and standing up.

"Chase?" Mom asks, looking up at him.

"This is the worst Thanksgiving ever," he says, storming out of the room. We watch him go, hearing his pounding footfalls as he stalks up the stairs. When his slamming door reverberates through the house, Dad sighs.

"I'm fast losing patience with that boy," he says. "Acting like he's fifteen again, and the whole world is out to get him."

I actually agree with my dad, but I remember what Jack

pointed out. "I can make a pie, at least. Apple was always Chase's favorite—maybe that will soften him up."

Dad points his fork at me, looking stern. "Don't you be taking responsibility for your brother's poor attitude," he says, "You've got enough to worry about as it is."

My face relaxes. "I won't. But I feel bad, you know? He'd been looking forward to Marilee coming for Thanksgiving. I know the day will be hard for him because of that."

"Who's Marilee again?" Mom asks, her voice trembling.

Dad shakes his head. "Like a durn fifteen-year-old boy and not the man I raised him to be," he grumbles again. He wipes his mouth with a napkin, then sets it on the table and gets up from his chair. "Do what you like, sugarplum, but he's got to pull himself together, and no one's going to be able to do that for him but himself."

Chapter 26

W e spend a miserable, wet day on Tuesday stringing lights and setting up the decorations around the farm. The sky hangs low and heavy, the clouds a dull, unbroken sheet of gray. Cold rain falls in a steady drizzle—soaking through our clothes and chilling our hands until we can't feel our fingertips. Every breath puffs out in a faint white cloud, reminding us that winter is just around the corner.

Chase was planning to take care of paperwork in the office, but when I mentioned that I was worried we wouldn't get all the lights and signs set up in time, he bundled up and followed me outside.

"Thanks for helping with the lights," I say when we're finished, blowing on my hands as we head back to the house for dinner. "I really appreciate it."

He shrugs. "It needed doing."

We walk in silence for a bit, shoulders hunched against the drizzle. "I ordered us an Asian feast from Fong's for Thursday," I venture. "Including a dozen egg rolls," I add, knowing they're his favorite.

He makes no reply.

We skirt a large puddle as we pass the barn, and I make one final attempt to draw him out. "What were you and Jack arguing about on Saturday?" I ask. "You sounded upset."

He makes a noise in his throat, somewhere between a growl and a laugh. "Ask your *boyfriend*," he spits. "I'm sure he'd love to tell you."

I love my brother, but my patience with him is beginning to wear thin. "I'm asking *you*," I say, "but you don't seem to want to talk to me anymore. Why? We used to talk about everything, Chase. What happened?"

He stops and glares at me. "Jack happened," he says. "Ever since you guys started seeing each other you've been oblivious to everyone and everything else."

"That's not true," I say, stung by his words.

"Well, it certainly feels true," he says, turning away, "although Jack will be gone soon enough, and then maybe things can go back to normal."

He stalks away, leaving me standing cold and alone, wishing I'd just kept my mouth shut.

Chase stays in his room the rest of the night. I'm afraid that if I try to talk to him again he'll bite my head off, but I decide to risk a text message before bed.

EMILY

I'm sorry if I've been ignoring you. I haven't meant to.

I get a response almost immediately, which surprises me.

CHASE

I wasn't being fair when I said that. You've
been working hard for the family and the farm,
same as me. I'm sorry if I hurt you.

The words blur on the screen as my eyes fill with tears.

EMILY

Thx 🤍 love you Chase

CHASE

Love you too

The next morning I head to the store to pick up some
apples and strawberry ice cream. I consider grabbing a
premade crust as well, but I figure if I'm going through the
trouble of making a homemade pie, I'm going to do it right.
Checking out at Safeway, I drive across the parking lot to *The
Jitterbug* to grab a coffee and say hi to Sophie.

I pull into the drive thru and roll down my window. The
roar of the engine is too loud to make an order, so I turn off my
truck. After a moment I hear Sophie's voice on the speaker.

"Merry Christmas from *The Jitterbug!* What can I get started
for you today?"

"I'll take a tall gingerbread latte, please," I say.

There's a pause. "Emily?"

"Hey, Soph."

"Hey yourself! Anything else I can get you?"

"No, that's all, thanks."

"I'll have your total at the window."

I start up my truck and creep around the building. I can see
that it's busy inside, so it's a few moments before she opens the
window. A Santa hat is perched jauntily on her head, matching
her crimson nails and bright red lipstick.

"Hey, you," she says. "$7.41."

I hand her my card and she swipes it before handing it back. "How are things with Chase?"

I sigh. "Not great. But we'll manage."

She gives me a commiserating grimace. "Sorry." She hands me my drink and a white paper sack. "On the house," she says with a cheery wink.

My face softens into a smile. "Thanks, Sophie. You're the best."

She waves, and I pull away from the building.

It's been cold and rainy all week, with misty fog and low-hanging clouds covering the area. As I drive home I wonder idly when we might get snow, and make a mental note to check the weather and see.

I take my purchases into the house, kicking off my boots in the mudroom and dropping everything in the kitchen. The house is quiet. Chase is supposed to be out working with Jack, but I decide to investigate where my parents are.

Their bedroom is the last door on the left at the end of the hall, and where my mom has been spending most of her convalescence. The door is shut, so I knock on it quietly, in case she's sleeping. There's no answer. Slowly I turn the knob and peek inside, letting my eyes adjust for a moment to the dim light.

Mom is curled up on her side of the bed, the lines of confusion erased from her face as she sleeps. Beside her, his body curved in a careful embrace, lies my father. He has one arm draped protectively over her, his face slack in sleep—more peaceful than I've seen it in weeks. A lump forms in my throat at the sight of them, and I allow myself to remember how they once were, early in my childhood: young and in love, healthy, strong, and full of life and plans. Plans that never came to fruition. Some that never will.

I close the door quietly, swallowing the ball of emotion lodged in my throat and tiptoeing back down the hall. After blowing my nose, I tidy up the kitchen and connect my phone to the bluetooth speaker we keep by the fridge. Selecting my Classic Christmas Playlist, I roll up my sleeves and get to work.

There's a reason that Dad took over the cooking when Mom was no longer able, and it's not because I don't know how. By the time I've sung along with half a dozen Christmas carols, I'm a mess. There's flour on my cheek, on the floor, and somehow in my hair—even though I haven't touched the top of my head since I started. I look like a Sugarplum Fairy who got a little tipsy making bonbons—one who maybe shouldn't be allowed unsupervised in the kitchen. But it's too late now; I'm already elbow-deep in apples and ambition.

Half a dozen Granny Smiths are piled high in a mixing bowl, peeled and sliced into uneven crescents. I sprinkle cinnamon and sugar over them and add a dash of nutmeg. Well, maybe more than a dash. I'm not the best judge when it comes to appropriate amounts of holiday spice.

As I stir everything together, the sugary syrup starts to coat my fingers, making them unpleasantly sticky. The apples squeak against the side of the bowl as I mix, and I hum along to the tune of *Little Drummer Boy* coming from the speaker.

The pie crust is already rolled out, and I lift it carefully into the pie dish. I pile the apple filling high into the shell, scraping the bowl to get every last, sticky drop. I dot the top of the mound of apples with tiny chunks of butter—possibly too many, but is there really such thing as too much butter?

Then comes the best part: the lattice. Or, what will *hopefully* resemble a lattice. I cut the strips carefully, then begin weaving them over the apples. Some strips are wide, some are thin, a few are thick and others barely thick enough—but I make it work. It's not perfect, but I'm sure it will taste delicious.

I decide to wait to bake it until tomorrow, so it will be warm and fresh when we eat it. Pulling out some plastic wrap, I carefully cover the top and sides of the pie, then take it out to the garage to chill in the extra fridge.

Balancing the pie in one hand, I pull on the handle of the fridge with the other until the door opens. As I make room for the pie on one of the shelves, I notice an opened case of hard cider tucked in the back. I frown. While Dad or Chase sometimes indulge in a beer or two, we found out a couple years ago that cider makes my brother (and myself, to be honest) a little too drunk, too fast, so we rarely buy it. Chase must be more stressed out than I realized.

Setting the pie carefully on a shelf, I shut the fridge and head back into the house. Taking off my apron, I sit down at the table and survey the damage.

A rolling pin lies abandoned on the counter, speckled with bits of dough. Apples peels are everywhere. The sink is piled high with dirty dishes, and flour coats nearly every surface in a fine, white dust. Looking around, you'd think an army of unskilled elves had attempted a full course meal, not merely a simple apple pie.

As I'm trying to find the motivation to clean up the mess, the mudroom door opens and Jacks comes into the kitchen. "Whoa," he says, pulling up short. "What happened in here?"

"Compassion with a side of crazy," I say with a sigh, getting up from the table. When he looks confused, I add, "I made an apple pie for Chase, since it's his favorite."

Jack's look softens. "That's very thoughtful," he says, putting his arms around me, then laughs at the amount of flour that transfers from me to him.

"Sorry," I mumble.

"Don't be sorry," he says, pressing a kiss to my forehead. "You're adorable. Like a Christmas kitchen elf."

I snort. "I don't think Santa would hire me anytime soon," I say, indicating the mess around us.

"Let me help," he says. "Chase and I are finished anyway."

"Already?"

"Yeah." He rolls up his sleeves and turns on the faucet. "We finished marking and tagging the rest of the trees for You-Cut, and got the baler moved down closer to the parking lot."

"Oh good, thanks." I drop my apron into the laundry basket in the mudroom, then look down at myself. "I'm going to go clean up a bit," I say.

"Take your time," Jack calls. "I can manage in here."

I head upstairs, stopping in at the bathroom to rid my face and arms of flour. Pulling out my ponytail, I brush through my hair to get out what I can without having to shower. Satisfied, I pull my hair into a messy bun and head to my room to change. Swapping my jeans for some comfy joggers and pulling on a clean t-shirt, I switch off my light and return downstairs.

Just as I reach the second to last step, I hear Jack's voice in the kitchen.

"I told you I will, Chase. Don't worry about it."

There's a pause, in which I expect my brother to answer, but there's only silence. Then Jack speaks again.

"No, Chase, you can't."

Huh, Chase must be on the phone. I wonder where he went?

"Please," Jack says, his voice earnest. "I promise, it will be soon. I have it all planned out."

What are they talking about? What is it that Jack doesn't want Chase to worry about? I wrack my brain, trying to piece together some sort of explanation. I remember the phone call Jack got last week when we were prepping the saws, and the argument with Chase afterwards. Jack said something about he and Chase not agreeing on relationships... but what does Jack mean? What does he have all planned out?

A jolt courses through me as an idea drops into my head—one involving a diamond ring and Jack on one knee. My heart swoons, and a rush of excitement thrills through my body, sending tingles from the top of my head clear down to my toes. We haven't discussed marriage at all, but could Jack be planning to propose?

Jack sees me the moment I appear in the doorway. "I gotta go," he says, hanging up his phone. He smiles at me. "You look delightfully cozy," he says.

I smile, walking up to him and kissing his cheek. "You're wonderful, you know that?" I say.

He lifts his brow, surprised. "Thanks. What brought that on?"

"Oh, nothing in particular," I say, the bliss of anticipation giving me a decidedly happy buzz. "But cleaning the kitchen for me certainly helps."

He laughs. "I'll clean the kitchen for you anytime," he says.

I grin. "I'll be sure to take you up on that."

Chapter 27

I wake to the sound of a text notification on my phone. Rubbing the sleep from my eyes, I reach for where it sits beside the bed.

JACK

Happy Thanksgiving! I hope you have a great day with your family.

I smile, rolling onto my back as I reply.

EMILY

You too 🙂

JACK

Oh, you're up! Good morning, beautiful.

My heart thrums in response, wishing he was here so I could kiss him.

EMILY

Good morning 😊

JACK

I know it's Thanksgiving, but do you have plans for this evening?

EMILY

Nothing beyond gorging myself on Chinese food and annihilating Chase at Scrabble.

JACK

If you're willing to postpone the bloodbath, would you like to spend some time with me tonight?

EMILY

I would love to. Where? When?

JACK

I'll pick you up at eight

EMILY

Can't wait ☺

Climbing out of bed, I glance out the window. A freezing fog crept in overnight, coating the ground and the trees with a delicate crust of ice. I shiver at the sight, grateful to be snug and warm inside.

The smell of frying sausages drifts upstairs, luring me out of my room. Pulling on a sweatshirt, I walk downstairs to the kitchen, where Dad is standing at the stove.

"Happy Thanksgiving, sugarplum," he says when I come in.

"Happy Thanksgiving," I reply, smiling at him.

I kiss him on the cheek before pouring myself a cup of coffee. Sitting down at the counter, I blow across the top of my mug.

"Hungry?" he asks.

I nod, and he hands me a plate with two linked sausages

and a pile of steaming hash browns. He makes another plate for himself and comes to sit beside me.

"I saw the pie you made in the fridge outside," he says.

I nod. "I'll bake it this afternoon."

We eat in silence for a few minutes, but a question I've had tumbling around since yesterday comes out.

"When I put the pie in the fridge yesterday," I say, keeping my voice level, "I saw an open case of hard cider."

Dad huffs. "Your brother brought that home last week. So long as he keeps his nose clean about it I won't say anything, but his surliness is wearing on me. The sooner he gets this through his system, the better."

"I'm hoping the pie will cheer him up," I say, biting into a sausage.

Dad shakes his head. "I told you before, you're not responsible for your brother's bad mood."

"I know. But he seems so... depressed. Angry, actually, but I think that's just a mask for the stress and sadness he's feeling about everything."

"You mean about that woman from Oklahoma."

"Marilee," I say, taking another bite. "But I think that's only part of it."

I share with him what Jack told me, and Dad nods, thoughtful. "Jack may be right," he says, "but your brother is still responsible for his attitude and actions. He's acting like a child, and he knows better."

We finish breakfast and I offer to clean up the kitchen while Dad checks on Mom. Halfway through doing the dishes, Chase appears. His hair is tousled and his eyes are red, as if he's been crying, or drinking, or staying up *way* too late. Maybe all three.

"Hey," I call, setting a plate in the dishwasher.

He grunts and pulls a mug from the cupboard, then pours himself a cup of coffee. I watch him as he sits at the counter, bleary-eyed and unkempt, looking for all the world like a mall Santa on Christmas Eve—overworked, undercaffeinated, and questioning every life choice that led him there. He doesn't say anything, just wraps his hands around the mug and stares into the dark liquid.

"Marilee was supposed to be here today," he finally says.

I dry my hands and sit down beside him, pulling my half-empty mug toward me.

"I thought she liked me. I really liked her," he says.

I take a sip of my lukewarm coffee, then lean my head against his shoulder, just letting him know I'm here. He doesn't say anything else for a long time.

"You have every right to gloat," he says eventually, shifting beside me. "I know you saw it coming."

I sit up, frowning. "Why would I want to gloat?"

He shrugs but doesn't look at me, and we lapse into silence once more. I get up and rinse a rag at the sink, wiping off the counters as he broods over his coffee.

"The bill from the hospital came yesterday," he says at length.

I close my eyes, knowing it won't be good news. "And?"

He stares into his cup. "It's more than double what we anticipated."

I take a slow, deep breath before I open my eyes, then continue wiping the counters. "We'll manage. Tim and Jesse still owe us half of their invoices. Plus, we're about to open for the season, and we always get—"

"It won't be enough."

I look at him, but he won't meet my eyes. "Then we'll sell off the forty-five acres," I say levelly. "Or offer it to the bank as collateral."

But Chase just shakes his head, finally looking at me. "You don't get it, Em," he says, his voice growing more surly with every word. "It's not going to work. None of it is. All this nonsense that Jack has rigged up for us isn't going to make a bit of difference. When all is said and done, we'll be right back where we started. Worse, actually, because all of my savings will be gone."

I swallow, trying to remain calm. "It's already made a difference."

He laughs—a cold, bitter sound that shoots through the quiet kitchen like a well-aimed snowball. "Oh, that's right, Jack can do no wrong, can he? But he doesn't care about this place, and he doesn't care about you. If you knew what he—"

"That's enough."

Dad's voice cuts through the room, angry and commanding. He stands in the doorway, scowling at Chase. "We didn't raise you to speak like that to any woman, let alone your sister," he says.

Chase glares at him, then abruptly shoves the stool back and storms out of the room. The garage door slams behind him.

I stare after him, my pulse slowing down as my eyes fill with tears. Dad sighs, coming over to where I stand by the sink. His arms come around me, steady and sure, as the fragile façade I've been keeping in place all summer crumbles. The sobs come hard and fast, like a sudden winter storm. He doesn't say anything, just holds me as I fall apart.

I don't know how long we stand there, but as the ache in my chest starts to shift I pull away, wiping my eyes.

"Do you think he's right?" I whisper, the words catching in my throat. "Do you think everything we've done won't make a difference?

"I don't know, sugarplum," he says. "But we'll get through this together."

I don't see Chase the rest of the morning. He must have come back for his coat and shoes at some point, because they're not in the mudroom when I take out the trash a little while later. His car is still here though, so he must have taken off on foot. Dad isn't surprised when I tell him and he doesn't seem worried, but I send Chase a text anyway, hoping he'll respond.

He doesn't.

Dinner is a subdued affair. I head into town to pick up our meal from Fong's, but when I get back Chase still isn't home. My parents and I watch *It's A Wonderful Life* together while we eat, which does little to assuage my concern for my brother's welfare. I pull up his location on our family sharing app, and I'm relieved to see that he appears to be camped out in the lower shed. Or at least, that's where his phone is. I consider putting on my boots and tromping down the hill to check on him, but remembering his attitude this morning, I decide to leave him alone.

After dinner I turn on the oven so I can bake the pie. But when I go to retrieve it from the fridge in the garage, my heart sinks.

The case of cider is gone.

Trying not to worry, I take the pie inside and set it on the counter. I spread the egg wash on the top crust and give it a generous sprinkle of sugar before popping it in the oven. Then I go in search of my dad.

His face is solemn when I tell him what I've deduced from the location app and the missing case of cider. "This nonsense has gone on long enough," he says. Pulling on his coat and boots, he heads out into the fog.

I sit down at the table with my sketchbook after he leaves so I can keep an eye on the oven. The last thing I want to do is burn my peace offering. I pull out my fineliners and start inking a landscape while I wait.

Thirty minutes later I hear the door to the garage open. I look up from the page in time to catch a fleeting glance of Chase heading for the stairs. My heart unclenches, even as I hear his bedroom door slam above me. *At least he's home. At least he's safe.*

Dad walks through the kitchen shaking his head, just as the timer on the oven goes off.

It's been the worst Thanksgiving in my memory. Mom and Dad join me in the kitchen for a game of Uno and a slice of warm apple pie with strawberry ice cream—a favorite family combination Chase discovered when we were kids. He doesn't join us, though, even after I text him.

We're in the middle of our third game when the sweep of headlights across the windows causes us all to look up. I glance at my watch—it's only 6:13, so it's too early to be Jack. But he's the one that walks through the door a short time later.

"Happy Thanksgiving, Kenworth family!" he calls.

"Happy Thanksgiving," we chorus.

"You're early," I say, getting up from the table.

He answers with a mischievous grin. "That's because I'm actually here to talk to your dad."

My eyebrows shoot up, and my dad turns around in his seat to look at us. "You want a word with me, Jack?"

"If that's all right."

"Certainly." Dad gets up from his seat, pausing to kiss my mother on the forehead, then motions for Jack to follow him toward the office. Jack tosses me a smile and I sit back down, the familiar flutter in my stomach making me feel as if I'll float away.

A short time later (far shorter than I would have expected), Dad comes back into the kitchen alone. He grabs his plate and takes it to the counter for another piece of pie.

"Where's Jack?" I ask when he doesn't say anything.

"He went out the office door. Said he'll see you in a couple hours."

How Jack expects me to survive the next ninety minutes is beyond me. For a while I wander aimlessly from task to task, my mind preoccupied with thoughts of Jack and what he might be planning. Finally I sit down at the table with my sketchbook and watercolors, determined to finish Mr. Tumnus.

I've completed the painting and am waiting for it to dry when the doorbell rings. It makes me startle, and then I laugh —I can't even remember the last time someone rang the doorbell.

Mom and Dad are in the living room watching a show, but since they know who it is, they let me get the door. I pull it open to find Jack standing on the porch, holding a single red rose, the petals just beginning to open.

His smile comes slowly, and as it breaks across his face,

something inside me shifts. Looking into his eyes, I feel the pull of home. *I love him,* I realize, and the thought fills me with heat, like gulping hot chocolate too quickly.

"Hey," he says, his voice soft in the darkness.

"Hey," I echo, my newfound revelation making me feel suddenly shy.

He holds the flower out to me. "This is for you," he says.

I take it from him, and our fingers brush against each other. Tingles spread up my arm and throughout my body, causing my heart to race. "Thanks," I say. "Come in while I get my things."

He steps inside so I can shut the door. "Evening, Jack," Dad calls from the couch while I head to the kitchen.

I place the rose in a glass of water, rinse out my brushes, and check on my painting. It's dry enough to safely move it to my room, where I set it carefully on my desk to dry completely. I grab my coat and shoes from the mudroom and put them on. Hurrying back to the front room, I wrap a scarf around my neck. "Will I need a hat and gloves?" I ask, unsure of what he has planned.

"I don't think so," he says. "Besides," he adds, stepping closer so as not to be overheard, "if you get cold, I can keep you warm."

I laugh to hide my flush, then turn to call a farewell to my parents. As Jack opens the door, Chase comes down the stairs. He stops at the bottom, folding his arms over his chest, staring across the room at us.

"Hey, Chase," I say, unsure of his mood. "Did you get my text about the pie?"

He ignores me. "It's about time, McKinley," Chase says, and

I frown. Since when has he been calling Jack by his last name? I look up at Jack, whose jaw is clenched.

"Emily and I are just heading out for a bit," he says, sounding remarkably calm, "but you and I can chat when we get back if you'd like."

Chase scowls. "I don't think—"

Dad gets up from the couch, moving toward the stairs. "You kids go along," he says, nodding to Jack and I. "I'll have a word with Chase."

I cast my brother a pleading look, but he's not paying attention to me. With a sigh, I follow Jack out into the cold, dark night.

Jack takes my hand, stopping just off the porch to look at me. "Has Chase been like that all day?"

"He's actually been missing most of the day." I tell him briefly about the argument this morning, and my Dad confronting Chase down at the shed this afternoon. Jack sighs.

"I'm sorry you've been dealing with that today," he says, pulling me into an embrace. "But maybe we can forget about him for a bit and just enjoy being together. I've been waiting all day for this," he murmurs against my hair.

"Me, too," I say, nestling into his arms.

He brushes a kiss against my cheek. "Come on," he says, releasing all but my hand and pulling me gently across the lawn.

"Where are we going?" I ask.

"You'll see," he says.

We walk around the side of the house, but instead of heading toward his car, he turns and leads me to the barn. I give him a quizzical look, but he just shakes his head, smiling at me.

At the barn doors, he stops. "Close your eyes," he says.

I do so, and a moment later I hear the sound of the small side door opening. The faint warbling of Bing Crosby singing *White Christmas* floats from somewhere nearby, as well as some kind of fan. As I turn my head, I catch the fleeting scent of cinnamon.

Jack takes my hands. "Watch your step," he says, leading me forward into the barn.

"Can I open my eyes?" I ask.

"Not yet," he says.

He drops my hands, and I hear the sound of the door closing behind us. As soon as it does, I realize it's much warmer in here than it should be. The fan I heard must be some kind of heater.

"All right, open your eyes," Jack says.

I open my eyes and let out a delighted gasp. A space has been cleared amid the tangle of tools and equipment, and a large, thick blanket has been spread out on the dusty floor. Multicolored Christmas lights are strewn across the tractor and mowers, hanging from the windows and beams, winking and flashing in the dark. Several dozen candles in jars and hurricanes surround the intimate space, their flickering warmth lighting a flame inside me.

"Oh, Jack," I say. "It's beautiful."

"*You're* beautiful," he says, kissing me softly. He takes my hand and leads me to the center of the blanket, pulling me down to sit beside him.

"Is this what you came over earlier for?" I ask, thinking of his brief talk with my dad.

He chuckles. "Yes. I wanted to make sure it was okay for me

to take over the barn for the evening. I didn't want anyone thinking there was a thief in here." He reaches up and brushes a strand of hair away from my face. "Or interrupting us," he adds.

His hand cups my face, his touch tender, as if I'm the most precious thing he's ever held. I close the distance between us, and his lips are warm and sure, his kiss more a statement than a promise. *I see you,* it says. *I need you.* Not in a desperate, clingy way, but in the same way that one needs air to breathe.

I kiss him back, letting him know that I need him, too. Slowly the kiss deepens, his mouth moving against mine with a quiet urgency that makes my heart flutter.

Suddenly my phone alerts: a jolly *Ho, ho, ho!* rings through the barn, indicating that I have a text message. We break apart, staring at each other in surprised silence, then our faces split with laughter at the same time.

I pull the phone from my pocket, glancing at the screen. "It's just Chase," I say. "He can wait."

Jack chuckles, moving closer once more, until another *Ho, ho, ho!* interrupts us again. I sigh, seeing anther notification from my brother. I switch my phone off and set it aside.

"There," I say. "No more distractions."

"I highly doubt that," Jack mumbles.

Before I can ask what he means, *his* phone pings, and with a groan, he reaches for it.

"Three guesses who it is," he says.

I giggle.

He turns off his phone and tosses it aside. "Sorry about that."

"I wonder what he wants?" I muse.

"I'm pretty sure I know," Jack says, his look darkening. "But he's just going to have to wait."

I give him a curious look, but he shakes his head, letting his expression clear. "Forget about Chase," he says. "I want tonight to be about us."

"Mmm, I like that idea," I say, snuggling closer to him.

I tip my head up, wordlessly asking for a kiss, which he gives me. Electricity zings through me, and I sigh against his lips.

After a moment he pulls back, and I curl up under his arm. Jack traces a finger lazily over and across the back of my hand, making the hairs stand on end.

"Emily," he says after a long pause, "you make me happier than I ever imagined I could be."

I laugh lightly. "Jackson McKinley," I tease, "are you saying there's actually something in Echo Ridge that you *like*?"

My tone is playful, but when he doesn't respond, I sit up, looking into his face. "Jack?" I ask.

The side door to the shop suddenly opens, startling us both. A frigid gust of air blows in, along with my brother. Jack scowls and gets to his feet.

"Not now, Chase," he says.

"Yes now," Chase says, slamming the door behind him. His eyes are bloodshot and he sways slightly on his feet.

My stomach plummets. He's been drinking.

"She deserves to know," he says, glaring at Jack.

"Know what?" I say, confused. Jack looks at me, and a flash of something close to panic crosses his face. It frightens me, and I scramble to my feet. "What's going on?"

"Jack has something to tell you."

"Leave it, Chase," Jack says, his stance defiant. "Go back to the house."

"No," Chase says. "Not until you tell my sister the truth."

An icy stone drops into my gut. "What is he talking about, Jack?" I ask, looking between them.

"Chase, don't," Jack says, his voice low. "Please."

"Tell her."

"Tell me what!" I shout, but they ignore me.

Jack lifts his chin, a glint of anger flashing in his eyes. "I know you're upset that Marilee broke up with you," he tells Chase, "but that doesn't give you the right to make trouble for us."

Chase curls his lip. "I have every right. She's my sister."

I stare at him, wondering who replaced my brother with this angry, bitter man. For the first time in my life I don't even recognize him, and it scares me. I reach for Jack, but Chase sees the movement and turns on me.

"He's been lying to you, Em," he says. "Just ask him."

Jack looks at me, forcing a calm I know he can't possibly feel. "Emily, please don't listen to him."

"Jack took the job in Baltimore. He leaves next week," Chase says, spitting out the words.

"No!" Jack's eyes are dark, his look venomous as he whirls around. "Shut up, Chase, you're not helping."

The blood drains from my face, taking all my warmth with it. "Baltimore? But... they hired someone else."

Jack takes my face gently in his hands, forcing me to look at him. "Emily, listen to me. Please, just listen."

But I can't listen. I can't focus. His voice is coming from far away. So, *so* far away.

Baltimore.

"She doesn't *want* to listen Jack, can't you see?" Chase sneers.

But Jack ignores him. "I was going to tell you, Emily, I swear. Their initial hire fell through and I was offered the job last week, but that doesn't mean I'm going to accept. I planned all this tonight because—"

"He's telling you goodbye," Chase cuts in, his face twisted in malice. "I told you this wouldn't last, I told you he'd break your heart, and you—"

But Chase doesn't get a chance to finish his thought. In one swift, fluid motion, Jack rounds on him, slamming a fist into his face. I scream as Chase drops to the floor, blood pouring from his nose.

Jack stands over him for a moment, his chest heaving, before turning back to me. "I'm sorry you had to see that," he says, his voice remarkably calm. "Are you okay?"

I nod numbly, my eyes frozen on my brother, who stirs and tries to sit up. He lifts a hand to his face, feeling the warm, sticky blood, then drops his arm, swearing. Jack crouches down with a sigh.

"Sorry man, but it had to be done," he says, helping Chase sit up. My brother groans, cursing again. Jack looks around, and I quickly unwrap the scarf from my neck, handing it to him. Wordlessly he takes it, holding it gently against my brother's face. Chase moans.

Jack sits beside him, supporting his back and making sure he doesn't fall over. A minute later Jack shakes out his hand, stretching his fingers, and for the first time I notice how red and swollen it looks. "You've got a hard head, Chase—I'm pretty sure you broke my hand," he says.

Chase mumbles something unintelligible, and suddenly it all becomes too much.

"You idiots!" I wail, bursting into tears. "I have half a mind to hit you *both!*" Jack looks up at me, surprised, but I turn and run from the barn.

The cold air instantly chills my tears, which sting my eyes and face like tiny pricks of ice. I stumble, crying, through the dark, heading toward the cheerful colored lights of the house and some semblance of rational thinking.

"Emily, wait!"

I hear Jack's voice but don't stop. In a moment he reaches my side, then steps in front of me. "Please, Emily, let me explain."

"It's fine, Jack, you don't have to explain anything," I say, swallowing a sob and wishing I had some Kleenex.

"Yes, I do. Please, Emily."

It's the *please* that gets me. I stop, wiping the tears from my eyes, and finally look at him.

His face is ashen. "I'm so sorry," he says, "about everything. About the job, about hitting your brother, about not telling you before. I was just afraid that if I told you about Baltimore, you'd break up with me."

I look down, shaking my head. "Why did you think I'd break up with you?"

"Because... well, you knew I was looking for work. That I would probably be leaving." His voice sounds confused at first, and then resigned. "Because if I take the job," he says, swallowing, "I'll be moving across the country."

The words sound so final, and the shock of hearing them causes me to wince. He sees it, and his shoulders slump. "I'll be moving across the country," he says again, softer this time, "and you'll be staying here."

I want to tell him he's wrong. That it doesn't have to be this way. But what if it does? Jack's right—I've known all along that he was looking for work, and that when a job offer came, he was going to leave. Just like he knew that the only reason we even met was because he was helping us save the farm. My home. The one thing I can't ever imagine living without because it's so much a part of me, it would kill me to leave it.

"So I guess Chase was right," Jack says, looking back toward the barn. "I guess this is goodbye."

"No, it's not."

My voice is steady, and he looks at me. "This isn't goodbye, because I'm not breaking up with you."

His face lights up like the star atop a Christmas tree. "You're not? But what about—"

"I don't know," I say, rubbing my forehead. "I haven't figured out what all this could mean. But unless you're breaking up with me, this isn't goodbye. Not yet."

His look softens, and he starts to lift a hand to my face. But then he winces, and I remember what happened, and what he said.

"Do you think it's broken?" I ask.

He makes a face. "Probably. Your brother has a *really* hard head."

His words force a half-laugh, half-sob out of me. "You need to get that taken care of."

"Chase needs help more. I just couldn't..." He swallows. "I couldn't stand to see you run away from me."

His words and his look melt the ice in my gut. Gently I reach up and press a kiss to his cheek. "Thank you for coming after me," I say. "But I'm not going anywhere." I gesture to the house. "You go inside. Tell my dad what happened, and after he sees about your hand, send him out to the barn."

"What are you going to do?"

I set my jaw. "I'm going to have a few words with my brother."

Chapter 28

Chase is still sitting on the barn floor when I open the door. He glances at me for a moment before lowering the scarf. He looks terrible. Blood is smeared all over his swollen face, his nose like a squashed tomato.

"You're still bleeding," I say.

He glares at me. "Is that all you have to say?"

I fold my arms across my chest, narrowing my eyes. "Oh, no. I have *plenty* to say to you, believe me."

"Save it," he mumbles. "I'm not in the mood." He presses the cloth to his face again, moaning.

"And what mood would that be?" I ask, my temper rising. "Angry? Annoyed? Because I'd *love* for you to not be in *that* mood anymore," I say. "For two weeks, Chase, you've been a surly, bitter, beast, and I'm sick to death of putting up with you. And I *know* it's more than just you being upset about Marilee."

His eyes dart to my face, but I don't give him a chance to respond.

"I know you're worried about the farm," I say, "we all are. And I know you feel a lot of pressure to turn things around here. But it's not all on your shoulders, Chase. This is *our* home. Yours, mine, our parents—and we're all in this together."

He doesn't say anything. I sigh, my anger fizzling out like a wet firecracker, and sit on the ground beside him.

"You remember when Mom first got sick? And we didn't know anything about what Parkinson's was or how it would affect her or our family?" I take a slow breath. "I was so scared."

He doesn't reply, but I can tell that he's listening. Remembering.

"I didn't know what to do," I say slowly, measuring my words, "because I didn't know what it was. But you told me that we didn't have to know everything right then, that we would figure it out like we always did, together."

I let out a shaky breath. Christmas music is still playing softly from some hidden speaker, and the candles are still casting their flickering light over us.

I nudge his arm. "You've got me, okay? Every step. You're not doing this alone."

He makes a noise, but his voice is muffled by the scarf. I lean in. "What was that?"

He pulls the scarf away from his face. "I said, it doesn't feel like it, now that you've got Jack."

I sigh. "You're my brother, Chase. Nothing and no one could ever replace you." I pause. "Is that part of it? Have you been jealous of Jack?"

"I knew he was leaving," Chase says, his voice distorted from his broken nose. "He told me last week. But he wouldn't tell you."

"He told you he was leaving, or he told you he was offered the job?"

Chase shrugs. "What's the difference? He was hiding it from you."

I let out an incredulous laugh. "Chase, there's a huge difference!"

"You deserved to know."

"Yes, but Chase, it was never your place to tell me. Jack wanted to do it in his own way."

"Yeah, well..." He doesn't finish the thought, and I sigh.

"I know you were trying to look out for me," I say. "But you don't get to decide how I live my life or who I spend my time with. I'm sorry about what happened with Marilee, but Jack is right—that's no excuse for barging in and trying to break us up, too."

He doesn't answer. Blood is still oozing from his right nostril, dribbling down his chin and soaking into his shirt. It's very macabre, and it makes my stomach turn.

"Look," I say, "I don't know what's going to happen between Jack and I. But you have to trust me and the choices I make for myself."

"I don't want you to get hurt," he says sullenly.

I bark a laugh. "Yeah, well, I'm not the one who got hurt, am I?" He looks over at me and I lift an eyebrow at him. He tries to smile, then groans.

"Jack has a stronger punch than I expected," he mumbles. Gingerly he touches his face, wincing.

"Were you expecting him to hit you?" I say, amused.

"No, but I guess I'm not surprised he did."

"You deserved it."

"*I* deserved it? He lied to you!"

"He did *not*. He was going to tell me tonight, but then you barged in and ruined everything."

The door to the barn opens and Dad walks inside. He takes a look at Chase on the floor, then pushes the door shut.

"You look a fright, son," he says. "How're you feeling?"

"Like I got my face smashed in by someone I thought was my friend."

I roll my eyes and get to my feet. "I'm going to see how Jack is doing," I say.

"He's icing his hand in the kitchen," Dad says. "I'll get Chase on his feet and take them both to get checked out."

I move to the door but Chase's voice calls me back. "Emily?" he says.

I turn. "Yeah?"

"I'm sorry."

We look at each other for a long time, and I see a glimmer of the Chase I know looking back at me. "I'm sorry, too," I say.

He nods, and I head out into the night.

Dad takes Chase and Jack to the ER while Mom and I wait at home. When we finish the Christmas special she and Dad were watching, I ask if she wants to watch something else or get ready for bed.

"Neither," she says, looking up at me. "I want some hot chocolate. The *real* stuff."

I chuckle. "Sure thing, Mom. Peppermint?"

"What else?"

I help her into her wheelchair and push her into the kitchen, so we can chat while I fix our drinks. It's been her most lucid day since her fall, and I can't help but smile at the irony of her being more in her right mind on the same day that Chase seems out of his.

After putting some milk on the stove to simmer, I pull out some Hershey bars and a block of semi-sweet baking chocolate.

"Where do you see yourself in five years, Emily?" Mom asks while I chop up bits of chocolate.

I shrug. "Here. Running the farm for you and Dad, celebrating Christmas all year long. Just like you," I say with a soft smile.

"Do you see yourself alone?"

I pause while chopping, but don't look up. "Maybe. I haven't given it much thought," I say, even as my heart calls my bluff.

"You never minded being alone," Mom muses, and I transfer the chopped chocolate bits into the pan of milk. "Even as a child. Chase always wanted to be the center of attention, surrounded by friends and family, but you were happy with your pencil and paper, or a book. Quiet and alone."

Her words make me uncomfortable. They're true, of course —I did spend a lot of time alone as a child. I never felt lonely, though. I always knew where my mother and father were (and Chase, of course) and could go to them whenever I needed. But suddenly I picture my life now and realize that isn't the case anymore. Chase went off to school, and he'll be moving on with his life again soon. Dad's getting older, and Mom is... well. We don't know how much time she has left. But she and Dad won't always be here for me.

The thought is sobering.

I whisk the milk slowly, watching it turn muddy as the chocolate melts. Pulling a spoon from the drawer I taste it, then turn around to chop a bit more chocolate.

"Jack told us about the job," Mom says, breaking the silence. I don't reply.

"It sounds like a great opportunity," she continues.

"It probably is," I say, not looking up.

"Is he going to take it?"

I shrug. "I'm not sure. We haven't had a chance to talk about it, thanks to Chase. But probably—he's been looking for a job for months." I go back to chopping, though my insides tremble.

Mom watches me in silence for a moment. "You don't have to stay here, Emily," she says.

I look up, confused. "What?"

"Here. On the tree farm. You don't have to stay."

"Of course I do. I love it here. Besides, we've spent the last six months doing everything we can to save the farm—I'm not about to pack up and leave it now. It's my home."

"Home isn't always a place, Emily," she says. "Sometimes home is a person."

I laugh lightly. "Exactly. Here with you and Dad and Chase, I'm home." I scrape the additional chocolate bits into the pot and begin stirring it again.

"Emily."

I don't turn around, afraid that if I do I'll fall apart, and I don't want Mom to see that. To see *me.*

I taste the chocolate again, and this time it's perfect. Pulling it off the stove, I add a couple drops of pure peppermint oil and stir it again. Taking two mugs from the cupboard, I divide the steaming liquid between them.

"Sweetheart," Mom says, her voice soft, "do you love him?"

I don't have to ask who "him" is, nor do I want to answer her question. Saying the words out loud would be even more terrifying than thinking them in my head. So instead of replying, I pull the whipped cream out of the fridge and give each mug a healthy foam topper.

"Candy cane bits?" I ask, pulling out the small container from the cupboard.

"None for me, thanks."

I sprinkle them on top of my cup, then take both mugs over to the table where Mom is waiting. She takes her cup carefully in both hands, trembling as she lifts it to her mouth. I watch her to make sure she doesn't need assistance before taking a sip from my own mug.

"You know what the opposite of love is?" she suddenly asks.

I lick the foam from my lip. "Hate?"

She shakes her head, forcing it through her tremor. "Fear. It's a powerful motivator, just like love, but for all the wrong reasons."

I take another sip of my cocoa, my heart trembling in my chest.

"I don't want you to choose to stay on the farm because you're afraid, sugarplum," Mom says. "You should stay because you love it more than anything else."

"I do," I say quickly. "I love it here. More than anywhere else in the world. This place is a part of me; the trees are a part of me. And everyone I love is here, too."

"Everyone?"

I look down at my cocoa, at the tiny bits of red and white striped candy floating atop the cloud of cream. "I can't leave you," I say, my voice breaking.

"Sweetheart," she says gently, "we'll be okay."

"You don't know that," I say, shaking my head and

dislodging the tears that had built up in my eyes. I brush them quickly away.

"No," she says, "I don't. But I do know this: you shouldn't stay because you're scared. Staying just because it's safe... that's not living, sugarplum. Not really."

I drop my head into my hands. "But what if—and I'm not saying I will, or even that I want to—but what if I leave, and wherever I go, whatever I do..." I swallow. "What if it doesn't work out? What if I uproot everything, and... and..." I can't even bring myself to say the words.

"Then you come home," she says simply. "You come home and we make up the guest room, and we'll cry with you on the couch and then ask Sophie to come over and do your nails."

I laugh, and the movement shakes more tears loose, sending them streaking down my face. "You make it sound so easy."

"It's not easy," she says. "But it's right. It doesn't mean you love us any less, it just means you're trusting yourself more. And whatever the next part of your life is supposed to be." She reaches across the table, taking my hand. "You have so much love to give," she says. "Don't hide it here just because this is all you've ever known. You deserve to be terrified and thrilled and alive."

And loved, my heart adds.

I am loved, my brain argues.

Not in the same way, my heart persists.

I sigh, squeezing Mom's hand. "Thanks, Mom. I love you."

"Love you too, sweetie."

I hear my phone go off in the other room, and I get up from the table to retrieve it.

"It's a text from Dad," I say, coming back into the kitchen. "Chase's nose is broken, but Jack doesn't have any fractures in his hand. Just soft tissue damage."

Mom sighs. "Well, at least one of them is okay," she says. "And who knows? Maybe Chase will meet a cute nurse and put this whole messy business behind him."

Chapter 29

The day after Thanksgiving is always the busiest day of the season. While some people opt to go shopping for Christmas gifts and new electronics, dozens of families choose to spend the day wandering the fields, looking for the perfect tree to take home with them.

By eight A.M. I've caffeinated and bundled up against the cold. The morning air is sharp and smells of fir and frost. I can see my breath in little clouds as I walk between the rows, boots crunching over thin crusts of ice on the grass. The trees—hundreds of them—stand at attention, tall and full and glittering in the early light like they've been waiting all year for this moment. All their lives for this moment.

I stop in the middle of a field, reaching through the branches of the nearest tree to touch its trunk. It's cold and steady, but I close my eyes and imagine the thrum of excitement pulsing beneath the bark.

"Are you ready?" I whisper.

Of course, it whispers back. *It's what I was born for.*

I open my eyes, stepping back from the tree. I walk slowly along the row with my arm extended, letting my gloved fingers brush each tree as I pass. The needles rub against each other, the branches swaying with mirth and excitement. *Our turn! It's our turn at last!* they seem to cry.

A table near the shed where we handle the sales is set up for complimentary serve-yourself cocoa and cider. Dad will be bringing the large insulated drink dispensers down a bit later. I make sure we have enough cups and lids ready, then head across the parking lot to the entrance.

I tie a large red bow to the welcome sign, then unlock the gate and pull it wide, officially opening for the season. Red ribbons flap from fence posts, tangling in the Christmas lights that will make this place glow like the North Pole by tonight. I look up the hill, across the fields of trees to the greenhouses, knowing our home is tucked up there, too. "Please have let all this be enough," I plead to the heavens.

A family of four arrives just before ten, bundled in coats and scarves. "Welcome to the Kenworth Christmas Tree Farm," I say, greeting them as they climb out of their car. "Is this your first time here?"

"Oh, no," the mom says, a short, plump woman with a kind smile and flaming red hair. "We came in July for the summer event you had," she says. "Which reminds me..." She digs in her pocket, then holds out a slip of paper. "We adopted a tree and got this coupon."

I take it from her, feeling a thrill run through me. "Thank you so much!" I say. "Have you been enjoying the updates?"

"Very much so," she says. "It's been fun and educational for the whole family."

"I'm glad to hear it."

I hand her husband a saw and point them in the direction of the available trees. The youngest girl skips ahead, pointing to trees twice as tall as she is. The mom smiles as she wraps an arm around her other daughter's shoulders, following after the first.

"Remember, nothing taller than the van!" she calls.

More cars trickle in over the next hour—old sedans, minivans, a couple of pickups with dogs in the back. People pour out into the crisp air, stepping out of their vehicles and into a Christmas card. Rebekah arrives and opens up the boutique, and between handing out saws and directing the foot traffic, I turn on the stereo, filling the air with the sound of classic Christmas carols.

Shannon arrives to stay with Mom, allowing Dad to come down with the drink dispensers. He offers to help the new arrivals, leaving me free to bale and tie the freshly cut trees. I whisper to each one as they pass through my hands, wishing them luck and encouraging them to stay fresh and green until New Year's.

I help an older couple find a tree with "strong branches for heavy ornaments," and offer to cut it for them as well. They thank me profusely, recounting past years' Christmas trees as if reciting a family genealogy. Another family asks for two trees— one for the family, with homemade ornaments and colored lights, and the other "for show," to hang with strands of pearls and designer baubles.

"Do you offer flocking?" the woman asks, her high-heeled boots looking incredibly out of place in the icy mud at her feet.

"I'm sorry, no," I say. "It's not good for the trees or the environment."

She presses her crimson lips together in a line, then turns

away and starts directing her husband toward the tree she wants. I shake my head and walk away.

By noon things are humming right along. Chase is up at the house, nursing a killer hangover and massive headache from his broken nose, but Dad and I and a couple temps manage to keep things moving among the trees. I pop into the boutique to see how things are going, but Rebekah has it well in hand. After checking the cocoa and cider levels at the self-serve table, I sit down on an upturned stump to rest.

"Merry Christmas," a voice calls, coming up behind me.

I turn with a smile, the familiar feeling of warmth, of home, filling me up inside. "Jack! I wondered when I'd see you."

"Not as early as I'd planned, but hopefully you'll forgive me," he says, pressing a kiss to my cheek.

"Always," I say, turning my head so his lips meet mine. He chuckles, then takes a seat on the log next to me.

"How's the day been?" he asks.

"Great so far. Oh, and guess what? The first family that showed up were here in July for the big event, and came to use the coupon they got from adopting a tree!"

"That's fantastic!" Jack says. "That's exactly what we were hoping for."

His smile is so big and genuine, I forget for a moment that he might be going away. But then his smile fades, and a shadow of worry crosses his face.

"About the job..." he says.

I sigh. So much for it being a great day.

He takes my hand in his, and I notice that his other hand is wrapped in a loose bandage. "Does it hurt much?" I ask, nodding at it.

He glances down, lifting his right hand and flexing the

fingers a bit. "It's sore, and stiff, but the doctor said it should be fine. Ibuprofen and ice for a few days, and try not to use it."

I nod, and the silence falls between us, tense and full of fear.

"A few months ago," he says, "I would have taken the job without much hesitation. But even knowing it's a great opportunity, every time I consider it now, all I can think about is how far away I'll be from you."

I look down at our gloved hands, wishing I could feel his skin against mine. His fingers would have callouses now, from working beside me all summer long. Painting the workshop. Mending fences. Driving a mower. I turn my hand over, cupping his fingers with my own.

"When do you have to give them an answer?" I ask, looking up at him. He lets out a heavy breath, and it puffs in the air around him like a steam engine.

"I told them last week that I needed some time to think about it. I wanted to talk to you first. But then I kept putting it off, because I thought... well, I told you last night what I thought. I was afraid it would mean the end of us." He swallows. "But they called me on Wednesday afternoon with a new offer: come out to Baltimore for a week or so and see what I think. They'll put me up in a hotel and show me around the company, so I can make a more informed decision." His voice lifts slightly, and I can tell that he thinks it's a good idea.

I can also tell that he wants me to think so, too.

"That's great," I say, offering what I hope looks like a real, albeit small, smile. "When do they want you to come out?"

"Monday," he says, his shoulders and voice both drooping. "They want to have things squared away by Christmas."

Christmas. It's been the unspoken deadline all year. Every single idea, each new implementation, all our hard work—all of it culminating on the one day that defines us as a business and a family.

"Monday," I repeat, looking out across the fields. Children dart between the trees, laughing and playing, and somewhere I hear a man singing along with the music. This place is magical for me every day of the year, but today it's magical for everyone else, too.

Jack is watching me, so I try to keep my expression neutral. He reaches an arm around me and I lean into him, knowing what comes next.

"I'll only be gone a week or so," he says. "Then I'll be back, and we can discuss the job then."

A tiny puff of laughter—or is it a sob?—escapes me, and I shake my head. "This is a decision you need to make on your own, Jack. It's your life; you need to do what's best for you, and what will make you happy."

Tucked against his side like I am, I can't see his face, but I can feel his intake of breath, as if he wants to say something. But no words come, and the moment passes.

"I need to get back to work," I say, sitting up.

"How can I help?" he asks.

"Can you just walk around and see if any of the guests need anything?" I ask. "That way I can focus on baling the trees so we don't get backed up."

He chuckles. "Anything to avoid talking to people," he says, bumping me on the shoulder. I narrow my eyes at him.

"I have talked to *dozens* of people today, I'll have you know," I say.

He laughs again, and in one swift motion swoops in to kiss

my pouting lips. Startled, I laugh, but he's already turned away, smiling as he heads off into the trees.

The laughter drifts away, and the smile on my face follows, replaced by an ache in my chest that makes it almost impossible to breathe. Jack is leaving, and something inside tells me that he won't be coming back.

Chapter 30

"Excuse me, do you have any greeting cards?"

I'm helping Rebekah take orders in the boutique on Sunday afternoon when a woman asks the question.

"Like, Christmas cards?" I say.

"Yes. Not those mass-produced boxed sets, but individual ones. Something special and handmade, you know."

I *do* know, but somehow, in all our planning for the boutique, we neglected to find or stock any stationary. Inwardly I cringe at the oversight. "I'm sorry, we don't," I say, giving her an apologetic smile.

The woman sighs. "That's too bad. This would be the perfect place to sell them."

She takes her purchases to the counter for Rebekah to ring up, and I go back to folding shirts and tidying the shop. It's nearly time to close the boutique for the night, but her comment keeps coming back to me. *This would be the perfect place...*

That night, alone in my room, I pull out my sketchbook. Flipping through the pages, I stop and stare at the painting of

Mr. Tumnus. His bright eyes are focused intently on his snack, the gentle washes of paint softening his features. A few turns later, a half-finished sketch of a barred owl looks up at me from the page. I look through the whole book, pausing to examine and critique the various sketches and paintings I've done. An idea begins to form in my head, and when I come to the very end of the book I set it aside. Pulling out some loose sheets of watercolor paper, I begin to draw.

By Monday morning Jack is gone, and Chase is back to work. His face looks a fright—two black eyes in shades of purple and blue, turning green and yellow around the edges. The swelling has gone down a bit, but his nose is definitely crooked now. I wonder if it bothers him or not.

The biggest change, however, has been in his attitude. I'd like to think it was the pie (which he finally ate), but I'm pretty sure it was the talk we had after Jack hit him. Or maybe it was actually the punch that Jack threw. Whatever the cause, it feels nice to have my brother back in his right mind. Not only that, but he's been tripping all over himself to make up for his belligerent attitude the last couple of weeks.

The day passes slowly. I try not to think about Jack flying further and further away from me, and instead focus on the coming weekend and the massive Winter Wonderland event we'll be hosting. It's nice to have Chase by my side again as I make phone calls, set up more decorations, and prepare for what will hopefully be the biggest crowd of the season.

On Tuesday morning I send a text to Jack. It's a photo of the temporary reindeer pen we've set up by the parking lot. *Can't wait to meet Santa's reindeer!* I say, then feel my chest begin to ache. Renting reindeer for the season was one of Jack's ideas, and I wish he could be here to see it. I tuck my phone away, but as I move about my chores and preparations, I keep waiting for his reply.

It never comes.

Things are slow in the afternoon, and I spend some time working on the set of notecards I started. A squirrel, a deer, a raccoon, a fox, and an owl—each animal hand-painted in a simple forest setting, wearing jaunty little Santa hats. I take my time with the watercolors, making sure they look realistic, with only a touch of whimsy. I let them dry overnight, and on Wednesday I take my fineliners to add pen-and-ink details, carefully erasing my sketch marks when needed.

"What's that you're working on, sweetie?" Mom asks as Shannon wheels her into the kitchen for a snack.

"Some notecards for the boutique," I say, a flutter of nerves bursting in my belly. I hold up the fox for her to see.

"Oh Emily, it's wonderful!" Mom says, reaching a shaky hand out to touch the paper.

"You think so?"

"I do. Are you going to sell them as a set or individually?" she asks.

"I think individually for now. There was a guest on Sunday asking for a handmade, artisan greeting card. I can't believe we didn't think of it sooner."

"I bet they sell out the first day," Mom says. Shannon nods in agreement.

"Then I better plan on making more," I say with a grin.

. . .

On Thursday morning I wake up to a text from Jack.

> **JACK**
>
> The reindeer pen looks great! Man, I wish I was going to be there this weekend.
>
> The company has kept me running since the minute I touched down. But I miss you. How is everything else on the farm? How is your mom? How's Chase?

I roll over onto my back, typing with my thumbs.

> **EMILY**
>
> Chase is fine. You must have knocked the sense back into him because I feel like I have my brother back. So thanks. ☺
>
> The farm is great and Mom is doing well—I'll tell her you said hi

I chew on my lip as I consider what to type next.

> **EMILY**
>
> I decided to take your advice and sell some of my artwork. Not as actual art, but I've been working on a set of watercolor notecards for the boutique.

Three little dots appear on the screen, and I wait nervously for his reply.

> **JACK**
>
> Good for you! Will you send me a picture? I'd love to see them. And I can't believe we didn't think of notecards when we were stocking the shop. Good call.

EMILY

Me either. A guest asked for some on Sunday, which gave me the idea.

JACK

Your solution is perfect. Proud of you, Em.

His words cause a lump to form in my throat. I wish he was here. My hands hover over the screen, itching to tell him that I miss him, that I don't want him to take the job, that he should come home to be with me. But I can't tell him all that. It wouldn't be fair.

EMILY

Thanks. Looking forward to Christmas

I almost said that I was looking forward to seeing *him* at Christmas, but even if he comes home for Christmas, I know he won't be staying. The minute I saw his face light up when he told me about the job, I knew he would take it. Even if he said he didn't want to, even if he made excuses or tried to pretend it wasn't the right fit, I knew it was. Because it has everything he wants.

Except me.

When I was eleven years old, my family went to Leavenworth, WA in January. It was only a couple years after Mom's diagnosis, and her only symptom was a slight tremor in her right hand, so after the busy holiday season, we packed up and went on vacation. It was absolutely magical. Even though it was after the New Year, all the Christmas lights and decorations were still up, all over the city, and the glittering snow made it feel like we were at the North Pole. I've never forgotten that trip. In fact, the memory of that experience and the wonder I felt there is what inspires me when decorating the property every year.

By Friday the tree farm has been transformed into a glittering winter wonderland. Strings of lights glow like tiny golden stars amid the trees, winking and flashing in the night. Carols play softly from unseen speakers, mingling with the sound of sleigh bells and children's laughter. Dozens of families meander through the trees, searching for the perfect specimen to take home and make their own.

I wander over to the far side of the lot, where a large pen has been set up to house the two female reindeer we're hosting for the season. Prancer and Vixen trot over to greet me, and I rub their noses affectionately. The two have quickly stolen my heart, and I've already started researching the possibility of adding a small herd to the farm. The forty-five acres we've kept in reserve will be the perfect home for them, I'm sure of it.

I turn around and see Chase walking toward me. It's been over a week since the argument with Jack, but he still looks a fright. He tried to convince me to let him play Santa this weekend, but I argued that a Santa with two black eyes would terrify the children.

He stops beside me, his hands propped on his hips. "Not a bad turnout," he says, surveying the scene around us.

"Think it was all the advertising you did?" I ask.

He shrugs. "That's probably part of it. And I'm sure the mailing list from the July event has helped a lot."

I glance behind me at the reindeer. "Prancer and Vixen have been popular."

"And the market," Chase adds.

"Think it will be enough to save us?" I ask, almost afraid of the answer.

He blows out his breath in a long exhale. "Who knows. I think it might, barring any catastrophes."

I grimace. "Like an unexpected hospital stay?"

He doesn't respond, but I can tell he's just as worried as I am. Mom's rising medical costs are what sunk us in the hole in the first place—are they going to prevent us from climbing out of said hole as well?

I slip my arm through his as we walk to the little shed in the far corner, so Chase can get back to work. "I wish Jack was here to see it," I say. Chase stiffens beside me.

"Is he coming back at all?" he asks with forced politeness, though I'm sure he's fighting the urge to say *I told you so.*

"He said he is."

I can feel his eyes boring into my face, but I don't want to get into it with my brother, not again. I notice the line at Sophie's booth has finally dwindled, and I let go of his arm. "I'm going to get some hot chocolate. Want me to bring you any?"

"Nah, I've got a thermos of cider in the shed. Thanks, though."

He continues on as I turn and make my way to where Sophie works in a cozy little market stall made of wood. While we still have complimentary cocoa and cider for guests, those who want coffee or a gourmet beverage can order from Sophie. And provided that we stay in business past the new year, we've invited Sophie to be our official food and drinks vendor for all our events going forward. She was happy to oblige.

The air is crisp and cold, heavy with the smell of woodsmoke from the bonfire across the lot, and as I draw close to Sophie's booth, the rich aroma of coffee and chocolate fills my nostrils. She sees me approaching and offers a smile.

"What'll it be, boss?" she asks. "A gingerbread latte or a peppermint hot chocolate?"

"Mmm, peppermint hot chocolate, please."

"You got it," she says, grabbing a cup and adding a pump of peppermint syrup to it. "You're overdue for a manicure," she says. "Want to come by this week?"

"Sure. Can you do something festive for the season?"

"Of course." She fills the cup with dark, steaming cocoa.

"How are you and Matt?" I ask.

She grins. "He invited me to go on a cruise with him in February." I gawk at her, and she laughs. "What? Is that so surprising?"

"Uh, yeah! Didn't you guys break up?"

She waves a hand dismissively in the air. "Old news, Em. We've been back together and better than ever since the bonfire."

I shake my head, chuckling. "You and Matt really are meant to be, I guess."

"What do you mean?"

"Who else would be willing to put up with the other's shenanigans, over and over again?"

She rolls her eyes. "Whatever. How're things with Jack?"

I don't answer right away. She adds a generous amount of whipped cream to my cup of cocoa, then sprinkles a spoonful of crushed candy canes over the top.

"Lid or no lid?" she asks.

"No lid, thanks."

Handing me my drink, she watches as I take the first sip.

"Delicious," I say, licking the creamy foam from my lips.

She starts cleaning up from my order. "So... Jack?" she reminds me.

I sigh. "It's fine."

"Just fine?"

"Well, he left for Baltimore Monday morning, if that tells you anything," I say, taking another sip.

Sophie's mouth drops open. "He took the job?"

"Not exactly," I say, trying to ignore how the thought of him clear across the country sends stabbing pains into my chest. "They flew him over there so he could check out the company and the area. That way he can make an informed decision, you know?" I smile blandly at her.

"Hmm." She presses her lips together, one hand on her hip. "So they can wine and dine and convince him to take it, you mean." She looks at my stricken face and grimaces. "*Ay, lo siento.* That was a bit blunt."

I look down at my cup, trying to ignore the churning in my gut. "It's fine. I've come to that conclusion myself, actually. But Jack swears it's only temporary. He said he'll be back next week."

"And if he isn't? Are you going to do the long distance thing?"

"I don't know. I want to at least try to make it work, but for how long? What happens a year from now? Five years from now? If we only ever live apart, what's the point?" I sigh. "Jack couldn't wait to get out of Echo Ridge. He didn't want to come back in the first place, and now that he has a chance to work and live in a big city, what is there to keep him here?"

She eyes me pointedly, and I give a half-hearted laugh.

"Jack's not *that* into me," I say, thinking of Thanksgiving and the proposal that didn't happen. "He doesn't like me enough to live somewhere he hates."

"Are you sure about that?"

"Of course I'm sure! Would he even be considering Baltimore if he did?"

She ignores my question and asks one of her own. "What about you then? Are you that into him?"

I dodge the question by answering an adjacent one. "Are you suggesting I leave Echo Ridge? Soph, we've spent the last eight months doing all that we can to save the farm. I couldn't possibly walk away, not when things are finally turning around for us."

"But what if they don't?"

Her honest question feels too raw, too possible, for an equally honest answer. I steel myself, taking a brittle breath. "If the farm fails and we have to sell, then so be it. But that doesn't mean I have to leave Echo Ridge. I can't, Sophie. I won't do it," I say, setting my jaw.

She lifts her brow and steps back, folding her arms. "Then you're probably right," she says, "there's not really any point in continuing a relationship with Jack."

She watches me, but I don't respond. After a moment I take another sip of my drink. "Thank you for the cocoa," I say. "I'm going to check on the boutique."

Without another word, I turn and head up the hill.

Chapter 31

The weekend is nearly perfect. More people come than we could ever have hoped for. The Santa we hired this time is a master, delighting children and adults alike with his acting skills, passing out candy canes and speaking to the reindeer as if they really belong to him. Sophie sells out of almost everything halfway through Saturday, and has to shut down the booth temporarily to run into town for more supplies. And our inventory in the boutique runs dangerously low, what with everyone buying hostess gifts, souvenirs, and presents for their friends and families. Mom was right—all my notecards sell on the first day, which feels crazy and wonderful at the same time. I'm already planning to do more.

The Winter Wonderland event was only one weekend, and I know we still have two weeks left until Christmas, but I'm so anxious about everything that on Sunday night I ask Chase to give me a loose financial update.

We head into the office first thing Monday morning, and Chase sits down to run the numbers and balance the books after the big event. I watch him closely, chewing on a hangnail as I wait for his verdict. Finally I see his face relax.

"It's going to be enough, Em," he says, slumping back in his seat. "It will be close, but we'll make it work," he says.

"Will we need to sell off the extra land?" I ask.

"I don't think so. At least, not right now. We'll see how much we bring in over the next few weeks, and how much is left after the mortgage and bills are paid in January. But barring any other catastrophes, the farm should be safe—for another year, at least."

I collapse into a chair, relief washing through me. "And Jack said it will only get better from here," I say, more to myself than to Chase. "The first year is always the hardest."

Chase watches me from the corner of his blackened eye. "So where do you and Jack stand, anyway?" he asks. "I get the feeling that things aren't really over, but how do you expect this to work?"

I look at him, and a slow smile stretches across my face.

"What?" he says, clearly alarmed at my expression.

"Oh, nothing," I muse, "it's just interesting to hear you say that after what you told me when I questioned you dating Marilee."

It's the first mention of her between us since The Altercation™, and I'm a little nervous about how he might react. But he merely rolls his eyes, turning back to the computer.

"Yeah, well, you live and learn, right?" he says, lifting an eyebrow at me. Combined with his mottled skin, the effect is quite ghastly, and I tell him so. He laughs.

"I can always count on you to tell me the truth," he says, amused.

I smile at him. "Always."

"Speaking of the truth," he says, "did you sell some of your artwork? Mom said you put some stuff in the shop and they sold right away."

"Not really artwork—just some notecards I painted. But yeah, I did."

"That's great, Em." He nudges my arm. "See, I told you you were a real artist."

I smile. "Thanks. I'm not sure I'll ever be brave enough to sell my work as *actual* art, but it's nice to know that it's appreciated."

We get up from our seats and Chase gives me a hug. "Whatever you decide, Em, I'm proud of you."

Jack calls me later that night. He took a trip into Washington, D.C. over the weekend and spent an afternoon wandering through the Smithsonian.

"You should have seen it, Em, you would have loved it," he says.

"Why, did they have a Christmas exhibit?" I tease.

"No."

"Was it full of trees, then?"

He laughs. "You know, I gotta admit, I *am* kind of missing the woods."

I give an exaggerated gasp. "Jackson McKinley, did you just say what I think you said?"

I can hear the smile in his voice when he responds. "Shocking, right? But hey, they kinda grew on me over the summer."

I laugh with him at his lame pun. "Well, now you know how

I feel," I say. "And you'll be back in a few days, right? You can get your fill of trees then."

He doesn't respond, and my heart drops.

"Actually," he says, "I wanted to talk to you about that." He sighs. "They've offered me a deal I can't refuse, Em. It's more than double the salary I've seen for any other job I've applied to, and includes a cost of living allowance. The company is stable and there's room for growth. Everything about it seems perfect, except..."

His voice trails off, and I wait for him to say it, wait to hear if I mean as much to him as he's come to mean to me. But he doesn't say anything.

At last I clear my throat. "Congratulations," I say. "That's great, Jack. So will you start after the New Year?"

"I start on Wednesday, actually. They've already lost so much time, trying to find the right candidate, that they want me working as soon as possible."

"So you're not coming home? At all?"

"Not for a while, no."

I pause. "You're going to miss Christmas."

"I will, yeah."

A broken smile tugs on my lips. "You don't like Christmas much anyway, though. So it's not like it's a big deal."

"Emily, I'm so sorry. I honestly didn't come out here planning to take the job, I swear."

"I believe you," I say, my voice more calm than I feel. I want to scream and cry and rant and rave, but I can't. I won't.

At least I still have the farm.

My hand trembles as I hold the phone to my ear, striving for serenity. "We knew this day would come—we've known it all along. I'm sure you're going to love it there. And I've got the farm, thanks to you. So we both got what we want. No regrets."

There's a pause, and then he asks, "What do you mean? Are you saying... is this goodbye, then? Didn't you mean what you said to me outside the barn?"

I close my eyes, rubbing my forehead. "Of course I meant it, Jack. But even then I admitted that I didn't know how it would work. I still don't know, to be honest. There's just so much going on right now. It's the busiest time of year for us, and with my mom's fall and you being gone..."

I release a long, drawn-out breath. I think about what Sophie said, and I wonder if she's right. Is it even worth it to try? What would be the point? "Maybe..." I say, hesitantly, "maybe we should take a break. 'Till after the new year, at least. So things can settle down here on the farm, and you can get used to your new position."

"A break." There's a pause, and then, "All right."

A thick, uncomfortable quiet falls, my stomach sickening as the silence stretches between us. My heart is begging me to take back the words, but I can't.

"I guess I'll talk to you later, then," Jack says, his voice oddly strangled.

"Yeah. I guess so," I reply, desperately trying not to cry. "Good luck with the new job," I say.

"Thanks. Good luck with the farm. And your notecards."

"Thanks."

Silence. Then, "Will you tell me how it turns out?" he asks. "All our plans, you know? If, after all is said and done, it was enough to save the farm."

Tears spring to my eyes. "Chase ran the numbers, and all

the early figures look good. Better than good. He said it's a sure thing—the farm is safe."

There's the slightest pause, and I wonder if he has to keep taking deep breaths like I do so he doesn't choke on his tears. "That's great, Emily," he says. "Really great." There's another pause, and when he speaks his voice is softer, lower than before. "Now... now you'll never have to leave," he says.

I hear what he doesn't say. What he *won't* say. Because he knows—he's always known—that this is my home.

"Yeah." I say.

The line goes silent again, and after a minute I realize the call has ended. Did Jack hang up? Or did I? I honestly don't know, and I feel sick thinking about it. But maybe it wasn't either of us. Maybe some magical, reverse-Cupid creature has been hovering between us, ready to cut the line the moment he saw an opportunity.

I pull the phone away from my ear, watching the screen for any final text, any sign that maybe he's changed his mind, maybe he'll be coming home for Christmas after all.

Home.

But nothing comes. I set the phone on the table beside my bed and curl up under the covers, feeling as if I could fall apart with a single breath.

Jack's right. Now that my home is safe, I'll never have to leave.

The funny thing is, suddenly it feels a lot less like home.

Chapter 32

Contrary to popular belief, the most magical day in the whole year for a child isn't Christmas—it's the day of the first snowfall.

It's been cold for weeks, and even below freezing a few times. But the icy drizzle doesn't give us so much as a hint of snow until the week before Christmas.

It starts just after breakfast—soft and tentative, like the sky isn't quite sure the world is ready. But I'm ready. I breathe in the cold, sharp air, letting it prick the inside of my nose. The trees in the surrounding woods stand tall and silent, their branches completely still as they await their coronation.

And then, the first flake lands on the sleeve of my coat.

I hold my breath, studying the tiny, perfect crystal as it clings to my arm. After a moment it's joined by another. And another. I look up, and suddenly the air is filled with broken bits of frozen sky.

Within minutes, the trees in the fields are wearing it like lace, each one bedecked like a bride on her wedding day. I tilt my face up toward the sky and close my eyes. The flakes are cold against my cheeks, but it's the good kind of cold—the kind that lets you know you're still alive.

I haven't felt very alive for the last few weeks. Ever since Jack left, my world has felt dull and lifeless, like a dried out Christmas tree left on the curb after New Year's. But the snow rekindles something of the magic I usually feel at this time of year.

I hear the crunch of boots behind me and turn to see Dad coming down the road from the barn, bundled in flannel and smiling like a kid who's never seen snow before.

"Father Winter finally decided to make an appearance," he says, nodding at the sky.

We stand there together in silence, watching the snow fall around us. But soon a minivan pulls into the parking lot, breaking the spell.

"And so it begins," I say, heading down to meet them.

Dad chuckles. "Just one more week, sugarplum," he says, following me down the hill.

The cold sinks into my fingers even through my gloves, but I keep tying the twine anyway, looping it around the thick trunk of the Douglas fir and cinching it tight to the roof rack. The family thanks me, all warm smiles and laughter, their little boy bouncing up and down like a jack-in-the-box. I smile back, wish them a Merry Christmas, and wave as they pull out of the parking lot.

"Hey." Chase's voice comes from behind me. "You've been baling and loading trees for four hours straight. Take a break. Have some cocoa."

"I'm fine," I say, turning away.

But he doesn't buy it. That's the blessing (and curse) of being a twin: there's no way to hide how you're feeling from the one you shared a womb with.

"You've barely smiled all day," he says.

I lift an eyebrow. "Did you see me just now? I was all smiles for that family."

"Faking it for customers doesn't count."

"I'm not faking it."

He gives me a look, and I sigh. "Fine. I was faking it. But I'd rather not talk about it."

"You don't have to talk. But you also don't have to pretend it doesn't suck."

I stare at him. "I thought you were *glad* Jack's gone."

He looks down, kicking his toe at the frozen ground. "I'm not glad, per se. Especially considering how miserable you are."

"I'm not miserable," I say automatically. "We knew all along he was looking for work and would be leaving eventually. You were constantly reminding me of that fact, remember?"

Chase doesn't say anything for a moment. Then, "You're still allowed to think it sucks, though."

I look out across the fields, at the snow falling in slow, drifting spirals. It's enchanting, but I can't *feel* how enchanting it is. I can't really feel anything but this dull ache in my gut since Jack went away.

"Fine, it sucks. But I don't regret fall—" I stop, and Chase lifts his brow. "I don't regret the time I had with Jack," I amend. "I just... miss him."

Chase exhales in a long puff, his breath billowing around us in a white cloud. He looks up the hill into the vast fields of trees —some empty from the wholesale harvest, others puckmarked with gaps where guests cut down their own trees. "Are you actually in love with him?" he asks, not looking at me.

My heart beats a staccato in my chest, and I consider the implications of whatever answer I give. At last I decide that it's not worth pretending to Chase. He knows me too well for me to get away with it, anyway.

"Yes," I say, and suddenly my vision blurs. "But he's not in love with me."

"Did he tell you that?"

"Of course not," I say, dashing the tears from my eyes with the back of my gloved hand.

"Then how do you know?"

My eyes fill up again, and this time I let the tears overflow, running down my cheeks like tiny frozen rivers. "He left, didn't he?"

He frowns. "Not because he wanted to, Em. Do you think I'd have a broken nose if he did?"

I make a noise somewhere between a sob and a laugh, and a tiny glimmer of hope starts burning within me. "Do you really think so?" I ask.

"I do. He'd be crazy not to love you."

The silence settles between us like the snow, soft and light. I dry my eyes and look around, aching with a loss I've never felt here before. The tree farm is all I've ever known, and all I ever thought I wanted. But it's different this year. Somehow it's not enough anymore.

A family comes down the incline with a Noble fir, laughing and chatting about where it ought to go in their house. I start to move toward the baler, but Chase puts a hand on my arm.

"I'll take this one," he says.

"It's fine, I can do it."

"Please, Emily."

It gets me, every time, and finally I sigh. "Fine. But what am I supposed to do?"

He looks at me long and hard. "That's up to you," he says, "but if I were Jack, I'd want to know how you feel."

He claps me on the shoulder and moves away, leaving me to stare after him, wondering if I have the courage to do what he suggests.

Chapter 33

C hristmas Eve has always been as wonderful a day for me
as Christmas. The excitement of the season, the joy of
anticipation, the gifts and traditions—both days are full to the
brim with magic and delight. Which is why it feels completely
surreal to be walking through the SeaTac airport on December
24th, towing a small carry-on suitcase with a gift box tucked
under my arm.

It was Mom who convinced me. After Chase took over the
baling I went up to the house and cried on her shoulder,
agonizing over what to do. She squeezed my hand and
reminded me of what she said at Thanksgiving: *don't stay
because you're afraid. Home is more than just a place, it's the people
you love.*

I purchased a plane ticket within the hour.

I thought about texting Jack to let him know I was coming,
but I didn't want to explain my reasons why over the phone. So
instead I packed a bag, kissed my family goodbye, and prayed
he'd be willing to meet me when I landed in Baltimore.

Once past security, I pulled my suitcase along slowly,

marveling at all the movement around me. I feel helpless and small, a tiny snowflake lost in a massive winter storm. I've never flown on a plane before, but I'm just as nervous about getting *to* the plane as what will happen once I'm *on* the plane.

As I move through the terminal, I notice a large sign advertising Maeve Chocolate. Recognizing the rebranded name, I pull my suitcase into the shop, hoping my favorite chocolate candy will help to settle my nerves.

"Hi, welcome in," the cheerful attendant behind the counter calls. I smile at her and move toward the large back wall covered in chocolate, searching for the hazelnut butter crisp bonbons. I move slowly along the shelves, bending down to see if perhaps it's near the bottom.

"Hi, welcome in," the attendant calls again, assumingly to another customer. "Can I help you find something?"

"I'm looking for your hazelnut butter chocolate," a masculine voice says, and I freeze.

It can't be. It would be *impossible.*

But as I turn my head to face the attendant, who is now headed directly for me, the man turns, and Jack McKinley looks me straight in the eye.

He jolts, like I did. "Emily?" he says, his voice incredulous.

I straighten, blinking. "Jack."

We stare at each other, and the attendant looks between us. "Um, the hazelnut butter crisp is right over here, sir," she says, indicating a spot to my right.

"Thanks," Jack says, not taking his eyes off me. The attendant moves past us, back to the register, while Jack and I continue to stare at each other.

Jack breaks the silence first, chuckling. "Of all the things I expected today, seeing you here never even crossed my mind," he says.

I smile, a puff of laughter escaping from me as well. "Same."

"So, what are you doing here?" he asks.

"Um," I glance around, "buying some chocolate?"

He laughs, long and loud, and the sound thaws the last bit of icy awkwardness lingering inside. His eyes sparkle as they look into mine, and in that moment I know that I made the right decision.

"I meant at the airport," he says, his eyes dancing.

I smile. "I know what you meant. But seriously," I say, grabbing a package of hazelnut butter crisp bonbons, "this conversation will be better over chocolate."

He chuckles, following me to the register, and pays for the candy. We thank the attendant and leave the store together.

"This way," Jack says, heading back toward the central terminal. But then he stops. "Unless you need to catch a flight somewhere?"

I laugh. "Not anymore I don't," I say, and his face lights up.

We move toward the large glass wall of the central terminal, the world outside the windows an enormous, misty white. Finding a couple seats tucked away from the hustle and bustle, we sit down.

He shakes his head, half a smile on his face. "I still can't believe it," he says. "And to think I almost missed you! It's a good thing I decided to stop and pick up some of your favorite chocolate to take with me to your house," he says, winking at me.

I smile back. "And I'm glad I decided to stop and get some to calm my nerves before my flight."

"Have you ever flown before?" he asks.

I shake my head. "Nope. I figured a cross-country flight on one of the busiest travel days of the year would be a great way to ease me into it."

He laughs again, reaching for my hand. I meet him with both of mine, my heart filling up as he lifts my hands and kisses first one and then the other.

"You were coming to see me in Baltimore?" he asks.

"I was, yes."

"Why?"

And suddenly the time has come. My heart hammers in my chest and my mouth suddenly goes dry. "Because there's something I need to tell you."

His face instantly sobers. "There's something I need to tell you, too."

"You first," I say, desperately trying to find my courage.

He nods, then takes a deep breath. "When I left for Baltimore, I didn't think I'd be taking the job. I fully intended to come home and keep looking. But once I was there, it was easy to acknowledge that it was the perfect opportunity. And it was, in every way but one."

I look down at our hands, at his thumb tracing circles across my knuckles.

"I'm not going to lie—when you suggested that we take a break," he says, "it hurt. A lot. At first I thought I'd get over it, that once I got busy the ache inside would let up, but it didn't. And that ache made me realize that the one thing the job didn't have was actually the most important. I guess what I'm saying is..." Jack swallows. "I love you, Emily Kenworth. I was afraid to say it sooner, because I wasn't sure if what you felt for me was as strong as what I feel for you. And I didn't want you to feel obligated, you know?" He reaches up, cupping my face with his hand. "But the fact that you're willing to spend Christmas in Baltimore, away from the farm and everything you love, that tells me quite a lot."

My look softens. "Actually, I wasn't going to spend Christmas with you," I say.

He frowns. "You weren't?"

"No." I grin. "I was going to spend your *birthday* with you. So happy birthday!"

He laughs, and the sound loosens the knot in my gut. "Emily Kenworth, I know I just said it, but I'll say it again: I *love* you."

He kisses me, soft and slow, and my insides melt like molten chocolate. But there's something I still need to say, so I pull back, my nerves tangling into knots.

"I have a gift for you," I say, reaching for the premade gift box beside me. "It requires an explanation."

He takes it in his hands, and surprise flits across his face. "It's got some weight to it," he says. Lifting the lid off the box he peers inside. With a quizzical look, he pulls out a terra cotta pot filled with dirt.

"I'm glad you said it comes with an explanation," he says, "because if this arrived in the mail I'd be terribly confused."

"It's a Christmas tree," I say, forcing the words out before I lose my nerve. "Or it will be, someday. I planted one of the seeds from the cones we harvested together."

His eyes register surprise, and I look down, embarrassed.

"I realized after you left that it wasn't just love for the trees and the farm and my family that was keeping me in Echo Ridge. It was fear, too—fear of the unknown, fear of what I might find, or not find, somewhere else. But I clung to the belief that it was for love," I swallow, my voice growing softer, "until I realized that the thing I loved most wasn't there anymore."

I look up, and what I see in his eyes gives me courage. "So I'm here to say it too: I love you, Jackson McKinley. And I want to be with you. And since you've decided to make your home in Baltimore, I've decided to bring the Christmas Tree farm with me, to you. Because I can't live without either."

His eyes grow wide. "You... you would leave the farm? Your trees? For me?"

I try to smile, but the lump in my throat makes it more of a grimace. "I would," I say, nudging the pot he still holds. "I'm bringing what I can with me, but even if it doesn't grow, I'm still choosing you."

Gently he puts the pot down and reaches for me, and I fall into his embrace. He holds me close, not caring when I start to cry because I can't hold in the tears any longer. They leak down my face, soaking his shoulder, but he doesn't pull away. He whispers in my ear that it's okay to cry, that he knows how much I love the trees, and that he loves me. He cradles my head, stroking my hair until my sobs subside and my breathing slows. As I pull away, he gives me a soft smile.

"Sorry about that," I say, pulling a tissue from my pocket and wiping my nose. "I thought I was done crying about it."

His eyes are concerned as he watches me. "Are you sure, Em?" he asks, searching my face.

"I'm sure."

"After all the money and effort we put into saving the farm, to just... walk away?"

I choke on a sob masquerading as a laugh. "Are you trying to convince me to change my mind?"

He brushes his hand gently down the side of my face, his

eyes warm and soft, like fresh gingerbread. "No," he says, his voice husky, "I'm just in awe that you love me enough to make that decision."

I place my hand over his where it rests against my cheek. "I do," I say.

He leans forward and presses his lips to my forehead. I close my eyes, letting myself relax, trying not to think about all that I'm giving up, and instead, thinking of the life I will have with Jack. He sits back, and I open my eyes.

"When did you decide to come home for Christmas?" I ask. "Were you going to surprise me?"

His mouth pulls up in a lopsided grin. "Well, actually…"

Chapter 34

"Y̶ou quit your job?" Chase looks incredulous. "But, why?"

Jack is sitting on our couch, one arm curled around me and the other stretched out along the back. I'm tucked into his side, half reclining against him, not wanting to let him go. I haven't stopped smiling since we left the airport together.

"This is why," Jack says, and he leans down to kiss the top of my head,

Chase frowns. "I don't understand. Did you get another job, in Seattle?"

"No."

"Then what are you planning to do?"

Jack looks at me, and I sit up. "We were talking on the way back from the airport about that," I say, "and we have a proposition for the family."

Chase folds his arms across his chest, frowning. But Dad gives me an encouraging smile. "Go ahead, sugarplum, we're listening."

I clear my throat. "For the last several years the farm has

supported two full-time employees—me and Dad—as well as seasonal and part-time workers. But Mom is going to need round-the-clock care from now on, so we thought that if Dad stepped back from operations—"

"—then maybe I could step in as an official employee," Jack says.

"Leaving you free to go on to medical school," I say to Chase.

"And Emily here, doing what she loves," Jack finishes.

We look around the room, waiting for their reactions. Dad looks up at Chase, still standing in the doorway.

"That sounds like a lot of sense to me," he says. "Chase?"

Chase works his jaw, his eyes on my face. "Does this mean you're engaged?"

I flush. "What! No, not at all, it's just—"

"So what happens if you guys break up?"

My face is burning and I can't bring myself to look at Jack, who clears his throat beside me. "I wouldn't be a business partner, just a full-time employee. An office manager, if you will, who's not afraid to get his hands dirty. Emily or your parents would be free to fire me at any time."

"I'm not going to fire you," I mumble.

"But if it ever comes to that, Chase, I wouldn't leave your sister—your family—in a lurch. I swear to you, I would do everything in my power to ensure the success and stability of the farm before I left."

"Good," Chase says. "Because I owe you a black eye if you don't."

His scowl twists into a grin, and I finally relax. He looks at Dad and nods. "Sounds like sense to me, too," he says, "with only one problem."

"What's that?"

He lifts his shoulders. "There's no money for medical school," he says. "We sunk it all into the farm to turn things around. Which, to be clear, I don't regret at all. But there's nothing left. Not even for a single semester."

We sober at his statement, the weight of his words heavy in the silence. "Then we'll sell off the forty-five acres and you can use that," I say.

"That's a great idea," Jack chimes in.

Chase frowns. "What if this year was just a fluke and everything goes south again?" he asks. "The business doesn't have any savings. You could lose everything."

Jack shakes his head. "I won't let that happen."

Dad gets up and puts a hand on Chase's arm. "You deserve it, son. You've given up a lot to get us to where we are—it's only fair we help you get to where you want to go, too."

Chase looks at each of us, then finally he nods. "All right."

"Great," Dad says, clapping him on the back. "Let's go find the paperwork and see what we need to do to get the land listed for sale."

"What, now?"

"No time like the present, son," Dad says. He steers Chase toward the office, winking at me as they pass.

Jack gets up from the couch and turns, offering me his hand. I take it, and he pulls me up beside him. The way he looks at me causes my heart to swoon, and I wonder how I ever thought I could live without him. Taking my face in his hands, he presses a gentle kiss to my lips.

The lights from the Christmas tree cast a warm, flickering glow across the living room, bathing everything in golden light. His arms wrap around me and our lips meet again, gently at first, and then deeper, as if making up for all the kisses we've missed the last two weeks. My hands rest against his chest, his heart pounding beneath my palms.

"Happy birthday, Jack," I whisper against his lips.

"Merry Christmas, Emily," he says.

I laugh lightly. "Christmas is tomorrow," I say.

"*Every* day is Christmas with you," he says, pulling me even closer.

It's the nicest compliment I've ever received.

Epilogue

Three years later

The damp smell of earth and loam fills my nostrils, clearing my head and warming my heart. My knees are already wet from kneeling on the ground, but I don't care. It's been a soggy spring, and today is the first sunny day in a week —I wasn't about to let it go to waste.

Jack hands me the spade with a grin. "Ready?"

His excitement is tangible, and only slightly higher than my own. "Ready."

Taking the spade in my ungloved hand, I make a large opening in the earth. When it's wide and deep enough, I scoot over so Jack can place the seedling carefully in the hole. We use our hands to scoop the earth back into place around it, filling in the gaps and tamping it down. I sit back on my heels, satisfied.

"And that's it?" Jack asks, looking from the sapling to me and back again.

"That's it," I say. "Oh, wait, the fertilizer. Can you grab it? It's in the wheelbarrow."

As Jack gets to his feet, I lean in close to the little tree.

"Grow, little one," I say. "Grow up big and tall and healthy, until you're ready to be crowned for Christmas."

As if in reply to my words, I feel a swift kick from inside my abdomen. I press a hand to my stomach and laugh.

"What's so funny?" Jack asks, coming back with a small sack of fertilizer.

"The baby thought I was talking to her instead of the tree," I say.

Jack sets the bag on the ground and helps me get to my feet. He crouches down, cradling my round belly between his hands and pressing his cheek to my overalls.

"Don't mind Mommy," he says. "She talks to the trees more than she talks to me, too."

I laugh again and smack him playfully on the arm, but he catches my hand, standing up beside me and leaning in to kiss me. I turn and press my lips to his.

A chilly wind sweeps across the field, blowing tendrils of loose hair around my face. Jack reaches up and tucks a strand behind my ear.

"You've got dirt on your face," he says.

"So do you," I say, wiping my fingers down his cheek and leaving a muddy, brown streak. We laugh, and he kisses me again.

Jack spreads the fertilizer around the base of the sapling, then gathers our things and puts them in the wheelbarrow. I look down at the little tree, barely two feet tall, and my heart swells.

"What should we name her?" I ask, when Jack comes to stand beside me.

"I thought we decided on Kathryn, after your mother?" he says.

I roll my eyes. "Not the baby. The tree," I say, pointing at it with my chin.

"Do you name all the trees, too?" he says, incredulous.

"Of course not," I say. "But this one is special. This one is *ours*."

I twine my fingers with Jack's, leaning my head on his shoulder. We stare at the young tree, her branches swaying gently in the breeze.

"How about Noelle? It will be a tribute to Christmas, and to *you*," he says, kissing the top of my head.

I smile. "Noelle it is."

I pull a small piece of red-and-white striped ribbon from my pocket. Crouching down, I tie it loosely around one of the branches. "Merry Christmas, Noelle," I whisper.

Jack chuckles. "It's only April!"

But I shake my head. "It doesn't matter. For the trees, it's only ever Christmas."

He helps me up again, and hand in hand we walk back to the house. The ground is soft and spongy, and we skirt the bigger puddles in the road. The sky above us is impossibly blue, clearer than it's been in weeks. After the heavy gray winter, the high, cottony clouds are a blessed relief, since they don't carry any threat of rain. Robins call to one another from the surrounding trees, and somewhere off in the woods, a woodpecker taps out a steady rhythm.

As we come up to the barn, I turn and look out across the fields. A breeze moves through the trees, lifting my hair and bringing with it the smell of spring.

"Should we start on the rest of the planting, do you think?" Jack asks.

I shake my head. "Not yet. We'll give it another week, see if the ground dries out a bit more."

He nods, and we keep walking toward the house. "So what's on the agenda for today, then?"

"I think I'd like to paint today, Mr. Kenworth," I say.

Jack chuckles, shaking his head. "I still can't believe I let you talk me into changing *my* name when we got married," he says.

"Well, you couldn't very well help run the Kenworth Christmas Tree Farm and *not* be a Kenworth," I say, with mock severity.

"That's true. And I guess all the women who married into the family business had to change their names, too."

"Exactly," I say.

We reach the house and climb the steps to the door. "Well, Mrs. Kenworth," Jack says, "I'm going to put the wheelbarrow away and then see about fixing the front gate. Try not to paint me into any romantic landscapes this time."

"No promises," I say, grinning. "You're very paintable."

He laughs, pulling me into his arms. With our bodies pressed together, I can feel our daughter squirming inside of me, stretching her little body as she moves around. I close my eyes and curl my fingers into the fabric of Jack's shirt, wanting to memorize the feeling of this moment. I take a long, slow breath. He smells of cedar and musk, and something else I can't quite name, until my heart pulls out a dictionary and supplies me with the word.

Home.

Other books by Shaela Kay

Contemporary romance

Only Ever Friends
Only Ever Neighbors

Historical romance

A Heart Made of Indigo
Scoundrel In Disguise
The Rodenburg Girl

Christmas at Edgewood Park
Christmas at Cartwright Manor

To Train a Heart

*If you enjoyed the book, please consider
leaving a review!*

Acknowledgments

Glory goes first and foremost to my Heavenly Parents, without whose help and influence I could do nothing.

My infinite thanks go to my writing group, the Tumble-words, for continual encouragement and support while writing, and to Chalon Linton, Kim McCoy, and Cherika Hedengren for their help and feedback while I was working on revisions and edits. It really does take a village!

I appreciate the University of Washington School of Medicine and my wonderful husband, John, for help in answering my medical and school-related questions. I was overwhelmed while conducting research for Parkinson's disease at how varied the illness, treatment, and progression really is. With what I learned, I did my best to convey the seriousness of the disease and the magnitude with which it affects the life and loved ones of those diagnosed, without letting it overwhelm the story.

In all my research about Christmas tree farms, I'm extremely grateful to Patrick White and Lewis Hill for their invaluable information contained in their book *Growing Christmas Trees* as well as the dozens of families and farms that share information on their blogs and websites. I now want to start a Christmas tree farm, so it really can be Christmas all year long. John, we should get on that.

About the Author

Shaela Kay was born and raised near Seattle, WA. She studied theater and English at Brigham Young University-Idaho and is an award winning graphic designer. She and her family live in the Pacific Northwest with too many hobbies and not enough bookshelves. You can visit her online at www.shaelakay.com

www.ingramcontent.com/pod-product-compliance
Lightning Source LLC
Chambersburg PA
CBHW072126250626
47159CB00007B/2577

* 9 7 8 1 9 4 7 0 0 5 4 3 3 *